DOCTOR ONE NIGHT

DOCTOR ONE NIGHT

A Workplace Second Chance Romance

Doctor Feel Good

BLAKELY STONE

blakely
STONE
CONTEMPORARY ROMANCE

Foreword

One wild night with UAB's most irresistible surgeon. Now, I'm stuck working with him—and fighting every urge not to fall back into his bed.

I've spent years on my research, and the last thing I need is a distraction like Dr. Hunter Parrish.

Now the secret bad-boy doctor is my partner on a high-stakes, make-or-break clinical trial.

Our night together six months ago should have been the end of it—a scorching, forbidden secret.

Unfortunately, every time his smoldering eyes lock onto mine, it feels like he's daring me to forget the rules.

There's no way I'm letting this arrogant, too-sexy-for-his-own-good surgeon ruin everything I've worked for. But damn, keeping it together has never been this hard.

The real danger isn't letting him in—it's that once I give him a piece of my heart, I might never get it back.

*This is Frankie and Hunter's story. It mixes a **one-night stand, second chance, workplace romance, strong female, and a damaged MMC**. Frankie may be a falling for a grumpy, off-limits surgeon with a damaged past, but Buster differs from what meets the eye. While this story is 1 of 4 books set at UAB Hospital, each focusing on a different love story with a too-hot-to-handle surgeon, it is a stand-alone book filled with twists, challenges, and a guaranteed happily ever after.*

ONE

Frankie

Tuesday, October 3, 2023

UAB HOSPITAL

1802 6th Ave S, Birmingham

9:04 _pm_

ALONE IN THE LAB, I bend over the microscope, completely absorbed in the delicate patterns the cells form under the lens. That's how I prefer it and avoid coming in during the day if I can help it.

The hours have slipped away unnoticed, and I don't mind one bit. There's something almost meditative about this work—just me, the slides, and the steady cadence of my thoughts.

This newest discovery has me all excited about what this means for my research. I've pored over it for more than an hour now and I still can't get enough.

I jump when I hear the door open with a quiet click. I whip around, not expecting anyone. It's Dr. Hunter Parrish, fresh from the OR, looking like he's just been through hell and back.

His scrub cap is gone, revealing dirty blonde hair that's tousled as if he's run his hands through it a dozen times. His blue eyes have that tired but sharp look I've seen before —focused, intense, self-assured. He's a big deal around here, a cardiothoracic surgeon with a reputation as solid as the square jaw he's currently clenching.

But it's not just his reputation that makes my breath catch. He's not wearing his white coat, and for the first time, I can see the tattoos that cover his muscular arms.

I'm mesmerized by the intricate designs that snake down them. It's a side of him he usually keeps hidden, and the contrast between this inked-up, rugged version of him and the buttoned-up doctor I've seen around occasionally is overwhelming in the best possible way. "Dr. Renna," he says, his voice low and a little rough, probably from hours of barking orders in the OR. "What are you doing here so late?"

"I could ask you the same thing," I reply, managing a smile even though my heart's doing a weird little flutter in my chest. Maybe I'm the one who needs cardiothoracic surgery.

"Long surgery?" I ask casually, or at least that's what I'm aiming for.

He nods, stepping closer to the microscope station where I'm seated. "Transplant. It took longer than expected. I'm just here to pick up some blood work results for my patient before heading home."

I gesture to the computer. "They should be in the system now. I'll pull them up for you." I stand and walk over to the computer and he follows close behind.

As I navigate the lab's database, I'm hyper-aware of his presence next to me. He's close enough that I can feel the heat radiating off him, the essence of him seeping into me. He's within inches, so close that I can see the faint shadow of stubble on his jaw, the way it contrasts with his usually put together appearance.

God, he's handsome. The kind of handsome that makes you forget how to breathe for a second.

"Here we go," I say, finding the results and bringing them up on the screen. "Looks like everything's in order. I'll put them in MyChart now."

He leans in, scanning the data, and I catch a whiff of him —clean, with a hint of something darker, more earthy, an expensive smelling-cologne that suits him perfectly. "Good," he murmurs, more to himself than to me, it seems. Then his eyes flick to mine, and there's something staring back at me. It's something that wasn't there a moment before. A spark of interest, maybe, or curiosity.

"Do you always work at night?" he asks, his voice softening ever so slightly, like he's genuinely curious. He pulls up a stool next to me and leans in as if we are two old friends catching up. The truth is, I hardly know the man. I just admire him from afar every once in a while when I catch sight of him.

"Not usually," I admit, tearing my gaze away from him to focus on the screen, trying to regain some composure. "I normally work from home, analyzing data from my computer. But this," I gesture to the slide under the microscope, "was too fascinating to stay away from. I had to see it for myself."

He nods, and for a moment, the professional veneer drops just a little. "I get that. Sometimes you just need to be there, see with your own eyes."

I glance up at him again, and there it is—the tattoos, the tired but strong set of his handsome, broad shoulders, the way he's looking at me like he's actually seeing me... Something about him here, the late hour, that no one else is here, makes my my panties wet.

"You should see them," I say before I can think better of it. "The cells. They're incredible. Want to take a look? It's not every day you get to see medical advancement in real time."

He smiles, and it's not the polite, distant smile I've seen him out give a hundred times to patients, or coworkers. It's something warmer, something real. "Sure. Let me see what has you all excited."

Look in the mirror, I want to say. Instead, I move aside as he leans in. I have to resist the urge to run my hands through his messy dirty blonde hair. He straightens up, his interest clearly piqued. "What exactly am I looking at?"

I gesture toward the microscope. "It's cardiac tissue from a patient who's been on the new anti-inflammatory protocol. What you're seeing are the effects of early-stage myocardial infarction—heart attack. I've been tracking the inflammatory markers, and the results are… well, I think they could be groundbreaking."

His eyebrows lift slightly as he bends back down to the microscope. "Groundbreaking, how?"

I love when I meet someone as genuinely interested in this stuff as I am.

"Check out the reduction in inflammation around the damaged tissue. Normally, we'd see a lot more scar tissue forming by now, but with this treatment, the cellular response is completely different. It's almost as if the heart is healing faster, with less permanent damage."

He peers through the lens, and I watch as his expression shifts from curiosity to something deeper. He's more focused, almost reverent. There's a long moment of silence, and I can tell he's processing what he's seeing.

"This is impressive," he murmurs, still staring at the slide. "If this holds up in further trials, it could change the way we handle post-op care for heart patients. Faster recovery times, fewer complications."

"Exactly," I say, my excitement bubbling over. "We're seeing a significant reduction in the markers associated with chronic inflammation. If this pans out, it could mean less long-term damage and better overall outcomes for patients."

He pulls back from the microscope, turning those intense blue eyes on me. "I'm impressed."

His words send a thrill through me, and I can't help the smile that spreads across my face. It's not just the validation from someone like him, someone who's a leader in his field, it's the fact that he genuinely seems to understand how important this could be.

"Thanks," I say, flustered and breathless under the weight of his attention. "I mean, there's still a lot of work to do, but it's exciting, right?"

"Very," he agrees, his voice soft but firm. "You know, I might have to stop by more often, now that I know such amazing research is going down here."

I laugh, shaking my head. "You're always welcome, Dr. Parrish. Just don't blame me if you end up spending all your late nights in the lab."

"I could think of worse places to be," he replies. The teasing note in his voice sends another little thrill through me.

But before the moment goes on too long, he straightens up, all business again. "Seriously, though, I want to stay updated on this. Let me know when you have more data."

"Will do," I promise, watching as he steps back, preparing to leave. He turns to go, pausing for a final last glance over his shoulder. I clear my throat. My awkwardness about how to handle the moment seems like it's flashing like a neon sign, and I want to do anything to divert it.

I'm still reeling from the intensity of our conversation when Hunter turns around, his blue eyes locking onto mine with an unreadable expression. Before I can try to decipher it, he's moving toward me, closing the distance between us. My breath hitches as he stops just inches away, his gaze dropping to my lips.

There's no time for second-guessing, no chance to brace

myself before his hand cups the back of my neck, fingers tangling in my thick hair.

He leans in, and my heart thunders in my chest as his lips meet mine in an all-consuming kiss that's dizzying in its urgency. It's a jolt of pure electricity, igniting a fire within me I never knew was there smoldering.

I return his kiss with equal fervor. My hands find their way to his broad shoulders, clinging to him as the world around us falls away. The spark between us is a living thing, devouring us both with its hunger, and I surrender to it, to him.

Why the hell not?

Hunter's strong hands are on my waist, pulling me closer until there's no space left between us. I can feel the hard planes of his sculpted body as he effortlessly lifts me and places me on the edge of a nearby table. The slide of my bottom against the cool surface through my pants is a stark contrast to the heat radiating from him.

With a swift motion, he clears the table beside me, papers and lab equipment clattering to the floor. I gasp as he kisses me again, deeper this time, more demanding. His tongue sweeps against mine, and I'm lost in the taste of him.

My fingers fumble with the drawstring of his scrub pants, desperate to feel his skin against mine. He helps me, shedding the thin barrier along with his shirt, revealing the masterpiece of tattoos that adorn his chest and shoulders. I trace the lines of ink with my fingertips, marveling at the artistry, the beauty of the man before me.

Hunter's hands slide under my lab coat, sliding along the waistband of my pants and undoing the button. His touch sets my skin on fire. I've never felt so in tune with every sensation.

He breaks our kiss just long enough to remove my coat and pull the shirt over my head. Raking over me with a hunger that makes me yearn to be desired by him, he dives back into my mouth with his.

Leaning in, his lips graze my ear. His voice is a low growl that sends shivers down my spine. "Frankie, you're incredible," he murmurs, his breath hot against my skin. "I've wanted you since the moment I walked in here tonight."

I respond with a moan as his mouth finds the sensitive spot where my neck meets my shoulder, his teeth nipping at the delicate flesh. My hands explore the contours of his back, the muscles flexing beneath my touch as he grinds against me, the bulge of his arousal unmistakable.

In one swift movement, he unhooks my bra, freeing my breasts, his hands cupping them with a reverence that makes my head spin. His thumbs graze over my nipples, eliciting a gasp from me as they harden under his touch. He captures one in his mouth, his tongue circling the peak, and I arch into him, my body aching for more.

The sound of our ragged breathing fills the room, punctuated by the soft, wet noises of our kisses and the occasional moan. His hand slips between my legs, rubbing against the lace fabric of my panties, and I moan his name, my hips bucking against his palm, wanting more friction, more force.

"I want to devour you," he whispers, his voice hoarse with need. "All of you."

I nod, unable to speak, as he tugs at the waistband of my thong, pulling them down. His fingers trace the length of my inner thigh, teasing, until they find my center, hot and slick with desire.

He groans at the contact, his fingers sliding easily inside me, and I cry out, my body clenching around him. "God, you're so wet," he says, his voice filled with lust.

My response is incoherent. I'm lost in the sensation of his fingers moving inside me, his thumb circling my clit with just the right amount of pressure. With every stroke, the coil of tension within me tightens, and I'm teetering on the edge.

Hunter's gaze holds mine as he adds another finger, stretching me, preparing me for what's to come. With a commanding voice, he says, "I want to hear you come," and the raw need in his words pushes me over the edge.

My orgasm rips through me, pleasure crashing over me as I cry out his name. My inner walls clamp down around his fingers, and he watches me with a satisfaction that borders on smugness. But there's no time for complacency—not when the heat between us is still raging, demanding more.

He pulls his fingers out, and I whimper at the loss. He reaches into his pocket and pulls out a foil packet, and I grab his cock, hard and insistent against my thigh. I take the condom from him, and my hands shake slightly as I roll it onto his length.

With a low growl, he positions himself at my entrance. His gaze locks onto mine, teasing me with the tip of his head, rubbing gently on my wetness. "Tell me you want this," he says, his voice strained with the effort of holding back.

"I want this," I say, my voice breathy and eager. "I want you, Hunter."

With a groan, he thrusts into me, filling me completely. The sudden stretch makes me gasp, but the discomfort quickly fades into pleasure as he begins to move, each stroke of his massive body sparking new waves of ecstasy.

He sets a relentless rhythm, his hips pounding against mine, the sound of the meeting of our bodies echoing through the empty lab. I wrap my legs around his waist, pulling him deeper, wanting—needing—all of him.

Our bodies are slick with sweat, the air thick with the scent of sex and the sounds of our shared pleasure. Hunter's hand finds mine, our fingers intertwining as he drives into me again and again.

"Frankie," he gasps, his movements becoming more erratic, less controlled. "God, you are amazing. Fuck me."

Another orgasm is building, the pressure coiling low in my belly. "Don't stop," I beg, my voice barely more than a whimper. "Please, don't stop."

His response is a grunt of approval as he increases his pace, his shaft hitting that perfect spot inside me with every thrust. My body tenses, my toes curling as the world explodes. I cry out, my inner walls clenching around him as I come, and it's enough to send him over the edge with me.

With a final, powerful thrust, he buries himself deep inside me, his body shuddering as he finds his release. He collapses on top of me, both of us panting and slick with sweat, our hearts pounding in unison.

For a long moment, neither of us speak, too caught up in the aftermath of our passion. Finally, he lifts his head, his blue eyes meeting mine with a warmth that takes my breath away. "You're something else, Frankie Renna."

TWO

Hunter

_____

Friday, April 19

8:17 pm

THE HOSPITAL IS EERILY quiet at this hour, the kind of silence that presses in on you. It's broken only by the the distant beeping of machines. That and the hum of that creepy robot floor-polishing machine that makes its rounds unattended, like a rogue AI after-hours maintenance crew.

I've just wrapped up another grueling surgery, and exhaustion is settling into my bones. But instead of heading home, I find myself lingering in the staff room, thumbing through a white paper on Hodgkins lymphoma and letting the stillness of the night seep into me.

Or at least, I try to.

You'd be surprised what can happen on a ward when there's a quiet moment or two. As I sit here reading about HL and its relationship to heart injury—a subject that has become personal very recently—the commotion next door makes it clear that the rumors about residents screwing around aren't just urban legends.

To a lot of people, this is the stuff medical drama TV shows are made of, not real hospitals. One night in a quiet hospital hall would be enough to let them know that, yes, doctors and nurses get horny and bored, too, but not necessarily in that order.

Through the thin walls, I can hear the unmistakable sounds of what I believe is a resident and nurse making out in the custodian's closet next door. It's muffled but clear enough that there's no mistaking what's going on.

I roll my eyes and try to ignore it, but instead, my mind drifts to a night six months ago. Whoever is next door isn't the only medical professional getting his rocks off.

And suddenly my mind is right back there in that lab with Frankie.

Frankie, the hot researcher who managed to throw me off my game in a way no one else ever has. A quickie with no strings attached. I've done it a hundred times, just never in the hospital. So why does this one keep replaying in my mind?

I'm a cardiothoracic surgeon—a damn good one if you ask around. I take pride in what I do and work hard. Hell, work is my life—I'm obsessive like that.

I've spent years building a reputation as someone who can be counted on when it matters most. I'm the guy who stays late, takes the tough cases, the one who doesn't flinch when the pressure's on.

I don't do it for the accolades, though they come with the territory. I do it because I don't do anything half-ass. When I decided to go into this I knew I had to be the best. It's a heavy responsibility, but it's one I take very seriously.

I'm not a hero, not by a long shot. But I'm good at what I do, and that means something. It means everything, actually. It's why I've never had much time for anything else. Relationships, hobbies, downtime—they all take a back seat when you're in this field.

Maybe that's why I don't let myself get close to anyone. When I've already got so much on my plate, there's no room for anything else. The last thing I need is another person depending on me, another responsibility to add to the list. It's easier to keep my distance, to focus on the work, to keep my personal life—what little there is of it— compartmentalized and far away from the hospital.

I don't know what came over me that night, though. One minute she was showing me some slides, excited about some studies she had been conducting, and the next I was fucking her like a rabbit.

She's not the kind of woman you forget easily. One of those natural beautiful, no-frills, women. Something about her continues to pull me in. Those wide, intelligent green eyes, the way she speaks so animatedly about her research. Her passion and dedication is fucking hot.

That night, she looked at me like I was the only person who could understand what she was experiencing. Maybe that, along with the long and arduous surgery that preceded my visit, is why I lost control. Anyone who knows me knows that I never let myself get caught up in the heat of the moment.

Except with her that night.

It was quick, explosive, and over almost before it started. And afterward was awkward as hell. A couple of, "well, I'll see you around," and then I was out the door, running like I was trying to escape my own skin.

I've got to work on my exit moves.

Besides that, I've got these rules—I don't sleep with colleagues, and I don't sleep with anyone I might have to see again after. That was risky, going *there* with her. Luckily, I haven't seen her since that night forever ago.

The sounds from next door are fading now, and I sigh, scrubbing a hand over my face. I need to get out of here, get some sleep, and stop thinking about a woman that could get me in trouble.

"You're still here, Hunter?" The voice of Jonah Bellinger cuts through my thoughts. "You're not satisfied with being the top surgeon on the East Coast? Now you want to work the most hours, too? Keep all us mediocre surgeons behind you any way you can?"

It's kind of eerie how Bellinger can just glide into a room without making a sound. He's like a ninja, popping up with some smartass comment before I even know he's there.

The chuckle I hear as he opens the fridge is just barely audible because someone next door bellows, "Right there! Right there. Fuck, baby!" I guess things aren't winding down after all.

"Who's busting a nut now?" Jonah asks, shaking a bottle of juice as he comes to sit next to me on the couch. Like always, he doesn't so much collapse on the couch as he does float onto it like a paper airplane coming in for a landing.

How someone who is so the epitome of cool tolerates this environment is anyone's guess. It's like the college quarterback hanging with a bunch of tight-ass nerds.

"Not sure. I've been too focused on this to care," I wave the papers I've been perusing.

"Kind of quiet tonight," he says with a mild groan, leaning back against the faded leather couch used by so many of us in this place over the last five years. The last one was nearly down to the frame when it was finally replaced. Hopefully, we won't get to that point this time.

"Hey, earth to Hunter. What're you thinking about now?"

I sigh, "Too much, like always. Long surgery tonight," I sigh as I let my head fall to the back of the couch. "I need to get my ass up and head home, but I'm too intrigued by your handsome face."

"Fuck you, dork. Whatcha reading that's got you all hot and bothered?"

He holds his hand out, and I don't bother hesitating to pass the report over. There's enough medical jargon around here to keep us busy for a solid year if we read all of it.

"Hodgkin's lymphoma case, eh? Sexy. Last I heard, it was curable."

"Yeah," I reply, crossing my right leg over my left knee. "It typically is. But there's either a new strain out there, or there's a miniscule tweak in the RNA causing a risk to several people that we don't fully know about."

"Oh, even sexier." He continues to scan and seems moderately interested.

"This report was issued last year," I point to the page he is on currently. "It's been revised at least once. But so far, no one has nailed down the reason why the affected individuals are more susceptible and less likely to respond to treatment."

"How long has this been an issue?"

"I'm not sure," I say with a shrug. "I believe it's a fairly recent phenomenon. This case just caught my attention a few months ago. Things have been busy, but I've been reading up on everything I can get my hands on. Everything is just coming out, like water out of a fire hose."

I can almost sense his eyebrows raise, so I don't bother looking. He knows when I'm lying or not telling the whole truth. But Jonah doesn't grill me, which I appreciate.

"You mean Superman can't hear around corners?" His low, sardonic whistle would normally make me roll my eyes, but not now. "Damn, man. I thought you knew everything about everything."

"Eat shit."

"Lick nuts."

He laughs a little before he sighs, "We can't fix it all, man, you know that. But seriously, are you that riled up about this? This isn't even your focus."

Neither of us speaks as we hear the door to the supply closet unlock and then open. The light, padding footsteps that sneak out first likely belong to Ellen Sanchez, one of the newer, hot nurses. Her soft yet solid cadence in her clogs is unmistakable.

The next set of footsteps that comes out is a bit heavier and a little more cocky. Perhaps getting laid built up his confidence somewhat.

"Oh! I, ah, I didn't…" I recognize his distinct voice immediately: Teddy, the tall, lanky resident. He bursts into the staff room, expecting it to be empty, I'm sure.

"Just zip it up and move on, McFly," I say without turning around to face him. "I'm sure you've got rounds to do or something else you've been avoiding."

"Step to it, newbie," Jonah adds, "Make sure your dingle isn't dangling."

I ROLL my eyes behind closed lids, picturing the kid behind us checking his fly only to realize that he's wearing scrubs and doesn't have a zipper.

I'll admit it. Giving the residents shit is sometimes a nice change to the regular pace we set around here. It's like a sadistic form of entertainment for us and a rite of passage for them.

Jonah flips the page he was reading back up as we hear the footsteps trailing off toward the hallway. I know in a few moments, he'll ask me again why this report has me so fired up.

"Is Grace still out at the desk?"

"Yep," Jonah replies, smirking as he chomps on his gum. I hate it when people smack on chewing gum. "Big Mama's been looking for you, too. She wants you to try the caramel muffins she brought in."

"Big Mama" is an affectionate term we use for one of our oldest and most well-liked ER nurses, Grace Petit. She's a tough old woman who looks twenty years younger than her actual age, which is probably in her late sixties.

She isn't big at all. In fact, she is only five feet tall with her thick-soled shoes on and probably weighs a hundred pounds soaking wet.

Big Mama is not to be confused with Mama Bear, who is Maijka, our other mother-figure nurse, and the person who takes care of us all. We are a lucky bunch to have these two mom figures around to keep us straight and well-fed.

Grace recently had a medical complication, so we are all being extra protective of her. She has always been there for of us, so we are trying to do the same for her. We have to do it quietly, though, because she doesn't want anyone to fuss over her. Ever.

She likes Jonah the best. I'm sure it's because he showed up at UAB first. His calm and peaceful nature doesn't hurt. He's just one of those likable guy.

For years, she's been like a surrogate mother to him. That's cool, I guess, since his own mother was a piece of work from what little I've heard of her over the years. Come to think of it, I think mothering Jonah that is how she got the nickname "Big Mama."

"Caramel muffins, huh?"

"Oh yeah, sweet, sticky, and guaranteed to clog an artery or add a few pounds."

"Keeps us in business."

Surgeon jokes. They might be worse than dad jokes. But seriously, those fucking muffins are the epitome of food sin.

———

10:49 *pm*

"I'M OUT OF HERE, man. You're charming and all, but my bed is calling."

"Get some rest. I'm here for the night on call, so you know where to find me if you need me."

I act like I'm going to blow him a kiss but instead throw up a middle finger. We have a sophomoric sense of humor together, which is a nice break from the all-business approach I apply to life for the most part. Everyone needs a friend like Jonah to lighten the mood.

Pushing through the door into the hallway, my pace quickens as I make my way toward the parking garage. I round the corner, half-focused on my cases tomorrow, and suddenly, I slam right into someone. Papers go flying, scattering across the floor. Instinctively, I reach out to steady whoever I just ran into.

"Frankie?" The name slips out before I can stop it, and there she is, standing in front of me, her eyes wide with surprise. "Dr. Renna. I didn't see you coming."

Why the fuck did I call her Frankie? Fuck. Fuck.

"Dr. Parrish," she says, her voice calm, even though she's

kneeling down to gather her papers, clearly as caught off guard by our collision as I am.

She doesn't seem pissed, but then again, Frankie always seems as cool as a cucumber. She's got this easygoing nature, like nothing rattles her. Fuck if it doesn't throw me off.

I should say something, apologize maybe, but instead, I just stand there like an idiot, looking awkward as hell. I haven't seen her since I ran into her with my dick.

"Here, let me help," I mutter, crouching down to pick up a few papers, trying to keep my hands steady.

"Thanks," she says, her tone light, no indication that she is as ruffled as I am.

I hand her the two papers I managed to pick up while she picks up everything else. For a second, our fingers brush. It's just a touch, but it's enough to send a jolt through me. Damn it, why does she have to look so fucking hot?

"You're here late," I finally grumble, more to fill the silence than anything else. The words come out harsher than I intend, and I instantly regret it. That's the best I've got? Wasn't that my lead-in last time?

She smiles, that same easy smile I remember, and stands up, smoothing out her papers. "I just had to pick up some charts before a meeting tomorrow morning."

I clear my throat, trying to regain some semblance of control. "Look, about that night in the lab. I'm sorry I haven't reached out."

She cuts me off, waving a hand dismissively. "It's fine, Dr.

Parrish. Really. We were both caught up in the moment, and we stay busy. All good."

Her response is so simple, so unbothered, that it only throws me even more off-kilter.

Good. I will accept she is being honest. I nod, not trusting myself to say anything more. I shove my hands into my pockets, trying to find something—anything—to focus on besides her.

She tilts her head slightly, studying me in that way she has, like she's reading every thought in my head. "Everything else okay?"

I can't help the scoff that escapes me. "Long day. Always something. But yes, all good."

She nods, and for a moment, there's a hint of something in her eyes. It seems like she wants to say more. "Well, don't let me keep you. I'm sure you're eager to get home." It must have been wishful thinking.

There's no sarcasm in her tone, no bitterness, just a simple statement. And for some reason, that makes it worse.

I should be grateful she's not making this more complicated than it needs to be, but instead, I just get more annoyed. At myself, at the situation, at how damn perfect she's handling all of this.

"Yeah," I mutter, already turning to go. "Take care, Dr. Renna."

"You too," she replies. When I glance back, she's already walking away, back to whatever task she was so focused on before I ran into her.

As I head to the parking garage, the encounter plays over in my head, every word, every look. She's right—it was just a moment, nothing more.

———

HUNTER'S CONDO

The City Federal Building, Downtown Birmingham

11:31 *pm*

THE ELEVATOR DOORS glide open with a soft chime, and I step into the hallway of my building's top floor.

It's quiet, as it always is at this hour. I swipe my key card and push open the door to my condo, instantly greeted by the cool air conditioning. I keep it at seventy-two at all times.

Everything here is just as I left it—immaculate, organized, and undeniably high-end, but not in a flashy way. It's the kind of luxury that whispers rather than shouts.

The living room is spacious, with large, clear glass windows that offer a sweeping view of the Birmingham skyline. The lights of the city glitter far below, but up here, it feels like I'm a world apart.

The furniture is modern, with clean lines, soft leather, and polished wood. A low-slung sectional in a deep charcoal gray anchors the room, facing a sleek fireplace that I almost never use.

On the opposite wall, there's a built-in bookshelf filled with medical texts, a few novels I keep meaning to read, and a scattering of framed photos—mostly impersonal, like shots of places I've traveled or abstract art that caught my eye.

The kitchen is open, with granite countertops and high-end stainless steel appliances that gleam under the soft lighting. I make my way over to the fridge, grab a bottle of water, and lean against the counter, letting the silence of the space settle over me.

This condo is everything I thought I wanted. It's comfortable, it's luxurious, it's mine. It's small, but the view more than makes up for it. But sometimes, standing here alone, it's almost too empty. Like I've curated this perfect fortress and locked the world out.

I take a long sip, my mind drifting back to the path that got me here. My parents always pushed me to be the best. Excellence wasn't an option, it was a requirement. That pressure was both a blessing and a curse.

They drilled it into me that hard work was the only path to happiness in life and that there was no room for failure and no time for distractions. As much as I resented it and still do to this day, it's hard-wired into me now. That is how I live.

Their high-pressure campaign worked, I guess. I graduated at the top of my class, got into the best undergrad and med schools, and became the surgeon they always said I could be. But somewhere along the way, I lost sight of what I wanted, if I ever even knew. I was always told what I would be, and I just accepted it.

Trading happiness for perfection isn't necessarily the best bargain.

I'm sure it's why I am the way I am—why I bury myself in work, why I keep people at a distance. It's easier to focus on the next surgery, the next challenge, than to think about how I've built my life around expectations that were never really my own.

I'm good at what I do, but there's always that voice in the back of my mind, telling me it's not enough. That it will never be enough.

I love my parents, I suppose. But it's a distant kind of love, stretched thin over years of resentment and unmet expectations on both sides.

My father died a few years ago and it was both a relief and extremely painful. My mother blamed me for his death, in a way, and made it seem like I had failed by not saving him. That is the type of relationship we have.

We talk on holidays, mostly out of obligation. Mother will ask about my work, and I'll give her the highlights, the things that sound impressive enough to satisfy her. But we don't talk about the things that matter. There's no room for that in the world they built for me.

I finish my water and push off the counter to head toward the bedroom, kicking off my shoes as I go. Quickly, I strip off my clothes and head into the bathroom, turning on the shower. As the water heats up, I catch a glimpse of the dark bags under my eyes in the mirror. Damn, I look like shit.

The tattoos on my chest and arms are stark against my skin —remnants from my rebellion years ago, when I thought I could carve out a piece of myself that wasn't dictated by anyone else. But they seem distant now, more like reminders of a person I once wanted to be than who I am.

I step into the shower and let the hot water wash over me as I try to clear my mind. Even here, in the one place that's supposed to be my sanctuary, I can't escape the thoughts that keep circling back: the pressure to be the best, the constant drive to push harder, work longer, achieve more.

As the water pounds against my back, I can't help but wonder what it's cost me. And if, someday, it'll be too much. Can I keep this up forever?

My hand finds its way to my chest, tracing the lines of ink that adorn my skin. They're a part of me, a part of the rebellion that's been brewing inside of me since I was a kid. But that rebellion feels hollow tonight, because it's not the ink I'm thinking of—it's her.

Seeing her brought all of it back to the front of my mind. It's a good thing we don't see each other regularly because she's got my head all turned around.

I close my eyes, and there she is. I can see her humble smirk, hear the sound of her voice as she called out my name... It's been half a year since that night, since we lost ourselves in the lab, but the memory is so vivid like it was yesterday.

My hand slides lower, wrapping around my shaft, the water slicking my movements. I grip tighter, the pressure building as I think of Frankie, of the way her body felt against mine, the heat of her skin, the softness of her lips.

It's too risky to let her in, too likely to end in disappointment or heartache. But a man can always dream. Fantasy is safe and fulfilling enough for my needs.

I stroke harder, the friction sending jolts of pleasure through me. My breaths come faster, my pulse thundering in my ears as I picture her beneath me... Her green eyes looking up at me with that mix of challenge and desire that sets me off without even a touch.

The water pounds down, mingling with the sweat on my brow as I chase the release that's been building since the moment I saw her in the hallway, her papers scattering around us like fallen leaves. I remember the way she looked at me. The surprise in her eyes was quickly replaced by that quiet confidence.

My movements become more frenzied, my grip on reality slipping as I lose myself in the fantasy. I can almost feel her hands on me, her breath on my neck as our bodies move together in that rough, quick experience we shared.

"Fuck!" I yell out.

With a low groan, I come. The intensity of it washes over me as I lean against the cool tile of the shower wall. The water continues to pour down around me, a steady beat that mimics the rhythm of my heart before it gradually slows to its usual pace.

For a moment, I allow myself to bask in the aftermath, to savor the fleeting sensation of peace that wraps around me. But as the water starts to cool, reality seeps back in. I turn off the shower and step out, grabbing a towel and drying off.

I step out of the shower, wrapping a towel around my waist as I head into the bedroom. The steam follows me, clouding the mirror, but the cool air from the bedroom hits my skin, grounding me back into reality. My phone's screen lights up on the nightstand, catching my eye.

Missed call.

I swipe it off the stand, and my stomach tightens when I see her name—Mother. It's 11:30 at night here in Alabama, which means it's 9:30 on the West Coast. She has zero respect.

It's not necessarily an unreasonable hour in California, but she knows I'm two hours ahead. Shit like this is what really pisses me off. She knows I work long hours and that I'm usually exhausted by the time I get home. But that's my mother for you—always pushing, never aware, or maybe she doesn't care, what might be going on for me.

The tension is building in my shoulders again, the brief relief from the shower already fading.

I know I should call her back, even though it's the absolute last thing I want to do right now. It's probably nothing, some trivial update she could've waited until tomorrow to share.

But I can't shake the possibility that it might be something important. Something related to the Hodgkin's lymphoma she was diagnosed with just over a month ago.

The memory of our conversation about that is still fresh— her voice tight but trying to sound casual as she told me the news, the immediate cold dread that settled in my gut. I jumped into action mode, of course, because that is what I do.

I rattled off the tests she needed to have done, the scans, the blood work, but made a conscious decision to stay out of it beyond that. But there's this part of me that's been on edge ever since I got the news, waiting for the other shoe to drop.

I know I could reach out to her doctor directly, consult on her care, and make sure every step is being handled exactly the way I think it should be. But that's a line I won't cross. Not with my mother. If I get too involved, if I take on that responsibility, and something goes wrong… I'll get blamed again, just like with my father.

But I also can't ignore it. I need to stay on top of what's going on, and I need to make sure she's getting the best care possible, even if I have to do it in a way that keeps me at a safe distance.

With a deep breath, I press her name in the missed calls list and listen as the phone rings. Each ring is like a gut punch. She picks up after the third one.

"Hunter, darling," she says, her voice warm but tinged with her familiar evening slur. It's probably her second gin and tonic.

"Mom, it's late," I reply, trying to keep my voice neutral, even though irritation is bubbling just beneath the surface. "Is everything okay? Did you need something?"

There's a pause on the other end, and I can hear her take a breath. "I'm sorry, I realized after I called how late it is. I just got the results back from the tests you told me to get."

My heart skips a beat. I'm surprised she was listening and even more that she passed my suggestions on. Suddenly, the exhaustion I've been carrying all day evaporates, and is replaced by a desire to know more. "And? What did they say?"

"They're not terrible," she says slowly, like she's weighing each word before saying it. "But they're not great either.

The doctor said we need to discuss alternative treatment options."

I close my eyes, pinching the bridge of my nose. Of course it's not straightforward. Of course it's more complicated than I'd hoped, requiring me to analyze them. "Did he mention what kind of treatment? Chemotherapy? Radiation?"

"He mentioned both, and something about a possible clinical trial. I'm supposed to go back in a couple of days to talk it over with him."

I'm already calculating in my head, thinking about what I know and the options that might be on the table. "Send me what he gave you. I'll do some research on the trial. Make sure it's worth considering."

Fuck. Why am I doing this? I told myself to stay out of it.

"Hunter," she trails off, and there's that tone again, that hesitant, almost vulnerable tone that I'm not used to hearing from her. "You don't have to do that. I trust my doctor. You don't need to get involved."

Lies. All passive-aggressive lies. Take her up on it, Hunter!

"I'm not getting involved," I say, my voice sharper than I intended. "But you're right, your doctor knows what's best. I'm going to stay out of it so he doesn't think I'm interfering. I just thought you'd want me to look at them. Just let me know if anything changes."

I haven't said a word about my concerns to her or the possibility of a more aggressive strain. Hopefully her doctor is worth a shit and will explore all avenues.

Another pause. "I appreciate that, Hunter. Really, I do. But... you don't need to carry this, too. I'm going to be fine. My understanding is that this type of cancer is very treatable."

She says it like she's trying to convince both of us. But she doesn't know what I've recently learned about HL.

"Did the results come back on the specific strain?" I say, softer this time. I don't want to alarm her, but I want to know the answer, even if it is to quiet the chatter in my own mind.

"He didn't say specifically, but I'll call the office tomorrow and find out," she promises, and for a moment, it's almost like we have a normal relationship. Like we're just a mother and son talking about mundane things instead of life and death.

We exchange a few more words, but they're empty, just filler to avoid the silence that neither of us knows how to deal with. When the call finally ends, I let out a long breath. As much as tell myself to keep my distance, I'm worried. The stress of it settles back onto my shoulders, where it's lived for the last month, ever since she first told me.

I toss the phone onto the bed and stare out the window at the city below. A rage rises inside of me as I try to balance the need to protect my mother with the fear of getting too close.

And it's tearing me apart.

THREE

Frankie
_____

Saturday, April 20

Frankie's House

2620 11th Ave S, Birmingham

7:49 *am*

I JOLT AWAKE, my heart racing. The early morning breaks through the wood slats covering my windows, casting sharp yellow lines across my bedroom. Blinking away the remnants of sleep, I try to grasp at the fading wisps of my dream. It slips away like smoke, leaving only a lingering sense of something unresolved.

Hunter Parrish. His name echoes in my mind, bringing with it a strange mix of emotions. I can't recall the details of the dream, but his presence lingers as if he'd just been here in my room. Ridiculous, of course. We haven't spoken in months, not since that night in the lab.

Until our hallway crash last night, of course. Curious how seeing him brings all of that back into my consciousness.

I stretch, pushing away the covers, and swing my legs over the side of the bed. The plush rug that takes up most of the floor in my bedroom grounds me in reality, easing me into wakefulness. I can't shake this odd tingling all around me. It's like a phantom touch, a conversation half-remembered.

"Get it together, Frankie," I mutter to myself, padding to the bathroom. The face in the mirror looks back at me, green eyes still unfocused. I splash some cold water on my face, hoping to clear my head and brush my teeth. I can't do anything in the morning until I've brushed my teeth, not even take a sip of coffee.

As I go through my morning routine, flashes of the dream tease at the edges of my wakefulness: Hunter's intense and focused blue eyes; His tattooed sleeves peeking out from under his scrubs; His rare, genuine smile transforming his usually serious demeanor.

I shake my head, annoyed at myself. Why is he suddenly invading my dreams? The request, which is really a directive to me, from Dr. Theo Bench on Wednesday proposing a collaboration with him was probably the start.

And then seeing him in the flesh for the first time last night, running into that solid, broad chest, smelling him…

Curiously, neither of us mentioned the department head's proposal to pair up for the new pacemaker trial when we ran into each other. I wonder if he even knows, yet.

His possible involvement seems odd to me. He isn't a researcher—he is a surgeon. But, the truth is, there's no one else at UAB who knows as much about heart disease, pacemakers, and how they work as he does.

I pour myself a cup of coffee and try to focus on the day ahead. Today is not a work day. I have research to review and data to analyze, but it can wait until next week. Today, I have personal errands to run and laziness to catch up on.

———

ELMWOOD CEMETERY

600 Martin Luther King Jr Dr, Birmingham

1:16 *pm*

I KNEEL down on the soft earth, the scent of freshly cut grass mixing with the subtle fragrance of the flowers I brought with me.

The cemetery is quiet and peaceful, almost out of place, given the rush of life just outside its gates. It's one of the reasons I come here as often as I do. The world slows down here, giving me time to think, to breathe, to remember.

I start pulling at the small weeds that have cropped up around the headstone, determined to make it look as neat as possible. The stone is simple, just the way Mom would have wanted it. There are no frills and nothing ostentatious; just her name, the dates that mark the too-short span of her life, and the words "Beloved Mother."

"Hey, Mom," I whisper, the words catching in my throat like they always do. "I brought your favorites."

I place the bouquet of daisies and lavender at the base of the stone, carefully arranging them so they don't obscure her name.

She always loved daisies. She told me when I was itty bitty that they were the happiest flower and I always think of her when I see them. She also loved the smell of lavender. She would fill our tiny apartment with their scent, trying to make a home out of so little. She always had some growing around our house and in any outdoor spaces we had.

I sit back on my heels, letting my hands rest on my thighs as I take in the sight of her final resting place. It's been years since she passed, but the pain of losing her hasn't dulled much. If anything, it's just settled into a familiar ache, a constant reminder of what I've lost.

We grew up together, in a way. She was so young when she had me, barely more than a kid herself. Bill, the sperm donor, as I call him, left before I was born. He ran off to start a new life, a new family, without a second thought for the one he abandoned.

I've never had much of a relationship with him, and I don't think I ever will. He's just a name on a birth certificate, a ghost who haunts the edges of my life without ever really touching it. I haven't seen him since I was thirteen, and that was for about five minutes when he stopped by the apartment unannounced to "visit." We moved after that.

Weirdly, though, out of the blue, I've had a few voicemails from him recently. I don't even know how he got my number, but I eventually blocked him.

But Mom...she was everything. We didn't have much, but what we had, we shared. She worked two, sometimes three, jobs to keep us afloat, always smiling, always telling me that things would get better. She is the singular person that made me believe I could be anything I wanted to be. Even when I didn't believe in myself, she believed in me.

Mom was the first person in her family to even think about college, but she never had the chance to go. When I got accepted, it was like I was carrying both of us across that finish line.

When I earned my PhD, when I got to call myself Dr. Renna, I was the first in our family to hold that title. It was for her as much as it was for me. Unfortunately, she passed away before I graduated and earned the "D-R," but I know she was with me every step of the way.

I worked my ass off, not just because I wanted a better life, but because I wanted to honor everything she sacrificed to get me there.

My independence and my drive—they're not just traits; they're survival skills. Watching her do it all on her own, without a single complaint, taught me I couldn't rely on anyone but myself. Especially not a man.

My father's betrayal was a constant reminder of how easily someone can walk away and how devastating it can be to depend on someone who doesn't stick around. That's why I've always kept my guard up, why I focus on my work instead of getting caught up in relationships that could pull me off course.

When Mom got sick, it felt like the world was falling apart. Watching her fade, knowing there was nothing I could do, that I couldn't save her, was the hardest thing I've ever faced. She didn't have access to the kind of experimental treatments that might have made a difference, that might have given her more time. It wasn't fair. None of it was fair.

That's why I do what I do—why I'm so driven to make a difference in the field of medical research. I hope I can make a difference so other, maybe, won't have to go through what we went through, to lose someone they love because they couldn't afford the best care or didn't have access to the latest treatments. It's what keeps me going, even on the days when the work is overwhelming and the weight of it all seems too much to bear.

I run a hand over the smooth surface of the headstone, tracing the etched letters of her name with my fingertips. "I miss you," I say softly, the words falling into the quiet air. "I'm trying to make you proud, to do something that matters. I just wish you were here to see it."

A soft breeze rustles through the trees, carrying with it the faint scent of lavender, and for a moment, I can almost believe she's here with me, watching over me like she always did.

I sit there for a while longer, letting the silence wrap around me like a comforting blanket. This place, this ritual, is my way of staying connected to her, of keeping her memory alive in a world that moves on too quickly.

I know what it's like to love someone with your whole heart and then lose them, to be left with nothing but memories and a grave to visit. Love is both comforting and the one thing that can hurt you more than any physical pain I've ever experienced. A double-edged sword.

Eventually, I stand, brushing the dirt from my knees. "I'll be back soon," I promise, even though she doesn't need me to say it. I always come back. She knows my heart. She always has.

———

FRANKIE'S HOUSE

3:18 *pm*

I WALK INTO MY HOUSE, the familiar click of the door shutting behind me, echoing through the quiet space. It's a small, cozy place—nothing fancy, but it's mine.

The scent of the lavender candle I had burning before I went out still lingers in the air, mixing with the faint smell of coffee that's been a constant companion throughout the day. Oops. I didn't mean to leave it burning, but walking into is almost like Mom is here with me.

I toss my keys on the entry table and make my way to the kitchen, where a small stack of mail sits waiting for me. The usual—bills, advertisements, a flyer or two. I start flipping through them, not really paying much attention, just sorting the junk from the things that actually need my attention.

And then I see it.

An envelope, tucked between the electric bill and a coupon for pizza delivery. It's different, though. It's handwritten, the kind of thing you don't see often anymore.

I don't recognize the handwriting. The paper is plain, but the writing on the front is careful and deliberate. My name, my address. No return name, only an address that isn't familiar.

My fingers hovering hesitantly over the envelope. Something about it feels off. Or maybe just unfamiliar. I can't remember the last time I got a handwritten letter, much less one that wasn't from a friend or a colleague.

Curiosity gets the better of me, and I tear it open, unfolding the single sheet of paper inside. The handwriting is the same as on the envelope—neat, precise, like someone who took their time crafting each word.

But when I see the name at the bottom, my breath catches in my throat.

Dad. And not just "Dad," but "Love, Dad." Who the fuck does he think he is reaching out to me after all this time and calling himself dad? He's been nothing to me, and especially nothing resembling a dad.

For a moment, I just stand there, staring at the letter like it's something foreign, something I can't quite comprehend. I block his calls so he figures out where I live. I don't know if I should be creeped out or impressed by his attempt, even if it is a day late and a dollar short.

The man who walked out before I was even born, who left my mother to raise me on her own, who never once reached out, never once tried to be a part of my life, thinks we can be all chummy now. Shit. He better think again. He's dead to me.

I swallow hard, my heart pounding in my chest. Part of me wants to crumple the letter up and toss it in the trash where it belongs without giving it the attention it doesn't deserve. But another part, a part I don't like to admit exists, needs to know what he has to say.

With trembling hands, I smooth the paper on the cold stone countertop and start to read. The words swim in front of me, but I force myself to focus and take them in.

Frankie,

I know I failed you. I've lived with that knowledge for a long time, and there's no excuse for the choices I made. I wasn't there when you needed a father, and that's something I can never change. But I need you to know this: you were born from love. Despite everything, I've always carried that with me.

And I never stopped loving you.

You deserved so much better than what I gave you. I'm deeply sorry for abandoning you and for not being the father you needed. There's no way to make up for that, and I don't expect you to forgive me. But I hope you'll accept this apology for what it's worth.

I'm sick, Frankie. I don't say this to garner sympathy or to ask for anything more than a moment of your time. I might not have much time left, and before I go, I wanted you to know the truth about where my heart has always been.

I know I haven't earned the right to ask

anything of you, least of all your forgiveness. But if there's one thing I can offer before it's too late, it's my sincerest apology. I'm sorry, Frankie, for everything.

I want you to know that despite my absence, I never stopped loving you. I hope, in some small way, that matters.

Love,

Dad

Sorry? He's sorry?

Fuck you, you bastard.

A surge of anger rises in me, hot and fierce. Sorry doesn't make up for the years he left us struggling, for the way he abandoned my mother, for the way he made me believe I was never enough or worth sticking around for.

And yet, despite the anger, there's something else, too. Something softer, more complicated, pushes through me. A part of me that's always wondered about him, that's always wanted to know why he left, why he never tried to be a father to me pushes me outside of my comfort zone.

I read those words over and over, my mind spinning. I don't know what to do, what to think. Meeting him? After all these years? I can't even begin to process what that would be like. Would that be disrespecting my mother? He never had the time or desire to meet either of us when he wasn't dying or when she was—

The letter trembles in my hands as I set it back down on

the counter, my emotions a tangled mess of anger and confusion and unwanted longing.

I push that thought away. I've spent my whole life without him. I don't need him now. I've made it this far without him.

I leave the letter on the counter, staring at it as if it might suddenly provide answers, or vanish altogether.

Whatever happens next, I know one thing for sure: this letter, this man who suddenly wants to be a part of my life, has just stirred up a past I thought disappeared along with him.

———

MONDAY, *May 6*

7:18 am

MY PHONE RINGS just as I'm taking a bite of toast, the shrill sound cutting through the quiet of my kitchen. I glance at the screen and see Carly's name flash across it. She's the only person that would call me this early. I swipe to answer, holding the phone away from my mouth.

"Mmmph?" I manage to get out, still chewing.

"Frankie Renna, are you seriously answering the phone with your mouth full?" Carly's voice is teasing, but there's a hint of disappointment in it, too. "What have I told you about that, missy?"

I swallow quickly, trying not to laugh. "If you're going to call me at this ungodly hour, then you deserve what you get. What's up?"

"Just finished my night shift, and I was thinking about stopping by on my way home to say hi if you're up. You know, make sure you're still alive and all that."

I smile at her sarcasm. "Sure, you know I love the company. Odd hours and all."

"Great, because I'm pulling in now," she says, and I can almost hear the smirk in her voice.

I laugh, shaking my head at her audacity. "You're impossible."

"That's why you love me," Carly chirps, and a moment later, I hear a knock at the door.

I open it to find her standing there in her scrubs, looking as bright and cheerful as someone who hasn't just worked a twelve-hour shift. Her blonde hair is pulled back in a messy ponytail, and there's a mischievous sparkle in her eyes.

"Morning, sunshine," she says, breezing past me into the kitchen. "Got any coffee?"

"Always," I reply, grabbing a mug and pouring her a cup. "How was your shift?"

Carly takes a sip of coffee and sighs contentedly. "Shift was uneventful. Your coffee is the worst. You need to do better."

"Take it up with the manager."

"Noted. I'll file a complaint. So, what's going on in the world of Dr. Frankie Renna?"

"Well, as a matter of fact, I just got an email confirming I'll be working on a study with the insufferable Hunter Parrish."

Carly raises an eyebrow. "Wait, what? Hunter Parrish? As in the man you fucked sideways in the lab last year?"

I roll my eyes. "Yes, that Hunter Parrish." I choose to ignore her desperate attempt to bring this to the gutter. "It appears Dr. Bench had the bright idea to ask him to consult on the pacemaker work we've been doing, and I didn't exactly think like I could say no. You know, I didn't share with him the whole 'fucking sideways' sidebar."

Carly sets her coffee down, leaning forward with interest. "And now?"

"And now I just checked my email, and it's a go. We have a meeting this afternoon, the three of us."

Her eyes widen, and she gives me a knowing look. "Frankie, are you freaking out?"

I sigh, rubbing my temples. "Of course I'm freaking out. It's going to be awkward. Luckily, it won't be our first inter-action since our lab in-service. I literally ran into him at the hospital on Friday."

"What happened?"

"I was hurrying down the hall, looking down, and he rounded a corner at the same time. Bam. Like I said, literally."

"Fuck. Why didn't you tell me?"

"Exactly. That was Friday. We haven't spoken since then. Plus, no biggie. Until I get this email, of course."

"No biggie?! This is the first interaction since you two," she says, making a hand gesture with her pointer finger, going in and out of a circle created by her thumb and pointer on the other hand.

"You're disgusting and so juvenile, Carly."

"I know. But seriously."

"I know."

Carly reaches out and squeezes my hand. "Listen, just be careful with him, okay? He's a hottie, no doubt, but he's world's grumpiest. Plus, he has a reputation for the perpetual bachelor."

I nod, trying to keep my tone light. "Don't worry, girl. While we might have slept together that one time, I have no intention of ever going there again."

But as the words leave my mouth, a tiny voice in the back of my mind whispers the lingering essence of him from the dream the other night. I push it down, refusing to acknowledge the way my stomach twists at the thought of seeing him again.

Carly studies me for a moment, then nods, seemingly satisfied. "Good. Just keep your head on straight, and remember who you are. You're a brilliant, beautiful, and in-control-scientist-badass."

I force a smile, hoping it's convincing. "Yeah, I know all those things." Then I throw a dishtowel at her.

As we chat about lighter things—her patients, my latest research—I can't help the niggling doubt that keeps creeping in. The thought of being in the same room as

Hunter Parrish again, of working closely with him, has me on edge in a way I haven't been in a long time.

I tell myself it's just nerves, just the usual anxiety about bringing someone else in on my project, my baby. But deep down, I know it's more than that. I will have to deploy the universe's best self-control if he so much as brushes past me in a suggestive way.

"Are you pulling another night shift tonight?"

Carly stretches out on the couch, the wide sectional I bought just so I could spend time with my friends and have plenty of room. Right now, she's on the far left side, and I'm on the far right, our usual positions. I haven't changed out of my pajamas, and she's wearing a borrowed pair of joggers. I think she spends more time here than at her own house.

"Nah, they have me on-call for today. There was a big lull last night, not a lot going on, everyone covered, that kinda thing. It's nice, really. It's like my Friday."

"When do you go in?"

She shrugs, her eyes glued to the flatscreen hanging above the fireplace.

"They'll call if they need me. I'm not stressing over it too much."

"Who's running the desk?"

After stretching and showing her trim, athletic figure, Carly replies, "Grace is on the desk tonight, and she has her own little cadre backing her up."

"How is Grace doing, by the way?"

Twisting a strand of her short, blonde locks, which she does constantly, Carly blows out a breath.

"Well, that little scare she gave us last month is still getting her the side-eye from the folks upstairs. They want to be sure that one of their best ER nurses is still able to do the job without collapsing while on duty."

I nod a bit absently as I think about the issue Carly talked to me about a while back. When she told me she had a minor heart attack, part of my expertise, I've been keeping tabs on her.

"She's not working with any restrictions any longer, is she?"

"No," Carly replies, shaking her head as she stretches her legs, "They cleared her completely, but they're still watching. You know, company policy."

"Sill no idea what caused it?"

"Nope. Even bringing it up is a good way to get her growling, so I don't bother asking questions. A motherly Grace is better than a menacing one. Plus, I look forward to her home-baked goodies, so I'm not rocking that boat."

"So you do have some self-control when it comes to that mouth. Good to know."

"Rarely, but yes. She brought in apricot crumble cheesecake about a week ago," she says with a grin, licking her lips as she closes her eyes.

"And you didn't save me any, did you?"

Her shrug is answer enough. Meh, I don't blame her. I wouldn't save her any, either.

Just saying.

FOUR

Hunter

Hunter's Condo

8:12 *am*

THE WEIGHTS CLINK SOFTLY as I finish another set of deadlifts, the familiar burn in my muscles grounding me, pushing everything else out of my mind.

My home gym is quiet. The only sound is the rhythmic thud of my heart in my ears and the occasional rustle of fabric as I move. I can't find my Beats, so I'm going a cappella this morning.

The floor-to-ceiling windows in front of me offer a sweeping view of the city, the early morning light just beginning to creep over the skyline. This view never fails to remind me why I work as hard as I do and why I push myself to the edge every day.

I drop the weights and stand up straight, rolling my shoulders to shake off the tension.

There's no early morning surgery today, so I've got a little more time than usual. I could have slept in, but that's never really been my style. Instead, I'm here, sweating it out, trying to clear my mind before the day starts.

The workout helps—it always does. It's a way to keep everything in check, to control the things I can before I head into the chaos of the hospital.

My mind drifts once again to the email I got last night from Theo Bench, the head of research and development at the hospital. He asked me to collaborate on a pacemaker trial study they've been working on for years. I'm thrilled to be involved with something like this and honored he thought to include me.

He wants my input to push it over the finish line, to get it ready for FDA approval so we can start human trials. Being part of something like that, something that could change lives on a massive scale is exactly why I became a surgeon in the first place.

I've been involved in plenty of cutting-edge procedures and pioneering techniques that push the boundaries of what's possible. But this is something different. This is about creating something that could save thousands, maybe millions of lives, long after I'm gone. The idea of it sets my blood pumping harder than any workout ever could.

I grab a towel and wipe the sweat from my face, my mind already racing ahead to the late afternoon meeting I have with him after my last surgery.

I've got clinic patients to see first, a few routine cases, nothing too taxing. It's going to be a full day, but my brain shouldn't be too fried.

I've pushed myself just far enough this morning. Standing up, I grab the towel again, wiping the sweat from my face and neck before tossing it onto a nearby bench. I walk over to the mirror that spans one wall of the room, catching a glimpse of myself.

The reflection staring back at me is familiar—broad shoulders, defined muscles, the result of years of disciplined training, both physical and mental. But it's not just about staying in shape. It's about control, about having something in my life that I can command, something that's entirely mine.

My gaze drops to the ink covering my arms, dark lines and intricate designs that start at my wrists, wrap around my biceps and trail onto my chest and back. Most people don't know about the tattoos, I like to keep them to myself.

The tattoos are more than just art—they're my civil disobedience, a big middle finger to the life that was curated for me. I run a hand over the ink on my chest, tracing the familiar patterns. It's like armor, a shield I wear under my clothes, keeping the real me hidden from the world.

Outwardly, I play the game—I follow the rules, I do the work, and I deliver the results. But inside, there's always that simmering anger, that need to push back, to break the rules when I can get away with it. Occasionally I have to remind myself that I'm in control of my life, not anyone else.

Turning away from the mirror, I grab my towel and head for the shower. Today's another day for me to show up and do my thing. This new project has me excited, something new, something big. It's going to be a great day.

———

UAB HOSPITAL

10:47 *am*

THE ELEVATOR DOORS SLIDE OPEN, and I step inside, already running through the list of patients I've seen this morning. It's been a routine day so far, with no major surprises, but I could use a caffeine boost before the after-noon surgery.

I hit the button for the top floor, where the good coffee is, and lean back against the cool metal wall.

Just as the doors are about to close, a hand shoots out to stop them. The doors open again to reveal Shep Duncan, his familiar tall frame filling the space. He nods at me as he steps inside, his expression a mix of focus and mild irritation.

"Hunter," he greets me, and I give him a nod in return.

"Shep, brother, what's up?" Shep is a neurosurgeon here. We've been working side-by-side for years. I would consider him one of my good friends at the hospital.

"Got a second to talk about a patient?" he asks, his tone clipped, businesslike.

"If you can walk and talk. I'm heading up for a coffee," I reply, already mentally preparing for whatever discussion is about to unfold. "I've got a clinic patient in a few minutes."

"Sure," Shep agrees without hesitation, and we settle into the elevator's slow ascent.

"Who's the patient you want to talk about?" I ask, glancing at him as the numbers tick upward.

"Mrs. Falworth," he says, rubbing the back of his neck. "I know she's your patient for the arrhythmia, but she's been seeing me for some neuro issues—dizziness and a bit of memory loss. I'm thinking it might be related to her smoking, combined with her heart problems."

I stifle a groan. "Shep, I've told her a hundred times she has to stop smoking. That arrhythmia isn't going to get better if she keeps puffing away like a chimney."

Shep nods, his face grim. "I know. I've had the same conversation with her. She's not listening, though. I think it's more habit than anything at this point. She's in denial about what it's doing to her body."

"Denial or not, it's going to kill her if she doesn't quit," I snap, the frustration seeping into my voice. "We can treat her arrhythmia, but if she doesn't make some changes, we're just putting a Band-Aid on a bullet wound."

The elevator dings, and we step out into the hallway, heading toward the coffee shop. The smell of freshly brewed coffee greets us, and I make a beeline for the counter, Shep keeping pace beside me.

We start walking again, and I admit it, I feel a little bad about what I just said, but not enough to take it back. Some patients you can't reach. Either because they've developed destructive habits that they can't or won't break. Or because they're just incredibly stubborn and don't want to admit that someone else could be right.

"She's stubborn. I'll give her that," Shep continues, a hint of exasperation in his voice. "But if she's not going to quit, we need to figure out how to manage her symptoms before they get worse."

We start walking again and only make it about ten steps before we hear, "Good morning, gentlemen doctors." That accent could never be mistaken for anything other than Marijka, and it brings a smile to my face.

"Good morning, nurse," we say in unison, turning to face the lined but still-beautiful older Eastern European as she gazes at us from across her desk. It's not cluttered, it's not orderly, but it's somewhere in between. Marijka is our first-generation Mama Bear nurse who doesn't pull any punches.

"I trust my two little boy toys are on their way to something important, yes?"

"Always, Mama Bear," Shep chirps back. How is he always so fucking cheerful? I nod my head to her, holding equal affection, just not as syrupy in my delivery.

I order a black coffee and wait for Shep to finish ordering his before we find a spot to stand and talk. I have exactly three minutes. The hallway is relatively quiet, with just a few nurses and doctors passing by.

"She needs more aggressive treatment," I say, taking a sip of the hot coffee. "I think, at this point, we need to consider an ablation. It's not ideal, but it might be the only way to get that arrhythmia under control, which may help some of those neurological symptoms."

Shep nods thoughtfully, staring into his cup. "And on my end, I can monitor the neuro symptoms more closely, see if there's any direct correlation with her heart issues. Maybe if we can show her the connection between the smoking and the way she has zero energy, it'll be the wake-up call she needs."

I grunt, not entirely convinced. "Maybe. But I'm not holding my breath. We can only do so much, Shep. The rest is up to her."

He sighs, and for a moment, we both just stand there, sipping our coffee in silence. It's the same story with so many patients—doing everything we can to help them, only to watch them sabotage themselves. It's frustrating, but it's part of the job.

"Let's give it one more shot," Shep finally says. "We'll push for the ablation, and I'll keep hammering home the need to quit. If that doesn't work, well, we'll cross that bridge when we get to it."

"Agreed," I say, finishing the last of my coffee. "I'll talk to her about the procedure at her next appointment."

Shep gives me a curt nod. "Thanks, Hunter. I'll keep you in the loop on my end."

"Same here," I reply as we start walking back toward the elevators. "Good luck with her."

He smirks, but it's a weary one. "Yeah, I'll need it."

We part ways as the elevator doors close behind me, and I let out a long breath. Another day, another battle with patients who refuse to help themselves. But we keep fighting because that's what we do.

FIVE

Frankie

11:08 *am*

SITTING AT MY DESK, I'm surrounded by a sea of open files and papers, each one more critical than the last. The meeting with Dr. Bench and Hunter Parrish is later today, and I'm trying to make sure every detail is perfectly in place. The pacemaker trial is at a crucial stage, and this meeting could be the turning point that finally pushes it forward.

I glance at my screen, where an email draft to Hunter is open, the cursor blinking impatiently at me. It's just a simple follow-up that I'll send after the meeting this afternoon, but for some reason, I can't seem to find the right words.

"God, Frankie, are you actually emailing him?" Carly's voice breaks through my concentration. I turn to see her standing in the doorway, arms crossed, a teasing grin on her face. Her hair is still a little mussed from her nap on the sofa, but she looks as bright and energetic as ever.

I roll my eyes and lean back in my chair. "Carly, I already told you we're working together on this project. This is strictly business."

"Uh-huh, sure," she says, strolling over to my desk and peering at the screen. "Because business emails I write a draft and fuss over every single word and period. What are you saying? 'Dear Dr. Parrish, please give me a giant orgasm like you did last time'?"

"Ha ha," I deadpan, closing the laptop a little too quickly. "Yeah, just like that. You really have a way with words. So professional."

Carly flops down into the chair across from me, her grin not fading in the slightest. "Professional stuff, huh? Come on, Frankie, you can't tell me you're not at least a little bit flustered about working with him. I mean, the guy is like walking sex appeal with a stethoscope."

My cheeks warm slightly, and I quickly busy myself with straightening a stack of papers. "He's a surgeon, Carly. We have to work together. That's it. How he looks doesn't factor into any of it."

"Right," she drawls, clearly enjoying my discomfort. "And the fact that you guys slept together once has absolutely no effect on you?"

I shoot her a look. "Yep."

"Yeah, yeah, I know," she sighs, leaning back in the chair. "Just remember, Frankie, you're the boss in that room. You're the one with the expertise on this trial. Don't let his stupidly handsome face distract you from that."

I can't help but laugh at that, the tension easing just a little. "I won't. Trust me, I'm focused on the work. This project is too important to let anything—or anyone—distract me."

Carly smiles, softer this time. "I know you are. Just don't forget to take a breath, okay? You're going to do great."

"Thanks, Carly," I say, suddenly more grounded knowing her confidence in me. "I just need to get through this meeting, and then we'll see where things go from there. It's the unknown more than anything."

I lean over and pull the lighter out of the small drawer to light my lavender candle. Immediate peace descends on my anxious thoughts.

She stands up and stretches, clearly satisfied with our conversation. "Well, I'm going to go grab another coffee. Want one?"

I nod, grateful for the offer. "Yes, please."

As she leaves the room, I open my laptop again, staring at the email draft. I know Carly's right. I'm the expert on this trial, and I need to keep my focus on the task at hand. But as much as I try to convince myself that this is just another professional collaboration, I can't completely ignore the butterflies in my stomach at the thought of seeing Hunter again.

———

FIFE'S RESTAURANT

11:48 *am*

THE DINER IS BUSTLING with the lunchtime crowd, the clatter of dishes and hum of conversation creating a comforting background noise. Carly and I sit in our usual booth by the window, finishing up our meal.

She's been talking non-stop about the latest drama at the hospital, and I've been happily letting her fill the silence while I pick at the last of my salad. "So, what do you think?" Carly asks, suddenly shifting gears.

"About what?" I look up, realizing I've zoned out a bit.

"Dress shopping, duh!" she exclaims as if I should have been following along. "You have to come with me this afternoon. I need a second opinion."

I raise an eyebrow. "Isn't the gala still a month away?"

Carly rolls her eyes dramatically. "Frankie, you knuckle-head. It's just shy of three weeks away. May 25th. That's not a lot of time, and it's coming up fast. I need to find something soon. So do you! What if we need alterations? Or, what if we find the perfect dress but no shoes to match?"

I can't help but chuckle at her enthusiasm. "You fuss way too much about that kind of stuff. I'm just going to wear the same dress I wore last year. It fits, it got lots of compliments, and I don't have time to shop."

Carly looks at me like I've just suggested wearing a burlap sack. "You can't wear the same dress as last year! I don't care how fabulous it is. You need something new, something that makes you feel amazing."

I wave off her concern. "Carly, that's not really my style. I'm not going to stress over a dress. It's just one night. And, like I said, it's a lifetime away."

Carly crosses her arms, giving me a pointed look. "You'll never get a man with that attitude, you know."

I laugh, shaking my head. "Good thing I'm not interested in finding a man, then. God, you're something else. Do you think of anything else?"

She sighs, clearly exasperated with me. "Frankie, you're hopeless. But I love you anyway."

"Love you too," I reply with a grin. "But seriously, I can't go shopping with you, crazy person. Some of us have to work during the day, remember? And I have that big meeting this afternoon."

Carly pouts, but there's a twinkle in her eye. "Fine, but don't think you're getting out of this so easily. I'll find you the perfect dress, even if I have to drag you into a store kicking and screaming."

"Why don't you do that," I say dryly, standing up as we get ready to leave. "Find me the dress, buy it, and I'll Venmo you for the cost. You can be my personal shopper."

"Not a chance." Carly hands over her credit card for the tab, and I stuff a twenty in her bag. "Good luck with your meeting," she says, giving me a quick hug. "And don't let Dr. Hot Stuff distract you."

I roll my eyes again but smile. "I'll try not to."

We part ways, Carly heading off to whatever adventure she has planned for the afternoon while I head back to my office, mentally gearing up for the meeting ahead. I smile to myself. No matter how different we are, Carly always knows how to lighten my mood.

————

UAB HOSPITAL

5:14 *pm*

AS I WALK through the hospital's sliding doors, the familiar scent of antiseptic and the hum of activity hit me like a wave. Normally, it's comforting, a reminder that I'm in my element, where I belong. But today, there's an undercurrent of nerves that I can't quite shake.

My minds racing as I make my way to the elevator, my heels clicking softly against the hard, slick hospital floor. What is my problem? It's just a meeting, he's just a colleague.

I've had a thousand meetings before, and I've handled them all just fine. But this one is different. And this is exactly why you should never sleep with someone you work with.

I punch the button for the fifth floor, where our lab conference room is, watching the numbers light up as the elevator ascends. Maybe it's because I'm afraid Theo will be able to read all over my face that

Hunter had his dick inside of me in the room next door.

The night I've tried so hard to push out of my mind still has its claws in me. But it's not like I have feelings for him. We're both adults, and it was just one night. A momentary lapse in judgment, nothing more. Get it together, Frankie Renna. For fuck's sake.

My nervousness isn't about him—it's about the project. The pacemaker trial is something I've poured my heart and soul into for the last two and a half years. It's consumed me and driven me to push harder than I ever thought I could. That's all this is.

Hunter is a brilliant cardiothoracic surgeon, and his input could be the key to bringing everything together and seeing all my hard work come to fruition. This is a good thing. His expertise could be the missing piece we need to get FDA approval and make this trial a reality.

Protectiveness over the project! My apprehension isn't about the whole sex-with-Hunter thing at all. It's about his opinion—about whether he'll think my work is good enough, whether he'll see the potential I've been fighting so hard to bring to light.

I step out into the hallway, my stomach twisting into knots. What if he doesn't? What if he finds flaws I hadn't noticed, gaps I haven't filled? This project is everything to me, and the thought of it not being good enough, of me not being good enough, is terrifying.

Taking a deep breath, I remind myself that I've prepared for this. I know this project inside and out. I've put in the hours and done the research, and this is just another step in the process. I can't let my nerves get the best of me now.

As I approach the conference room, I force a smile, straightening my posture. It's just a meeting between colleagues, I've got this.

The familiar smell of whiteboard markers and the xylene solution used to prepare microscope slides lingers in the air. I take a deep breath and dive into getting everything set up. Where is my lavender candle when I need it?

First things first. I head to the projector, fishing my USB drive out of my bag. As I plug it in, I silently pray there won't be any technical hiccups. The last thing I need is for the presentation to crash right when we're getting started.

While the computer boots up, I pull out the printouts I've prepared for Hunter and Theo. I've gone over these a hundred times, making sure every detail is perfect. Carefully I place them in the men's seats, straightening the edges just so.

The projector whirs to life, and I pull up the presentation. Everything looks good and in order. I click through the slides, double-checking that all the animations and transitions are working smoothly.

Now for the hard part. I stand at the front of the room, running through the key points I want to discuss. "Okay, Frankie," I mutter to myself. "Start with the overview of the current pacemaker technology. Then move into the limitations we've identified."

I pace as I rehearse, gesturing to imaginary slides. "Highlight the improvements our design offers. Emphasize the potential impact on patient outcomes." My voice grows stronger as I go, my confidence building.

"Don't forget to mention the preliminary test results," I remind myself. "And make sure to stress the need for Hunter's surgical expertise in the next phase."

I'm so engrossed in my mental run-through that I blank out the sound of the door opening behind me.

"I got your surgical expertise."

I whip around to the source of the booming voice, and there stands Hunter in all of his fucking ridiculously handsome boyish looks glory.

SIX

Hunter

5:33 pm

WHEN I WALKED IN, I fully expected to see Theo Bench waiting for me with the usual stack of files and a laser focus on the pacemaker trial. Instead, I'm frozen in my tracks, because the person pacing the room isn't Theo. It's Frankie.

Goddamn.

For a second, I just stand there, stunned, trying to process what I'm seeing. She's muttering to herself—something about protocols and timelines and surgical expertise. She's completely absorbed in her thoughts.

She's not wearing her usual white lab coat. Instead, she's wearing a tight but professional pencil skirt that hugs her round, full curves, paired with a silk blouse that compliments the deep brown waves of her hair and those striking green eyes I remember all too well.

She's beautiful. Stunning, actually. And it hits me like a punch to the gut, knocking the wind out of me before I even have a chance to gather my thoughts. This caught me off guard. Seeing her again caught me off guard.

I step further into the room, trying to get a grip on myself, but my mind is spinning. Why the hell didn't Theo tell me she was involved in this project? I thought I was here to talk pacemakers and clinical trials, not to walk into a room with the one woman who's been occupying way too much space in my head for the past six months.

And now I just scared the shit out of her, breaking into her preparation with my smirky comment. She was too busy running through what looked like the entire agenda, flipping through files on the table, completely in her zone, to notice the door open.

I swallow hard, shoving down the nerves that are clawing their way up my throat. This isn't like me. I don't freak out. I don't get rattled. But Frankie, she's different. What the fuck?

"Hunter," she says, her voice a little winded, like she's also having to catch her breath. I'm sure I scared the shit out of her the way I came in and busted up in her preparation without her noticing my entrance.

"Frankie," I manage to get out, my voice sounding steadier than my legs at the moment. "I didn't realize you were part of this project."

She blinks, and for a moment, there's something in her eyes that stops me. Maybe it's nerves, or it could be something else. But she recovers quickly, straightening up and giving me a small smile. "Yes, this is *my* project. I've been running it for the past two-plus years. I thought you knew."

I shake my head, trying to wrap my mind around it. "Theo didn't mention it."

She nods slowly like she's processing that information, too. "Well, surprise, I guess." She holds up her hands dramatically and smiles. She's good, putting me at ease, diffusing my obvious discomfort.

I let out a breath, trying to dry my sweaty palms as I take a seat at the table. What I need is a minute to get myself together, to figure out how the hell I'm supposed to navigate this. I wonder if, at this point, it would be awkward to back out of my offer to assist with the trial.

She sits down across from me, and for a moment, we just look at each other, the air between us charged with something unspoken. I should be focusing on the project, on what this meeting is supposed to be about, but all I can think about is how close she is, how stunning she looks, and how utterly unprepared I am for this.

I clear my throat, trying to break the tension that's thick enough to cut with a scalpel. "Is Theo joining us?" I ask, my voice coming out a bit more clipped than I intend.

Frankie nods, her expression calm, unbothered. "Dr. Bench should be here any minute," she replies, glancing briefly at the door before turning her attention back to me.

She's composed, like this is just another routine meeting for her, while I'm sitting here like one of those dumbass newbie residents, fresh out of med school.

I lean back in my chair, trying to appear relaxed, but everything is off-kilter. I scramble for something to say, something to fill the silence. "How's, uh, everything going with the research?"

She smiles politely, that professional mask firmly in place. "It's going well. I think we are ready to soar. The data has been promising."

"Good," I grunt, nodding as I try to keep my thoughts straight. "That's great to hear."

There's a pause, the kind that stretches just a bit too long to be comfortable. "How about you?" she asks, her tone polite but distant. "How have you been? Recover from our collision Friday?"

"Busy," I reply, a little too sharply. "I don't stop, for the most part." Why didn't I keep with the lightness and comment on bumping into her on Friday? God, I'm such an idiot. All business and no play.

She nods, not missing a beat. "I bet."

The silence that follows is heavy, awkward. I should say something, but everything I can think of seems forced, like I'm trying to jam the wrong piece into a puzzle.

I'm not usually like this—small talk doesn't bother me, but right now, it's grating on my nerves. I am totally a fish out of water, and it's making me more irritated by the second. Where the fuck is Theo Bench?

———

TUESDAY, *May 7*

12:20 *pm*

. . .

I'M deep in the middle of charting, my focus narrowed to the screen in front of me when my phone buzzes on the desk. I glance at it and see a text from Jonah Bellinger, one of the few people who can pull me out of work mode.

Lunch in the cafeteria?

I check my watch. I've got some time before my next patient, so I shoot back a short reply.

Meet you in 5.

I finish up the note I'm working on, close out the chart, and push back my chair from my desk. It's been a long morning, and the idea of grabbing a quick bite with Jonah is a welcome break.

When I walk into the cafeteria, I spot him already seated with his tray, looking like he's just come off a double shift. I grab a burger, some steamed broccoli, and a bottle of water before making my way over to him.

"Hey," I say, sliding into the seat across from him.

"Hey, dickhead," Jonah replies, already halfway through his sandwich. "Busy morning?"

"Not too bad," I reply, taking a bite of my burger. We fall into the usual small talk, catching up on patient cases, hospital gossip, the kind of things that fill the gaps between surgeries and rounds.

After a few minutes, Jonah glances at me, a glint of curiosity in his eyes. "So, I heard you're working on a new research project. Something with Theo Bench?"

I nod, swallowing a mouthful of green beans. "Yeah, it's a pacemaker trial. They've been working on it for a couple of years, and Theo brought me in to help get it over the finish line to start the clinical trial."

"Sounds like a big deal," Jonah comments, taking a sip of his drink. "Who else is involved?"

I hesitate for a fraction of a second but quickly cover it up. "Frankie Renna. She's the lead researcher on the project."

Jonah raises an eyebrow, a slow grin spreading across his face. "Frankie Renna, huh? She's hot."

I shrug, trying to play it off like it's nothing. "She's good at what she does. The project's solid."But as I say it, I can't help the flash of memory that comes with her name. She's good at a lot more than research.

Jonah's grin turns a little wicked. "Come on, man. You've got to admit she's a knockout. And smart, too. The whole package."

I shake my head, trying to steer the conversation away from dangerous territory. "She's a colleague, Jonah. We're working together. That's it. You know we can't go there. Nothing but trouble."

But Jonah isn't letting it go. He leans in, his voice dropping to a conspiratorial tone. "We hardly see her. Not enough, if you ask me. I might have to tap that ass now that I think about it. She's got that whole sexy scientist thing going on."

A spike of irritation flares up inside me, but I keep my expression neutral, taking another bite of my burger to buy myself a moment. The idea of Jonah going after Frankie doesn't sit well with me, and that realization hits harder than I'd like. But I keep my mouth shut, knowing it's not my place to say anything.

Still, Jonah's eyes narrow, and I can tell he's picked up on the shift in my mood. "Whoa, hold up. Are you actually pissed I just said that? I was just kidding, dude."

I glare at him, more out of reflex than anything. "I'm not pissed, Jonah. Just saying we've got work to do, and I'm not looking to complicate things."

He chuckles, clearly enjoying this more than he should. "Uh-huh. Sure, that's all it is."

"Drop it," I snap, not in the mood to deal with his teasing right now.

"Alright, alright," Jonah says, holding up his hands in mock surrender, though the smirk on his face doesn't fade. "But seriously, Hunter, if you're not interested, maybe I should—"

"Jonah," I warn, my voice low and edged with a tone that tells him I'm not going there.

He laughs, shaking his head. "Relax, I'm just messing with you. But you might want to figure out what's got you so worked up before this project turns into a bigger headache than it needs to be."

I don't respond. Instead, I finish off the last of my green beans as my mind is already a mess of thoughts I don't want to untangle right now. Jonah's got a point, but that doesn't mean I'm ready to deal with it.

We finish lunch in relative silence, Jonah occasionally throwing me a look while I focus on getting through the rest of the meal without snapping at him again. I'm guessing he wishes he had invited someone else to join him.

By the time I get up to leave, I'm more than ready to get back to work. I'll gladly embrace anything to keep my mind off Frankie and whatever the hell is brewing under the surface.

———

3:01 *pm*

JILL, my assistant, buzzes through to my office, jolting me out of my focus on the documents about the pacemaker and all of the impressive strides Frankie has made in these studies in a relatively short time. "Yes," I answer, a little annoyed to be pulled away.

"Just a reminder, Doctor Parrish, that you have a three o'clock appointment with Mrs. Oppenstar. She's already here waiting for you in the front lobby."

"Great, send her into an exam room. I'll be right there."

"I've informed her, Sir. But, she insists that—"

"—I come to meet her in the lobby. Yeah, I remember. Thanks, Jill. Can you please inform the front I'll be right there?"

"Yes, Sir. So ten minutes?"

"Oh, you're funny."

Her girlish chuckle is cute, but it's kind of lost on me right now. "I'll let them know."

Did I mention that I really care about the people I work with? They're all sarcastic pains in the ass sometimes, but I appreciate the whole team.

Refocusing on what I was reading in Frankie's notes before being interrupted, I start to get a boner. Fucking hell. Better make that fifteen minutes, Jill.

Thankfully the hard-on goes away the moment I get to my feet. I give Jill a sarcastic smile on the way out, and she returns it right back. See, I'm not *all* grumpy all the time.

Mrs. Oppenstar was seventy-four when she first came to see me a little over a year ago. Her primary care doctor referred her after a routine check-up revealed something off with her heart. She had been becoming increasingly fatigued, short of breath, and had this persistent tightness in her chest that just wouldn't go away.

Tests confirmed what I suspected: severe aortic stenosis. Her aortic valve was narrowed, restricting blood flow from the heart to the rest of her body. It's a condition I see often in patients her age, but that doesn't make it any less serious. Without intervention, it would have continued to worsen, eventually leading to heart failure.

Surgery was the only option—a valve replacement. I've done it countless times, but every patient is different. And with someone like Mrs. Oppenstar, age and overall health add layers of complexity. We went over the risks, the benefits, and the expectations, and despite the gravity of it all, she remained calm and trusting.

The surgery went smoothly. I replaced her damaged valve with a new one, restoring the blood flow her body so desperately needed. But it's not just about the surgery for me. It's about what happens after. The recovery, the follow-ups, making sure my patients know they're not just case numbers on a chart.

Mrs. Oppenstar is one of those patients who reminds me why I do what I do. She is tough and resilient, and despite her age, she had a spark in her that made me want to fight even harder for her recovery.

Her makeup is on point, as usual, as is her sense of style. She is wearing a deep-blue sweatsuit that is no doubt the hottest item among her friends at her assisted care facility.

In truth, she's not bad-looking for a woman of seventy-five, and she's incredibly ambulatory.

But then again, I've never been the type to go for much older women, so being cordial and comforting with her is easy since I don't get the notion that she's wooed by my looks or youth, either.

Thank God for small favors.

"Hello, young man," she drawls as I make my way across the lobby. She's the picture of a quintessential grandmother: prim, proper, and ladylike to a tee. She's an old school Southern lady in modern times.

"Hello, Mrs. Oppenstar." I'm genuinely happy to see her. She gives me a wide smile when I approach her.

"Busy day, Doctor Parrish? You were a few minutes late by my watch."

"It's always busy when we least expect it, Mrs. Oppenstar," I reply. "They never let me rest, isn't that a shame?"

"Indeed, it is. Let me know who to speak for about that."

She reaches out gently with one hand for a lift. Being a gentleman, I offer her my hand as she expects. I've adopted her, in a way, as a sort of surrogate grandmother I never had.

As we walk toward the elevators, she regales me once again with everything that's been going on in her life. She loves her bridge and her grandchildren. These are subjects she never tires of telling me about.

SEVEN

Frankie

Saturday, May 18

TUPILANO *Boutique*

Mountainbrook Village

3:19 *pm*

I STAND in the middle of the boutique, completely out of my element. The racks of dresses surround me, all draped in silks and sequins, every shade of color imaginable.

Carly is buzzing around, pulling gowns off hangers with the enthusiasm of a kid in a candy store. I, on the other hand, am trying to remember why I let her talk me into this.

"This one, Frankie, you have to try this one!" Carly says, holding up a deep emerald dress that looks like it costs more than my mortgage. She practically shoves it into my arms before I can protest.

"Carly, this is a waste of time," I mutter, but she's already moved on, diving into another rack.

Shopping has never been my thing. Spending hours trying on clothes, especially ones that cost a small fortune, seems dirty to me. There are a million better things I could be doing with my time.

Besides, I'm not excited about this fancy party like Carly is. The only reason I'm even going is to woo potential sponsors for the pacemaker trial. That's it. The thought of spending the evening schmoozing wealthy benefactors is hardly thrilling, but it's necessary.

Carly, of course, has other ideas. She's convinced that she's going to meet her future husband—or at least a decent stand-in. She's boy-crazy, clothes-crazy, and just plain crazy sometimes, but I love her for it. She's good for me in that way.

I catch my reflection in one of the boutique mirrors, holding the emerald dress against myself. It's beautiful, but I can't help but think about how many other things I could do with the money it would cost. Still, I know Carly won't let me leave here without trying on at least a dozen dresses, so I head to the fitting room.

As I step into the dress and pull it up, I have to admit it's a good fit. The color brings out the green in my eyes, and the fabric clings in all the right places. I glance at myself in the mirror, and just as I'm about to shrug it off, Carly's pipes up from outside the fitting room.

"Let me see! I know that one's going to look amazing on you!"

I open the door, and Carly gasps, clapping her hands together. "Frankie, you look stunning! I knew that color would be perfect on you."

The shop attendant, who's been hovering nearby, nods in agreement. "Your skin tone is gorgeous, and your hair—so naturally wavy. You don't need much to look fabulous."

I smile politely, though inwardly, I'm rolling my eyes. Compliments are nice, sure, but I'm not here to be fawned over. I'm just trying to find something that will get Carly off my back.

As I turn in front of the mirror, Carly leans against the doorframe of the fitting room, watching me with a grin. "You know, Hunter Parrish is going to be at the gala," she says, her tone teasing.

I try not to let my expression change. "So?"

"So, you've been meeting with him a lot lately. How's that going, anyway? You never give me the juice I so desperately crave." She is clearly fishing for gossip, but she knows I'm about as exciting as the dress's hanger now lying on the floor.

I sigh, stepping back into the fitting room to try on another dress. "He's all business and a little moody," I tell her from behind the closed door as I shimmy out of the dress. "But he's really into the project. I have to admit, I'm impressed with how passionate he's gotten about it in such a short amount of time."

Carly chuckles. "Grumpy and passionate, huh? Sounds like the perfect combo."

"Don't start," I warn, pulling on a midnight blue dress. "He's just…really focused. And he's a damn good surgeon. You don't see that kind of dedication very often these days."

Carly peeks around the door, a mischievous glint in her eye. "That's not the only admirable thing about him, if you know what I mean."

I roll my eyes, even though she can't see me. "Yes, Carly, he's attractive. But that's not the point. Been there, done that, you know."

She laughs, leaning against the doorframe again. "Just saying. You're probably right to be leery of him. He's got a reputation. Thank goodness you're more sensible than I am."

I look at myself in the mirror again, considering her words. The green dress fits even better than the last one, and it somehow makes me feel more confident. Maybe this won't be such a waste of time after all.

"I know," I say, stepping out of the fitting room to show her the dress. "Hands-off. Strictly business."

"Good," Carly says, giving me an approving nod. "This is the dress. Now, let's find you the perfect shoes to go with it. We've got sponsors to impress and maybe a few hearts to break."

I laugh despite myself, shaking my head as we head to the cash register. I can't believe I'm buying this. She's a good saleswoman, I'll give her that. Maybe she's in the wrong line of work.

———

SAIGON NOODLE HOUSE

6:20 pm

I SINK into the chair at my favorite Vietnamese restaurant, suddenly aware I could fall asleep right here and now. Shopping all day has drained every ounce of energy from me, and I'm grateful to finally sit down and relax.

The warm, spicy aroma of Bún Bò Huế, my favorite dish, wafts through the air as the waitress places it in front me, bringing a small smile to my face despite my exhaustion. My mouth waters with anticipation.

Carly sits across from me, still buzzing with energy, even after dragging me through quite possibly every boutique in the city. She's scrolling through her phone, probably looking at more dresses or shoes, but I'm too tired to care.

"Thank you for today," I say, my voice coming out more tired than I intended. "Even though I spent way too much money, I appreciate you helping me."

Carly looks up and grins. "Of course! What are best friends for? Besides, you needed a new dress, and now you're going to look amazing so you can woo all of the rich guys to fund your trial. You know everyone falls for the hot scientist."

I smile back, feeling a pang of something deeper as I look around the cozy restaurant. "You know, this is something I wish my mom could have been here for. She would've loved shopping with you and me like this."

Carly's smile softens, and she reaches across the table to

squeeze my hand. "I know, Frankie. She would've had so much fun with us today."

The memories of my mom tug at my heart, a bittersweet ache that I've grown accustomed to but never fully shake. I glance down at the steaming bowl in front of me, the rich broth swirling with herbs and spices, and take a deep breath.

"It was a heart attack, right?" Carly asks gently, her tone cautious but caring.

I nod, picking up my chopsticks and stirring the noodles in my bowl. I pause for a second. "It was more complicated than that. But yeah, essentially, her heart failed, and it killed her. We were stuck with what was available back in twenty-twelve, and it wasn't enough. She was thirty-four, only six years older than I am now. As I approach that age, I realize more now than I did then, how young she was."

Tears well at the trough of my eyes as I think about how frustrating it was for me to know they couldn't do anything to save my mom, an otherwise vibrant and young woman with her life ahead of her. It still gets me everything I think about it.

Carly's brow furrows. "I didn't mean to pry. You don't have to explain if it's too much."

I shake my head. "No, it's okay. Awareness is key. Talking about it is how we advance research, how we save others. My mom had restrictive cardiomyopathy. Her heart muscle became too stiff, so it couldn't fill properly with blood. It led to heart failure."

Carly blinks. "I've heard of cardiomyopathy, but restrictive?"

"Yeah," I say, the weight settling in my chest as I talk about it. "It's rare. Her heart couldn't pump well enough, and by the time they figured out what was wrong, there wasn't much they could do. Back then it was so unknown and caught so late because of little research, the treatment options were almost nonexistent. It's why my passion now in research is on the heart. I want to make sure people don't go through what she did."

"Wow, I've known you all these years and I had no idea how this all unfolded for you. As a nurse, it is so frustrating when we have sick patients that we can do nothing for and we know it. It must be ten times worse when it's your mom."

I swallow the lump in my throat and take a sip of the broth, letting the warmth soothe me. "It is. It's hard not to think about what could have been. Knowing what I know now, there are procedures that might have saved her, or at least given her more time. But back then we didn't know."

Carly puts her hand on mine. "You're an amazing scientist and daughter. I know your mom is so proud of you."

I nod, as the familiar surge of determination rises in me. "I can't bring her back, but if my work saves even one person, it'll be worth it."

Carly doesn't say anything for a moment, just lets me sit with my thoughts as I take another bite of the noodles.

The flavors filling the place are rich and comforting, like home cooking, reminding me of the way the aromas of my mother's cooking filled the house. This gives new meaning to the phrase "comfort food."

We sit in comfortable silence for a while, just enjoying the food and the warmth of the restaurant. Moments like these remind me how important it is to have someone like Carly in my life—someone who understands, who doesn't push too hard but knows when to be there. She's a good friend, and I'm lucky to have her.

I start to tell her about the letter I got from my father last week, but I don't have the energy to go into all of that with her right now. I'm still not sure what I am going to do about it. My instinct is to do nothing, but with only one surviving parent and no siblings, there is a tiny part of me that wants to see if there is even a tiny connection there before he is gone, too.

Maybe we can choose our families. Carly is my family—I don't need to reach out to a man who abandoned me for over fifteen years, who only reaches out because he knows his time is limited and he some guilt he wants to assuage.

As we finish our meal, a sense of peace settles over me. The day might have been exhausting, but this moment, this connection with Carly, makes it all worth it. I'm grateful to have a friend that lets me bring my mom up and have a piece of her here with us.

We pay the bill and head out into the evening, the cool air a refreshing change from the warmth of the restaurant. As we walk back to the car, we lock arms. Finishing up a successful, full day together, even if we spent it shopping, brings me a deep sense of satisfaction.

7:42 *pm*

. . .

THE WATER IS STILL warm after a long bath. The scent of lavender and eucalyptus fill the bathroom as I sink deeper into the tub. It's been a full day. Shopping with Carly, trying on dress after dress, and then dinner that left me both physically full and emotionally spent... I've had enough extrovert activities to fill an entire month for me.

Now, in the quiet of my house, I can finally let the tension melt away. The Epsom salts soothe my tired muscles, and I close my eyes, letting the soft flicker of the candle and the calming fragrance of essential oils wash over me. This is my sanctuary, the one place where I can shut out the world and just be.

I stay there for a while, soaking in the silence until the water starts to cool. Reluctantly, I sit up, reaching for the towel I've draped over the side of the tub. The air is cooler than the water, and a slight shiver runs through me as I step out and wrap the towel around myself.

Just as I'm about to blow out the candles, there's a knock on the door.

I freeze, my heart skipping a beat. It's Saturday night, and I'm not expecting anyone. Who would be stopping by at this hour? For a moment, I consider ignoring it, but the knock comes again, a little more insistent this time.

Quickly, I slip into my robe, tying it tightly around my waist as I head toward the door. My wet hair drips onto the floor, leaving a trail behind me, but I barely notice. My mind is racing, trying to figure out who it could be.

I press my eye to the peephole, squinting to get a better look at the figure standing on the other side. When I see who it is, my breath catches in my throat.

It's him.

I only recognize him because of the commercials for his used car business—the same ones that play during late-night TV, with his face plastered all over them. The man standing at my door, the one I haven't seen in person since I was barely a teenager, is my father.

My hands shake as I back away from the door, my mind reeling. What is he doing here? At this hour? I'll give him one thing, he sure has gotten persistent. That would have been helpful when I was a kid.

Another knock, this one softer, almost hesitant.

I swallow hard, the knot in my stomach tightening as I try to make sense of what's happening. My father—this stranger—standing at my door on a Saturday night.

I don't know what to do, what to say. A thousand thoughts race through my mind, but I can't seem to focus on any of them. All I know is that everything I thought I'd buried, everything I thought I'd moved on from, is suddenly right in front of me, waiting on the other side of that door.

But I need to know why he's here before I call the cops.

EIGHT

Hunter

Monday, May 20

UAB Hospital

5:08 *pm*

IT'S BEEN a day that feels twice as long as the hours say it's been. Finishing my last appointment for the day, a routine post-op check-up that went smoother than expected when my phone buzzes in my pocket. I pull it out and see a message from Frankie.

> Still on for this evening? I'm pulling up to UAB now.

I can't help but smirk. Even though today was slower than usual, I know our meeting isn't going to be a cake walk. Working with Frankie has been interesting, to say the least.

The tension between us is like a live wire, buzzing with every interaction. And the more time we spend together, the harder it is to ignore.

> Yeah. Meet me in the lab room in 30?

I tuck the phone back into my pocket and head toward the elevator. Even though all I want to do is sit in my apartment and sip on an expensive scotch and do nothing, I'm not about to let that stop me from getting some genuine work done on this project.

The pacemaker trial is at a critical stage, and while my surgical schedule usually means late meetings, I'm not complaining. If anything, it's an outlet outside of my normal surgeries and patients.

The lab is quiet when I get there, the usual hum of the hospital replaced by the muffled sounds of the evening shift taking over. Frankie must have made another stop before coming because I beat her here.

I set up my laptop and start pulling up the files we'll need, trying to focus on the task at hand. Against all my efforts not to, my mind keeps wandering back to the last time I was in here with Frankie.

Our meetings have all been in the conference room. We are meeting here to look at some of her slides in person. I didn't prepare for the sense of déjà vu I'd have coming in here again. Damn, this woman should be paying me rent. She is taking up that much space in my head.

She walks in a few minutes later, looking as composed as ever. She arrives with her hair pulled back, dressed in her usual professional attire with a skirt peeking out of the bottom of her lab coat. The soft lighting catches the warmth in her eyes. I shake off these thought as she sets her things down and sits across from me.

"Long day?" she asks, a hint of a smile tugging at the corner of her lips.

"Not too bad," I reply, leaning back in my chair. "Slower than usual, but it seems like I've been here forever. I actually had time to breathe today. Only four routine surgeries."

"That's rare for you," she says, flipping through some notes. "Maybe that's why you actually aren't scowling tonight."

I raise an eyebrow. "I don't scowl," I say as I scrunch my forehead.

"If you say so, Mr. Grumpy Pants."

"Who says I'm grumpy?"

She looks up, her smile widening. "Literally everyone."

I let out a short laugh, shaking my head. "I'm just focused. There's a difference."

"Is that what you call it?" she teases, but there's a lightness in her tone that makes it hard not to smile back.

We get to work, diving into the data that's come in from the latest tests. The pacemaker is showing promise, but there are still a few hurdles we need to clear before we can move forward. Frankie is meticulous, pointing out details I might have missed, and I have to admit, her attention to detail is impressive.

As we go over the results, we shift the conversation to the technical aspects of what we will explore in the trial: how the pacemaker interacts with different heart conditions, and how we will monitor and chart the potential side effects.

It's fascinating work, the kind that reminds me why I love exploring and learning about how the heart works, and why, sometimes, it doesn't. But the more we talk, the more I realize how much I enjoy these moments with her—how much I look forward to our meetings, even when they're late and I'm exhausted.

"Okay, so if we adjust the algorithm to account for variable heart rates, we might be able to reduce the risk of arrhythmias post-implantation," Frankie says, tapping her pen against the table thoughtfully. "This was a big issue with our animal trials."

I nod, leaning in to look at the data on her screen. "That makes sense. But we'll need to test it thoroughly before we make any changes to the protocol. The last thing we need is for this to backfire in human trials."

"Agreed," she says, meeting my gaze. There's a moment of silence, the air between us thick with unspoken tension. It's like we're both waiting for something, though I'm not sure what.

"So, you think you can handle more evening meetings like this?" I ask, breaking the silence with a smirk. "It would be hard to cover all of this during day, although I can carve out little bits of time here and there."

She arches an eyebrow. "I'm not the one with the packed surgery schedule. Can you handle it?"

"Touché," I reply, chuckling. "But seriously, this project is important. I'm in it for the long haul."

Her expression softens, and for a second, I see something in her eyes that I can't quite place. "I know you are. And I appreciate it. This trial… it means a lot to me. This has been my main focus for over two years. You know, that night you came by…"

The mention of that night, the elephant in the room, is like stepping on a land mine.

"Those slides I showed you, they were from the animal subjects in this trial."

"Oh, I had no idea. That is cool, how things have come full circle."

What the fuck am I saying? I'm trying to be suave, but everything I say, every twitch of my eye, every clearing of my throat makes me seem like a complete novice.

There's a weight to her words, something deeper than just professional dedication. I want to ask her more, to dig into what's really driving her, but I hold back. This isn't the time, and I'm not sure I'm ready to cross that line with her.

Instead, I nod and say, "Now that I know the context, I'll have to take another look."

She smiles, and it's genuine, the kind of smile that makes my chest tighten just a little. "Of course. You can come by any time, even if I'm not here. I've got everything cataloged and painstakingly labeled."

With that, we dive back into the work. The banter between us lightens the mood, but the underlying tension never really goes away. It's there in the way our shoulders brush when we both lean over the data, in the way her gaze lingers on me a fraction too long, in the way my pulse quickens whenever she's near.

By the time we wrap up, it's late, and the hospital has settled into its nighttime quiet. I pack up my things, as does Frankie. The easy conversation from earlier gives way to a comfortable silence.

Walking out of the conference room together, I get the strong sense that something's shifting between us. It's subtle, but it's there in the way she looks at me, in the way I can't stop thinking about her.

I'm not sure where this is going, but for now, I'm content to let it unfold. One late-night meeting at a time.

———

TUESDAY, *May 21*

8:41 am

Hands in my pockets, I speed walk down the hall to grab a coffee after wrapping up a meeting when I spot Jonah Bellinger coming out of one of the ORs. He looks exhausted, which isn't unusual after surgery. There's something in his expression that tells me it didn't go as smoothly as he would've liked.

"Jonah," I call out, and he glances up, his shoulders sagging a little with the weight of whatever just happened. "Somebody kick your ass in there?"

"Hunter," he replies, offering a tired smile. "Just the man I wanted to see. You should see the other guy."

I slow my pace as I approach him, catching the tightness around his eyes. "Everything alright?"

He lets out a long breath as he joins me on my walk. "Had a complication during the surgery. The patient's heart started to go into atrial fibrillation halfway through. Threw off the whole rhythm of the operation."

Atrial fibrillation—an irregular, often rapid heart rate that can cause poor blood flow. It's a common enough issue, but during surgery, it can be a real nightmare. "Did you manage to stabilize them?"

We both get on the elevator together and I push eleven. He nods his head indicating he is going to the same.

"Yeah, eventually," Jonah says, leaning against the wall as if he needs the extra support. "But it took longer than it should have. I used amiodarone, but it didn't work as quickly as I expected. By the time we got the heart rate under control, we were already behind. I can't help thinking there might have been a better way to handle it."

I nod, understanding his frustration. "Amiodarone is a good first line, but in the middle of surgery, you don't always have time to wait for it to kick in. Next time, consider using an intraoperative cardioversion if the patient's stable enough. It's quicker and can reset the heart rhythm almost immediately."

Jonah's brow furrows as he absorbs the information. "Intraoperative cardioversion... Why didn't I think of that?"

"It's not always the first thing that comes to mind, especially when you're focused on the surgery itself," I reply, trying to reassure him. "But it's a good tool to have in your back pocket when you're dealing with something like this."

He nods slowly, his expression thoughtful. "I'll keep that in mind. That's a good one to file away. Thanks, man."

"No problem," I say, giving him a pat on the shoulder. "It happens to the best of us. And while you're the worst of us…"

"Nice one."

We make our way to the top floor, both of us in need of a caffeine boost for the morning. We grab our coffees from the counter and head out to the balcony, where the warm May air hits us like a wall. Even up here, with the breeze, it's going to be a scorcher—another reminder that summer in Birmingham is already here.

We lean against the railing, the city sprawled out below us, the hum of traffic barely audible from this height. I take a sip of my coffee, letting the bitter warmth wake me up a little more.

Jonah glances at me, a smirk playing on his lips. "So, you bringing a prostitute to the to the gala? Figured that's the only way you'll get a date."

"Hilarious. That's your style not mine, remember?"

"I just asked that hottie I've taken out a few times that I told you about. It's nothing serious, but it's always fun to get dressed up with a looker on your arm."

I shrug, not having given it much thought. "Funny you should ask. I hadn't really planned on it, but Theo Bench cornered me this morning. Apparently, there are going to be several potential sponsors there, and I need to be on my A game to try to help secure funding for this trial."

Jonah nods, taking a sip of his own coffee. "Makes sense. So, you should probably take someone who knows the ins and outs of the project as well as you do. If you know what I mean?" He waggles his eyebrows as he says it.

I snigger, sensing where he's going with this. "And who is that, oh, sage one?"

"Frankie," he says without hesitation. "Duh! She's been leading this thing from the start, right? Plus, she's easy on the eyes. Win-win."

I chuckle, shaking my head. "It's a gala, Jonah, not foreplay."

He grins, clearly not taking me too seriously. "Maybe not for you. Regardless, it wouldn't hurt to double-team your prospects. With your looks alone, you might scare them off. Add in her beauty, and boom, you close the deal."

I take another sip of my coffee, considering his suggestion, however sophomoric it is. He's not wrong. Frankie knows this project inside and out, and having her there could give us an edge when it comes to convincing potential sponsors to open their checkbooks.

"Maybe you're right," I finally say, glancing out over the city. "It could be a good move, my brawn and her beauty."

Jonah nods, satisfied. "If you call that dad bod brawn, sure. But, don't forget, she's smart, too. Trust me, man. You two make a good team. Just make sure you're on the same page before you walk into that room. You don't want any surprises."

"Good advice," I admit, even if the thought of spending more time with Frankie outside of the hospital gives me pause. But this is about the project, about securing the funding we need to take it to the next level. I can handle that. We both can.

As we finish our coffee, the heat settling into our skin, I can't help but think that this gala might end up being more interesting than I originally anticipated.

NINE

Frankie

9:17 *am*

THE SOUND of the mail slot creaking open breaks through the silence of my house, followed by the soft thud of envelopes hitting the floor. I barely register it at first, my eyes being glued to the screen, absorbed in the latest data analysis for the pacemaker trial. But the sound lingers in my mind, a subtle reminder that the outside world still exists beyond the endless stream of numbers and charts.

I sigh, rubbing my temples as I push back from the desk. I've been at this for hours, and my brain is starting to turn into mush. A break wouldn't hurt.

With that I head to the front door, bending down to scoop up the small stack of mail. It's the usual assortment of bills and junk, but one envelope catches my eye, stopping me cold. The handwriting on the front is neat, almost too careful, and my stomach flips as I recognize it. It's the same handwriting as the letter from my father that arrived over a week ago.

Immediately, my heart starts to race, the blood pounding in my ears. My hands grow clammy as I stare at the envelope, a wave of nausea washing over me. What does he want now?

When he made his impromptu Saturday night visit, I told him stopping by wasn't appropriate. When he asked if he could come in to talk for a minute I told him it wasn't a good time. I might have been more apt to let him come in if I weren't dripping wet, but I guess in fairness, I haven't been very welcoming in his other attempts to reach me.

I have an urge to tear it open, to see what he has to say. At the same time, I'm terrified of what I might find inside. I can't breathe properly, my chest tightening with anxiety. It's like all the emotions I've tried to bury since his visit are suddenly clawing their way to the surface, demanding to be felt.

Before I can decide what to do, my phone buzzes in my pocket, pulling me back to the present. I fumble for it, grateful for the distraction.

> Off work. Can I stop by before I crash? Desperate for a nap but could use some company first.

I take a shaky breath, my fingers trembling as I type out a reply.

> Please do. I could use a break, too.

A small sense of relief washes over me the moment I hit

send. Carly's timing couldn't be better. I need to get out of my own head, and she's always been good at helping me do that.

I place the unopened letter on the kitchen counter, trying to ignore the way it seems to stare back at me, taunting me with the unresolved pain it represents. I'll deal with it later. Right now, I just need to breathe.

Then I tidy up the living room, trying to focus on something—anything—other than the knot of anxiety twisting in my gut. Carly will be here soon, and I can push this aside for a little while longer. But even as I straighten the cushions on the couch, I can't help but glance at the letter again, my heart still pounding in my chest.

The knock comes quicker than I expect. I forgot to take off the deadbolt. Normally, Carly doesn't knock. Essentially, I have a roommate without the benefit of shared expenses.

"Hey, girl," she says, her voice tired but cheerful. "You look like you could use some fresh air."

I manage a smile, grateful for her presence. "That obvious, huh?"

Carly steps inside and hangs her purse on the hook just inside the door that used to hold my beloved Pokey's leash. "I've been cooped up in that freezing hospital all night. What do you say we go for a quick walk while it's still nice out? I need to feel the sun on my face before I pass out for the next twelve hours."

The idea of leaving the house, of putting some distance between myself and that letter, is suddenly incredibly appealing. "That sounds perfect, actually. Let me just grab my shoes."

As I slip on a pair of sneakers, Carly stretches her arms above her head, yawning. "You wouldn't believe the night I had. Three traumas in the ER, back-to-back. I swear, full moons bring out all the crazies."

I laugh, grateful for the distraction. "Well, you can tell me all about it on our walk. Maybe it'll help take my mind off... things."

Carly raises an eyebrow but doesn't push. That's one of the things I love about her—she knows when to pry and when to let things be. "Sounds like a plan. Come on, let's get out of here before I change my mind and fall asleep on your couch."

As we step outside, the early morning air is crisp and refreshing, although it is already pretty hot for so early. I take a deep breath, letting go of some of the tension when I exhale. Carly links her arm through mine as we start down the sidewalk, and I'm struck by a wave of affection for my friend. She may not know it, but her spontaneous visit is exactly what I needed.

The sun is making its way up, blaring directly at eye level as Carly and I step out onto the sidewalk. The air is thick with the promise of summer heat, but there's a slight breeze that makes it bearable. Carly stretches her arms above her head, letting out a content sigh.

"God, it's amazing to be outside," she says. "I swear, those hospital walls start to make you stir crazy after a while. I crave outside air."

I nod, though my mind is elsewhere, the letter from my father still weighing heavily in my thoughts. I'm trying to shake it off, to focus on the walk and the company, but it's not working.

Carly glances at me, picking up on my distraction. "You okay, Frankie? You've been awfully quiet since I got here."

I force a smile. "Just tired, I guess."

She gives me a sideways look, clearly not buying it. "Tired, huh? You sure you're not just sulking because you didn't get that dress at half off?"

I let out a small laugh, but it's hollow. "Yeah, that must be it."

We walk in silence for a few more minutes, the sound of our footsteps the only noise between us. Carly keeps sneaking glances at me, and I can sense her curiosity growing. Finally, she stops and turns to me, her expression more serious.

"Alright, spill it. What's going on? You're not yourself today. I'm not buying what you're selling about being tired. Cut the bullshit."

I hesitate, the words catching in my throat. Part of me doesn't want to talk about it, doesn't want to admit that he's getting to me. But the other part of me is tired of holding it all in, of pretending like everything is fine when it's not.

"It's my father," I finally say, my voice barely above a whisper.

Carly's eyes widen in surprise. "Your father? What about him?"

I take a deep breath, the emotions bubbling up inside me as I try to find the right words. "He showed up at my door. Saturday night, after we got back from dinner."

Carly's mouth drops open. "He what? Why didn't you tell me?"

I shake my head, the memory of that night still vivid. "I didn't know how to tell you. I didn't even know how to process it myself. It's been years since I laid eyes on him, Carly. The last time I saw him I was still wearing jelly shoes and listening to NSYNC."

"Holy shit, Frankie. What did he want?"

"I don't know," I admit, appreciating the sting of the truth. I refused to let him in. I just… panicked. I was at a loss of what to say or do. Fresh out of the tub, I was in a robe, and it was late. That's not all—he's been trying to call me for a few months and he sent me a letter."

Carly is silent for a moment, processing everything. "Wait, so tell me again. I know you weren't close with your father, or basically had no relationship with him. But what happened? I mean, if you want to share. You can slap me and tell me to mind my own business if you want."

We find a bench just ahead under a large magnolia tree. I pull Carly with me and we sit down. This could take a while.

I swallow hard. The anger and hurt I've been holding back rises as I find the right words. "He left us. He left my mom when she was pregnant with me and went off to live his own life. My mom was a young, single mother, struggling to make ends meet while he went on with his life, probably not giving us a second thought. He made a few pathetic attempts to connect with me when I was little, but it was never more than a few visits. I never knew what to say to him, and he never tried hard enough to be a part of my life."

"Why now? After all this time?"

Carly listens, her expression softening as I continue. "I haven't heard from him in over a decade, not a single word after my mom died. And now, out of nowhere, he sends me a letter telling me he's dying and wants to make amends."

"He sent you a letter?! Like, in the mail?"

The tears well up in my eyes as the pain of his abandonment hits me all over again. "Yes, a couple of weeks ago, but I just tossed it. I didn't want to deal with it. But he's being persistent and he's wearing me down. So he stopped by Saturday and now I have a new letter, one I haven't opened."

Carly looks at me with a mix of shock and sympathy. "Frankie, why didn't you tell me sooner? I'm so sorry you've been dealing with this all by yourself. This isn't something you can just ignore. I mean, hearing from your estranged father who's sick... that's heavy."

With a trembling voice, I wipe away a tear that slips down my cheek. Dealing with it was the last thing I wanted to do. I've spent my whole life trying to forget him, to move on. But now, he's back, and I don't know what to do."

Carly reaches out and takes my hand, her grip firm and reassuring. "Frankie, you don't have to decide anything right now. But maybe it would be good to talk to him. To at least hear what he has to say."

I shake my head, the thought of letting him back into my life terrifying. "I don't know if I can, Carly. He hurt us so much. I don't know if I can forgive him."

"I know," Carly says gently. "And I'm not saying you have to. But maybe this is a chance for you to get some closure, to say the things you never got to say before. It might be healing, for you."

The tears are falling freely now, and I don't bother to stop them. Carly pulls me into a hug, holding me tight as I let out all the pain and anger I've been holding inside for so long.

"I'm here for you," she whispers. "Whatever you decide, I'm here."

I nod against her shoulder, receiving the weight of her words. I'm not ready to make a decision yet, but for the first time, I'm seeing that maybe I can find a way to let him in. Even if it's just to say, "fuck you, you bastard."

"Thank you. That means a lot. I'm sorry I got all snotty on you."

We both laugh as Carly fake-wipes her shoulder.

"Come one. Let's get moving. I have to work, and you have to laze around all day."

"Good point." With that, we stand up and head back. It's freeing to have gotten that out. I realize I have been holding all of this in, trying to will it away. But I needed to talk, to process it out loud.

———

10:41 *am*

Frankie: Please give me fifteen minutes. I

can't give up, but if you'll meet with me and you want me to leave you alone after that, I will. Please.

205-634-1144

Dad

GODDAMMIT. I throw the letter in the trash can and walk out of the kitchen. It's time to get back to work. I've procrastinated enough this morning.

The familiar glow of my computer screen is a comforting sight after the annoyance of having to deal with this bull-shit drama. After reading it, diving into data is a welcome a relief—something solid, something that makes sense that fits neatly in a chart. I scroll through the latest results, noting patterns and anomalies, my mind slowly settling back into its usual rhythm.

Then, my email pings, the sound sharp in the quiet room. I glance at the corner of the screen where the notification pops up, and my breath catches when I see the sender.

Hunter Parrish.

I open the email, and as I read his words, I encounter that same inexplicable flutter in my chest I seem to get when-ever anything Hunter Parrish-related comes my way. He's telling me he identified some risks that he wants to run by me. He has everything listed, but the words are all running together.

My frustration is rising. This is why Theo wanted to bring him in. It doesn't make it any easier when I feel like I have to defend my work.

Even with my defensiveness, I have an affection for Hunter's mind and compassion in this space. He is truly a dynamic surgeon with so much knowledge about the personal side when all I look at are the lab markers.

I shouldn't let myself get this way; I know that. There's no reason for it, and yet... my heart skips a beat, and my pulse quickens. Am I angry or giddy? Apparently, the two emotions are indistinguishable for me at this juncture.

Why does he have this effect on me?

I lean back in my chair, staring at the screen, trying to figure it out. My logical brain knows there's nothing between us—there can't be, and I don't want there to be. We're colleagues, and that's where it needs to stay. But he has this way of getting under my skin, of inducing things in me I can't quite define.

I take a deep breath and start to type out a reply. Then I erase it, not quite sure how I want to come back. I know we need to address his concerns, but he can wait a minute while I figure out how, exactly.

My heart is still fluttering annoyingly in my chest. I tell myself it's just the residual tension from talking about my father, from the emotional weight of that conversation with Carly. It has nothing to do with Hunter. It can't.

Shaking off the thought, I return to the data I was reviewing before he so rudely interrupted me.

TEN

Hunter

UAB Hospital

3:56 pm

BACK IN MY OFFICE, I'm poring over research and trying to figure out what else I'm not seeing when it comes to this study. I finished my cases almost an hour ago, but I'm staying around to hopefully meet up with Frankie and review my concerns.

She replied to my email saying she would be in around 4:30 today. She didn't comment either way about what I said in my message to her, so I'm not sure what her position will be. But I'm confident in my concerns, so how she perceives what I said is irrelevant to me.

When I realize I have a little more time to kill, I pick up the phone to reach out to my mother's doctors to discuss my concerns about this strain of Hodgkins. I don't want to inject myself there for so many reasons, but it is eating me alive.

She doesn't understand what I'm trying to get from her and it appears her doctors either aren't aware of this, or aren't putting in the time to address her situation fully. I know if I call, they will be more on top of things. But that will open a whole hornet's nest I'm not sure I'm ready for.

I hang up the phone after thinking better of it and try to come up with a plan. The last thing I need to do it go into it all hari-kari.

The data from Frankie's trial is spread out in front of me, a sea of numbers and charts that I've been combing through for the past hour.

My attention-deficit disorder brain goes back to this.

There are some things that don't quite add up, a few red flags that need to be addressed before we move forward. My mind is already running through how I'm going to bring it up to her without sounding like an ass.

A soft knock on the door shakes me out of my madness. I look up to see Jill, my assistant, poking her head in. She's holding a folder, her usual end-of-the-day stack of paperwork for me to sign off on.

"Hey, Jill," I say, leaning back in my chair. "You heading out?"

"Yeah, just about," she replies, stepping into the room. "But I wanted to drop this off first. It's the updated schedule for next week's surgeries, and there are a few things that need your signature."

I nod, reaching out to take the folder from her. As I flip it open, Jill lingers by the door, shifting her weight from one foot to the other. There's something on her mind.

"What's up?" I ask, glancing up from the papers.

She hesitates for a second before speaking. "I saw the email come through about the meeting with Dr. Renna later today. Do you need me to print out anything for it? I noticed there were some revisions to the protocol that came in earlier."

I pause, considering her question. I had asked her to pull some of the initial data last week, and she's been helping me keep track of the revisions as they come in. But there's something about the way she mentions Frankie that catches my attention—like there's more she's not saying.

"Yeah, actually, could you print out the latest version? And the revised charts, too," I say, watching her closely.

"Of course," she replies, turning to leave. But just before she steps out, she glances back at me, a thoughtful look on her face. "Dr. Renna seems really dedicated to this trial. I know that is her MO."

Her words hang in the air for a moment, and I can't help but wonder what she's getting at. "She is," I agree, waiting for her to elaborate, wondering where she is going with this.

Jill gives me a small smile, but there's something else in her eyes—something almost like concern. "Just make sure you're on the same page with her, Dr. Parrish. These things can get complicated if there are misunderstandings."

And with that, she's gone, leaving me alone with my thoughts. I stare at the door for a moment, her words echoing in my mind. Jill's usually straightforward, so when she drops hints like this, I know there's something behind them.

I watch the closed door after Jill left my office, her words lingering in the air like a storm cloud that won't dissipate. I can't shake the notion that she knows something I don't, and it's grating on me.

What exactly does she mean by that warning about Frankie? I'm not one to let things slide, especially when it concerns my work, and this trial is too important to leave anything to chance.

I stand up, the chair scraping against the floor, and follow her out into the hallway. She's just down the corridor, gathering her things from her desk, clearly ready to head out for the day. I quicken my pace, my curiosity getting the better of me, and call out before she can slip away.

"Jill, hold up."

She turns, surprised to see me, her bag slung over one shoulder and her keys in hand. "Dr. Parrish? Is everything alright?"

I stop in front of her, crossing my arms. "What exactly were you referring to back there, about Frankie Renna? Dr. Renna."

Jill hesitates, her eyes flicking to the side before meeting mine again. "I was just saying that Dr. Renna is very... I think particular is the right word. She is very possessive about her work and doesn't like anyone interfering or questioning her methods."

I narrow my eyes, not satisfied with the vague explanation.

"Particular? That's not what it sounded like. You're worried about something. Don't hold back."

She exhales, looking uncomfortable, but I can tell she's weighing whether or not to say more. Finally, she speaks. "There was an incident a while back. I made a comment—honestly, I didn't think it was a big deal—but it set her off. She was working on a study, and she felt I overstepped by suggesting a different approach. It got heated."

"Heated?" I repeat, raising an eyebrow.

"Let's just say she's very protective of her studies, Dr. Parrish. She doesn't take kindly to anyone trying to tell her how to do her job, even if they're just trying to help. And you… well, you're not exactly the type to back down if you think something's wrong."

I process this, understanding now why Jill was so cryptic. Frankie's possessiveness over her work and my own dogmatic tendencies could be a volatile combination, especially if we're not careful.

Jill's warning isn't just about Frankie—it's about the potential clash between us, one that could jeopardize the trial if it's not managed properly. We are two people with strong convictions.

"I see," I say slowly, my mind already spinning with the implications. "Thanks for the heads up."

Jill nods, looking relieved that I've taken her concern seriously. "It's just I know you well enough, I hope I'm not overstepping my bounds by saying something. I know you care about this trial. I can see the way you have jumped in. And I know she must, too, just knowing the little I do about her. I'd hate for things to go sideways, you know?"

"I know," I reply, though my thoughts are already ahead, trying to anticipate how my meeting with Frankie is going to go. "I'll keep that in mind."

Jill gives me a small, tight-lipped smile before turning to leave.

Her warning plays in a loop in my head, making it hard to focus. I tap my fingers on the desk, glancing at the clock. It's almost time for my meeting with Frankie. The issues are minor, but they're there, and I want to make sure we're on solid ground before we push forward. Now, as I head to her office for our meeting, I'm curious to see how she'll respond.

When I step into Frankie's office, she's already sitting at her desk, the same calm, composed look on her face that I've come to expect. But there's something in her eyes—something sharp and focused—that tells me she's ready for this conversation.

"Dr. Parrish," she greets me, gesturing to the chair across from her. "I've had a chance to review your concerns."

"Hunter. Please." It seems silly I have to say that. I had my dick in her not even two hundred feet from here. We are professionals, I get it. But we don't have to go the whole nine yards with the professional titles with each other if we are going to be working so closely on this.

I sit down, noting the organized stack of papers on her desk, the same ones I've been analyzing. She's prepared, no doubt about it.

"I figured you had," I say, leaning back slightly, trying to gauge her mood. "What do you think?"

Frankie takes a deep breath, her eyes meeting mine. "Your concerns are valid, especially considering your perspective as a surgeon who deals directly with patients who need pacemakers. I understand why the data might raise some red flags."

I nod, appreciating her acknowledgment but waiting for the other shoe to drop. If Jill is right, she's not going to agree with me entirely, and that's fine. In fact, it's what I'm expecting.

She continues, her tone thoughtful. "I've spent a lot of time with this data, and I know this study inside and out. The deviations you pointed out, particularly in the patient response times and the variability in heart rate stabilization, are within the expected range for a trial of this nature. We're dealing with a smaller sample size and a lot of variables, and while the fluctuations might seem concerning at first glance, they're actually well within the acceptable parameters we've set."

She pulls out a specific chart, pointing to the data in question. "Here, for instance, you noted that the response times seemed inconsistent, but if you look at the breakdown by age group and pre-existing conditions, you'll see that the variations align with what we expected based on the initial projections. We anticipated these differences, and they don't pose a significant risk to the trial's overall integrity."

I study the chart, seeing the logic in her explanation. It's clear she's thought this through, and while I still have my reservations, I can't deny that her understanding of the data is impressive.

"But I understand your point," she adds, her voice softening just a bit. "These are people we are talking about, not just numbers on a page. Your perspective as a surgeon is invaluable, and it's important that we consider every angle before moving forward. That's why I'm open to rechecking the data with these concerns in mind, to make sure we're absolutely certain before we proceed to human trials."

There's a sincerity in her voice that surprises me. She's protective of this study, no doubt, but she's also willing to listen, to consider other perspectives—even when they challenge her own. It's a balance I didn't expect, especially after Jill's warning. It's both intriguing and, if I'm being honest, sexy as hell.

I lean forward, my gaze locked on hers. "I appreciate that, Frankie. I hope you don't mind if I call you Frankie."

"Of course not," she blushes. It's the first sign she isn't completely void of feeling.

"I know how much this study means to you, and I don't want to undermine that. My job is to make sure we're doing what's best for the patients who'll eventually rely on this technology. But it's clear you've already considered these variables, and that shows just how much command you have over this work."

For a moment, there's a flicker of something in her eyes—something beyond the professionalism she always maintains. It's gone almost as quickly as it appears, but it leaves me wondering. Is she remembering what happened between us on the other side of that wall like I am?

"Thank you," she says, her voice steady. "I want this trial to succeed just as much as you do, and I'm confident that with our combined expertise, we can make that happen."

I nod, garnering a newfound respect for her—not just for her knowledge, but for her dedication and her passion. It's rare to find someone who can match me in intensity, and I find myself drawn to that in ways I hadn't anticipated.

As we wrap up the meeting, the tension between us shifts. It's less about conflict and more about the shared goal, the mutual respect that seems to be there between us.

As I leave her office, the realization hits me that this trial is going to test more than just our professional abilities. It's going to test our ability to work together, to trust each other. If she's anything like me, that isn't going to be an easy feat for either of our personalities.

———

HUNTER'S CONDO

6:32 *pm*

THE CITY LIGHTS flicker through the floor-to-ceiling windows, casting a soft glow across the room.

I drop my bag on the kitchen counter and pour myself a glass of water, the meeting with Frankie still fresh in my mind. It went better than I expected—better than it had any right to go, considering the tension between us and our brief history of intimacy, which almost seems like a dream now.

But there's something about her that's making this trial extra important to me. It's not just another project. It's almost like a quest to make it soar.

I lean against the counter, staring out at the cityscape, my mind shifting gears to the work ahead.

Pacemakers have been crucial to cardiac care for decades, but like with all medical devices, there's always room for improvement. The standard pacemaker does its job—regulating heartbeats by delivering electrical impulses to the heart muscles—but it's not without limitations.

Most pacemakers work on a fixed-rate system or a demand mode, where the device only fires when it detects an irregular heartbeat. They're effective, but they don't account for the nuanced needs of different patients, particularly those with complex cardiac conditions. The device doesn't always adapt well to a patient's activity level or the natural variability of a healthy heart, leading to complications like arrhythmias or even heart failure in severe cases.

What Frankie discovered and what we will be testing with this trial is different. The pacemaker Frankie and her team have been developing is designed to be adaptive—smart, if you will. Everything these days is smart, and it only makes sense for medical devices to use the same technology to conform to individual quirks and needs.

It's equipped with sensors that monitor not just the heart's electrical activity but also the patient's physiological status in real-time. Things like oxygen levels, blood pressure, and even metabolic rate are taken into account, allowing the pacemaker to adjust its pacing algorithm on the fly.

It's a dynamic system, meant to mimic the body's natural responses more closely than any device currently on the market.

The potential here is enormous. For patients with advanced heart disease, this could mean fewer complications, fewer surgeries, and a better quality of life. It's not just about keeping the heart beating—it's about keeping it beating the way it should under a variety of conditions, responding to the body's needs as they change throughout the day.

This kind of innovation could change the standard of care, make pacemakers less of a blunt instrument and more of a finely tuned part of the body's overall system.

But with all that potential comes risk. This isn't a simple upgrade; it's a fundamental change in how we think about cardiac care. The trials are going to be rigorous and the scrutiny will be intense. Every detail needs to be perfect because one misstep could set us back years—or worse, endanger patients' lives.

That's where my role comes in. As a cardiothoracic surgeon, I've seen the limitations of current pacemakers firsthand. I've been in the OR when a patient's device failed, when their heart didn't respond the way it should have.

I've seen the fear in their eyes when they realize their lifeline might not be as reliable as they thought. That's why I've become so invested in this trial. It's why I didn't hesitate when Theo asked if I could consult.

It's not just about advancing the science—it's about making sure the next patient on my table has the best possible chance at a full, healthy life.

And it's why Frankie's perspective is so valuable. She sees the data, the patterns, the possibilities in ways I can't. But I see the patients, the real-world application, the human lives hanging in the balance. Together, we might just pull this off —if we can get out of our own way to listen to the other.

I'm all pumped up from the realization of the full potential of what we are doing. Got to burn off some of this energy. A sunset run is just what the doctor orders.

ELEVEN

Frankie

Frothy Monkey

7:11 *pm*

I SIT IN THE CAFÉ, staring down at the paper cup of peppermint tea with the craft paper koozie wrapped around it. I spin the corrugated sleeve around mindlessly, trying to ease my anxiety but only adding to it.

The steam stopped rising from it a while ago, but I still haven't taken a single sip. I wrap my hands around it to try to stop my fidgeting. It's strange being here, waiting for a man who's been nothing more than a ghost in my life.

When I got the second letter, I thought about ignoring it—just like I ignored the first one. But something in his words got to me this time. The way he basically begged me, promised to leave me alone if I would meet, I figured I would see what is so urgent.

Carly told me I'd regret it if I didn't at least hear him out, and I came to the realization that she's right. But as I sit here, waiting, I'm not so sure. Part of me wants to run before he gets here. Maybe this was a mistake…

The door chimes, and I glance up to see him walk in. It's like seeing a stranger, yet there's a familiarity in his face because I've seen him over the years in his commercials. He looks older, frailer than I imagined. Up close, there's no trace of the slick car salesman. He's just a tired man who doesn't seems out of place.

He spots me and hesitates, as if unsure whether to approach. I nod slightly, giving him permission, and he makes his way over to the table.

"Hi, Frankie," he says softly, almost as if he's testing the sound of my name.

"Hello," I reply, keeping my tone neutral. I'm not sure how I'm supposed to feel—anger, sadness, maybe even relief that he's here. But I'm not ready to let any of it show.

He sits down across from me, his movements careful, like he's afraid he might break something. There's an awkward silence, the kind that stretches on just long enough to make you uncomfortable.

"I wasn't sure if you'd come," he finally says, his voice laced with uncertainty.

"I almost didn't," I admit, staring at him directly. "But you said you were dying. And you've at least made a valiant effort, so I figured I'd give you a chance to say your piece."

He nods, looking down at his hands, which are trembling slightly. "I am. I didn't want to burden you, but… I couldn't leave without at least trying to talk to you."

"What is it?" I ask, my voice sharp with impatience. "What are you dying from?"

He looks up at me, and I can see the weariness in his eyes. "I have Hodgkin's lymphoma. It's a rare form, and it's... aggressive. The doctors haven't been able to find anything that works. It isn't responding to the traditional treatment methods."

The words hit me harder than I expected. Cancer. Of course, it's cancer. A part of me has a modicum of sympathy for him, but another part, the part that's been hurt by his absence, is numb. My mother, the woman he abandoned along with his child, also had a terminal illness. I didn't see him visiting while she was dying.

I'm not sure what to say, so I just nod, letting him continue.

"They've tried the usual treatments," he says, his voice faltering. "But it's not responding. They've mentioned some experimental options, but..." He trails off, the unspoken truth hanging between us. He's running out of time.

I swallow, trying to process the information. This man, who I barely know but who has shaped so much of who I am, is dying. And there's nothing anyone can do about that. Strangely, when it was my mom in his place, I wanted to do anything and everything I could to try to stop it, to fix her. With him, I don't have that urge.

"Why are you telling me this?" I finally ask.

"Because I needed you to know," he says, his voice trembling. "I know I haven't been there for you, and that's my biggest regret. But I couldn't leave this world without at least trying to make things right, to give you some kind of explanation."

I narrow my eyes, my defenses going up. "And what explanation could possibly make up for twenty-eight years of nothing?"

He flinches, and I can see the pain in his eyes. "I don't expect you to forgive me, Frankie. I just wanted you to know that... I never stopped thinking about you. I stayed away because your mother said that is what she wanted. I didn't fight hard enough, and that's on me. But I did care."

I shake my head, tears stinging my eyes. "Caring isn't enough. Caring didn't help my mom when she was struggling to raise me on her own. You know, she died twelve years ago, right?"

"I know," he whispers, his voice breaking. "I didn't find out until after her death, I'm so sorry. I know I failed you both. But I want you to know that I didn't stay away because I didn't care. I stayed away because... because I thought I'd already done enough damage. I wasn't healthy for you two, and you deserved more."

That sounds like a cop out to me. I don't know what to say to that. The anger I've held onto for so long somehow seems unnecessary now, but I'm not ready to let it go. Not yet.

"I don't know if I can forgive you," I finally say, my voice trembling. "But I'm here, and I'm listening. That's all I can give you right now."

He nods, tears welling up in his eyes. "That's more than I deserve."

We sit in silence for a while, both of us lost in our thoughts. I take a sip of my lukewarm tea because I don't know what else to do.

I came here expecting to give him a few minutes, tell him to leave me alone and leave, having finally closed that door. But now, I'm not sure what I feel. There's a part of me that wants to understand, to find some real closure before it's too late. There's still a part of me that's a little girl who wonders why her father didn't love her enough to stay.

The café feels too small, too stifling now. I need to get out of here to clear my head. Bill's words are still echoing in my mind, but I can't deal with them here, not with him watching me, waiting for a reaction I'm not ready to give.

"I think I need to go," I say, standing up abruptly. My voice sounds distant, even to me.

My father looks up at me, a flicker of something—disappointment, maybe—crossing his face. "Of course, Frankie. I didn't mean to keep you."

I nod, not trusting myself to say more. I grab my bag, not even bothering to finish the tea that's gone cold in front of me. My hands are trembling slightly as I turn to leave.

"Thank you for coming," he says quietly, his voice full of a sadness that tugs at something deep inside me.

I don't respond, instead, I give him a brief nod before I push through the door and out into the none-the-wiser Birmingham air. The street is happy and alive as if a complete shitshow isn't going on in my life.

The soft glow of streetlights cast long shadows on the pavement. I start walking, not really paying attention to where

I'm going, just needing to move, to get away from the heaviness that's back there in the café.

I round a corner too quickly, my mind still miles away, and nearly collide with someone coming from the opposite direction. I'm about to apologize when I realize who it is.

"Hunter?" I say, my voice tinged with surprise.

He looks equally startled, pulling out his earbuds. "Frankie? What are you doing here?"

"I—" The words catch in my throat, the emotions from the meeting with my father suddenly too much to hold back. "I just…had a meeting and wanted to clear my head. It's a nice night so I thought a walk would be nice. I'm so sorry that I didn't see you. My brain must be somewhere else."

He studies me for a moment, his expression softening. "No worries. I should say the same. Apologies. Rough day?"

I nod, sensing the tears that I've been holding back start to well up. "You could say that."

Without thinking, I take a step closer, the need for comfort outweighing my usual caution. Hunter seems to sense it, his demeanor shifting from surprise to concern. He doesn't ask any more questions, just takes a slow, steady breath, as if inviting me to do the same.

"Do you want to walk for a bit?" he asks gently, his voice low and comforting. "I've gotten my run in. I could use a cool down. Shain Park is amazing at night."

I nod again, grateful for the suggestion. We start walking together, side by side, the silence between us not uncomfortable but rather calming. It's nice to just be in the presence of someone who isn't expecting anything from me, someone who's just there.

We walk like that for a while, neither of us saying much, but his quiet companionship is exactly what I need. The night air is cool against my skin, and slowly, my lungs can finally expand to let more oxygen in, letting my shoulders gradually drop back into some semblance of healthy posture.

The paved path we've been walking on winds through a patch of trees illuminated by soft, amber lights. Hunter gestures to a bench, and we sit down, the world around us quiet and still.

He turns to me, his expression still full of that quiet concern. "This is my favorite spot in the park. I usually sit here after a run and watch people walk by. It's very soothing."

"This is quite nice. I wouldn't have pegged you for a people-watcher, Dr. Parrish. I've never done this, but I like it."

"I'm glad to share," he says kindly, even friendly. He is usually so rushed, so tense and busy. This is a nice side to Hunter. I'm enjoying the view of the passersby and my bench neighbor. Who knew he would be the one to rescue me after that face-to-face with my father? And he doesn't even know.

The evening air is lighter now, the weight of the earlier conversation with Bill slowly lifting as I sit beside Hunter on the park bench. We don't say much, and somehow, that's exactly what I need. The silence isn't awkward, it's… comforting.

After a while, Hunter stretches his arms, his muscles flexing under the thin fabric of his shirt. I admire the way his tattoos run the entire length of his forearms, intricate designs that enhance his powerful physique. I remember wanting to study them more carefully after our quickie all those months ago. They seem to tell a story, one I've never asked him about, but now I find myself curious.

"You've got some interesting ink," I say, the question slipping out before I can think better of it. "Do they have any specific meaning?"

Hunter glances down at his arms, as if he's forgotten the tattoos are even there. A small smile tugs at the corner of his mouth and I can tell the subject interests him. He points to a particular design on his right forearm—a koi fish, beautifully detailed, swimming upstream.

"This one," he says, tapping the fish with his finger, "is for perseverance. The koi fish is a symbol of strength in the face of adversity. There's a legend that if a koi swims upstream long enough, it transforms into a dragon. It's kind of a reminder that the hard stuff you go through can lead to something greater."

I'm surprised by the depth of his answer, and I find myself leaning in slightly, intrigued. "That's really cool. I don't have any tattoos, but I love knowing the significance of them. Makes me imagine what I would get and where. Are you a koi?"

He shrugs, looking a bit self-conscious, but not in an uncomfortable way. "I guess I've always felt like I was swimming upstream. My parents had pretty high expectations, and there was always this pressure to be the best. But it wasn't just about proving something to them—it was about proving it to myself. The koi is a reminder that the struggle is part of the journey, and that the end result, the 'dragon,' is worth it."

His thoughtfulness and emotional depth catches me off guard. I see a glimpse of something more behind the gruff surgeon I know at work. This is a side of Hunter that's thoughtful, introspective, and surprisingly open, and it's hard not to be drawn to it.

"It suits you," I say softly, my eyes lingering on the tattoo. "You've definitely got that perseverance thing down. You're a fighter, aren't you?"

He chuckles, a low, warm sound that sends a shiver through me. "I guess you could say that. It's a work in progress."

We fall into a comfortable silence again, the air between us charged with something unspoken. I notice how effortlessly handsome he is, especially now, outside of the hospital, without the usual tension that seems to cling to him.

The athletic fit of his shirt clings to his chest and arms, and I can't try not to stare at the definition of his muscles, the sheen of sweat making them glisten under the streetlights. His tattoos wrap around his biceps and forearms, and there's something so effortlessly sexy about the way he carries himself—confident but not arrogant.

I find myself lingering, just a bit, as we walk back toward the main path. There's something about seeing him like this, outside of the sterile environment of the hospital, that's both disarming and almost inviting. He's still Hunter —sharp, focused, intense—but there's a warmth to him now, a side I haven't seen before.

We reach a point where our paths diverge, and he turns to me, that same easy smile on his face. "Take care, Frankie. I'll see you at work."

"Yeah, see you," I reply, and as he walks away, I find myself watching him go, the way his broad shoulders move, the effortless grace in his stride. Dear Lord, he is a beautiful man.

When he's out of sight, I take a deep breath, acknowledging a strange mix of sentiments. The heaviness from my talk with my father is still there. But it's muted now, as if a softer, more manageable emotion has enveloped it. I realize that it was Hunter's presence, his calm and unspoken support, that helped ease the turmoil inside me.

I walk back toward my house, my mind still replaying the unexpected encounter. It wasn't anything monumental—just a walk, a shared silence—but it was the perfect buffer from my surreal sitdown and from reality.

And I can't ignore the fact that Hunter, of all people, was the one who provided it.

It's strange, this pull I have toward him. We're colleagues, nothing more, and yet... there's something there. Something more than a meaningless fuck six months ago. Whatever it is, it's real, and it's growing.

Tonight, the walls I've built up around myself since our encounter so long ago, feel just a little bit lower. And for the first time, I find myself wondering what it would be like to let someone in.

TWELVE

Hunter

Back Forty Beer Company

9:01 *pm*

I LEAN AGAINST THE COUNTER, and the familiar hum of the bar surrounds me. I take the final sip of my beer as the bartender slides my credit card back toward me. The cold, bitter last swallow goes down a little too easily. It's a quiet night. There are just a few regulars scattered around, filling the space with the low murmur of conversation.

As I sign the receipt, my thoughts drift back to Frankie. Running into her tonight was... unexpected, but not unwelcome. I've always known she was naturally beautiful —anyone with eyes could see that—but seeing her tonight, outside of work, without the white lab coat and the usual professionalism that surrounds her, she was different. More relaxed, more... effervescent, if that's even the right word.

But there was something else too, something that set her apart from other women I've known. Women I meet, whether in the hospital or outside of it, often seem to have this unnerving desire to fill every silence, constantly vying for my attention, as if the quiet makes them uncomfortable. They're always trying to impress, to keep the conversation going, to make sure they're the center of my focus. It gets exhausting, to be honest.

But Frankie… she's different. She's comfortable in her own skin, not needing to fill the silence with pointless chatter. She doesn't fight for attention or try to dominate the space. She's just there, present, and somehow that's more engaging than any small talk could ever be. It's refreshing, a breath of fresh air.

She had something weighing on her, though. It was in the way her shoulders seemed a little more hunched than usual, the way her eyes carried a heaviness that wasn't there before. If I didn't know better, she almost seemed emotional when we first ran into each other.

I don't know if it's the pressure from the trial or if it's something more personal, but I could sense it. I didn't bring up work because it didn't seem right—not tonight, not with that look in her eyes.

She didn't offer much, and I didn't push. I'm not the type to pry, especially when it comes to personal matters. I wanted to know what was bothering her, what was making her seem like she was carrying the weight of the world on her shoulders, but I held back, and maybe that was for the best. Whatever it was, I'm sure she doesn't want to talk to a coworker about it.

There was something nice about just being there, about walking through the park with her and not having to say much. It was a break from the usual grind, from the constant demands of the hospital, from the pressure of always having to be on. Of course, in our moments of silence, I couldn't help but flash back to slapping her ass and the sensation of her warm skin on mine. I wouldn't be human if I didn't.

There's more to her than that, more to my intrigue than our intense, unplanned soiree. Maybe there's a side to her that I haven't had the chance to explore yet. And maybe I want to find out what that side is.

As I push open the door of the bar, the cool night air greets me, a welcome change from the warmth inside. But something's off. A murmur, a low, anxious hum that prickles the back of my neck breaks the usual quiet of the street. I step out onto the sidewalk, my eyes scanning the scene ahead of me.

A crowd has gathered, a tight knot of people clustered around something, or someone, on the ground. My heart rate kicks up, instinct taking over as I start toward the group, the distant sound of sirens reaching my ears. Someone is hurt, and judging by the way these people are huddled together, it seems to be bad.

"Excuse me," I call out, my voice cutting through the noise as I push through the throng. "I'm a doctor. Let me through."

The crowd parts just enough for me to squeeze through, and that's when I see her—Carly Gunner, lying motionless on the pavement. The sight of her, so full of life and energy just hours ago, now crumpled and vulnerable, hits me like a punch to the gut.

"Carly," I mutter, dropping to my knees beside her, my hands already moving to check for a pulse. Her skin is pale, her breathing shallow and rapid, which is a sign of shock. Blood pools beneath her head, staining the pavement dark. I quickly assess her, years of training kicking in as I check her airway, her breathing, her circulation.

"Carly, it's Hunter," I say, my voice steady despite the rush of adrenaline surging through me. "Can you hear me?"

There's no response, just a faint flicker of her eyelids, and I feel a surge of urgency. This is bad, really bad.

I glance around, spotting a woman holding a phone, her face pale with worry. "Did anyone see what happened?" I ask, my hands still working as I try to stabilize Carly's head, careful not to move her more than necessary. Any sudden movement could make things worse if she has a spinal injury.

"She... she stepped off the curb," the woman stammers, her voice shaking. "A car... it came out of nowhere, hit her, and then just... drove off."

A hit-and-run. My jaw clenches, anger bubbling beneath the surface, but I push it aside. Carly needs me to focus, not to get lost in the injustice of it all.

I lean closer to Carly, carefully checking her pupils for a response. One of them is sluggish, a sign of a potential head injury. Damn it. My mind races through the possibilities: a concussion, a skull fracture, internal bleeding. I need to keep her stable until the paramedics arrive.

"Someone get me a towel or a jacket," I call out, and a man immediately steps forward, handing me his jacket. I roll it up and carefully place it under Carly's head, trying to minimize any movement. Her breathing is still shallow, but at least she's breathing.

"Stay with me, Carly," I murmur, glancing down at her face, so unlike the vibrant, peppy nurse I see at the hospital. Her energy is usually infectious, a bright light in the often dark and sterile halls of the OR. Seeing her like this, so fragile, feels wrong on every level.

The sirens are louder now, getting closer, giving me a small measure of relief. But I know we're not out of the woods yet. There's still so much that could go wrong.

The crowd is still murmuring around us, but I tune them out, my focus entirely on Carly. "You're going to be okay," I tell her, more for myself than for her. "Just hang on a little longer."

Finally, the paramedics arrive, their blue and white uniforms a welcome sight. I quickly relay what I know, stepping back just enough to let them work but staying close, ready to assist if needed. They move with the same urgency I felt, carefully loading Carly onto a stretcher, securing her neck to prevent any further injury.

As they lift her into the ambulance, one paramedic looks at me. "You coming with us, Doc?"

I hesitate for a split second before nodding. "Yeah, I'm coming." I climb into the back of the ambulance, settling beside Carly as the doors close behind me.

The siren blares, and the vehicle lurches forward, speeding through the city streets toward the hospital. I keep my eyes on Carly, watching her every breath, every slight movement, ready to act at a moment's notice.

But as I sit there, I can't shake the image of her lying there on the pavement, so small and helpless. And I can't help but take on the weight of responsibility to make sure she gets through this.

"Stay with me, Carly," I whisper, more determined than ever. "You're not going anywhere."

The ambulance races through the city streets, its sirens cutting through the night. Inside, the paramedics work quickly, assessing Carly's condition with the same urgency I felt when I first saw her on the pavement. Her injuries, while serious, don't seem to be immediately life-threatening, but we're not taking any chances.

"She's stable for now," one paramedic says, his voice calm but focused. "Pulse is steady, blood pressure's a bit low but holding. Looks like she might have a concussion, possible fracture in the clavicle, and some bruising on the ribs. No signs of internal bleeding so far, but you'll want to confirm with imaging."

I nod, my eyes never leaving Carly. The sluggish pupil's response still worries me, but at least her vitals are stable. "We need to get a CT scan as soon as we arrive," I say. "Let's rule out any intracranial hemorrhage. And check for any fractures in the cervical spine, just to be safe."

The paramedic nods in agreement, making notes as the ambulance sways with the motion of the road. Carly stirs slightly, her eyes fluttering open for a brief moment before closing again. It's a good sign—she's responsive, even if it's only marginal.

"We'll need to keep her neck immobilized until we can rule out spinal injury," the paramedic adds, adjusting the brace around her neck. "Once we get her to the ER, we'll run the full trauma protocol."

A wave of relief washes over me, but I know we're not out of the woods yet. Head injuries can be tricky, and we won't know the full extent of the damage until we get those scans. But for now, Carly's stable, and that's something.

The ambulance pulls into the hospital bay, and the paramedics move swiftly, transferring Carly from the ambulance to a gurney with practiced efficiency. I stay close, my hands hovering near her as they wheel her into the ER, ready to step in if needed.

As we move through the bustling corridors, the familiar sights and sounds of the hospital fill the air—doctors and nurses rushing by, the beep of monitors, the low hum of conversations. But all of that fades into the background as we push through the double doors and into the trauma bay.

"CT scan, stat," I call out to the nearest nurse as we position Carly under the bright overhead lights. "Let's get a full workup—head, neck, chest. I want to know exactly what we're dealing with."

The team responds immediately, moving with the kind of precision that only comes from years of experience. I step back slightly, giving them space to work but staying close enough to monitor the situation.

Carly stirs again, her eyes opening for real this time. She blinks up at the ceiling, her gaze unfocused before it finally lands on me. "Hunter?" she murmurs, her voice weak but unmistakable.

I lean in closer, my heart easing at the sound of her voice. "I'm here, Carly. You're in the hospital. You were in an accident, but you're going to be okay."

She frowns slightly, wincing as she tries to move her head. "Accident…?" she echoes, her confusion evident.

"Yeah, a car hit you," I explain gently, placing a reassuring hand on her arm. "But you're going to be fine. We're just running some tests to make sure everything's okay."

Her eyes fill with tears, and she lets out a shaky breath. "It happened so fast… I didn't even see it coming."

I squeeze her arm, my voice softening. "You're safe now, Carly. We're going to take care of you. I'm going to stay with you until we know what is going on. Is there someone I can call to let them know you're here?"

She nods weakly, her tears spilling over as she tries to process what happened. "Will you please call Frankie Renna for me?"

"Of course," I say, leaning in closer. "I'll call her right now."

"Thank you."

The mention of Frankie sends a jolt through me, but I quickly push it aside. This isn't about me—it's about Carly. "I'll call her right now," I promise, reaching for my phone.

As I dial Frankie's number, the weight of the moment pressing down on me. Carly's voice is shaky, her usual energy replaced with a vulnerability I'm not used to seeing. She's always been so strong, so full of life, and seeing her like this—scared, hurt—twists something deep inside me.

The phone rings, and I pray Frankie answers quickly. Carly needs her, and right now, that's all that matters.

Frankie picks up on the third ring, her voice coming through the line with a mix of surprise and concern. "Hunter? What's going on?"

"It's Carly," I say, my voice steady but urgent. "She's been in an accident. She's okay, but she's asking for you. We're at the hospital. UAB."

There's a brief pause, and I can hear the shift in Frankie's tone as she processes what I've said. "I'll be there as soon as I can get there," she replies, her voice firm with determination.

I hang up and turn back to Carly, who's watching me with wide, tear-filled eyes. "She's on her way," I tell her, my voice gentle.

THIRTEEN

Frankie

UAB Hospital

11:41 *pm*

I RUSH through the hospital corridors, my heart pounding in my chest. When I finally reach the room where Carly is resting, waiting for tests and scans, I lose it. The moment I see her, lying there with a neck brace on, her face pale and bruised, I can't keep my normally stoic facade up. I'm at her side in an instant, my hand finding hers, holding on as if that alone could keep her safe.

"Carly," I whisper, my voice trembling with emotion. Her eyes flutter open, and she gives me a weak smile, but it's enough to break my heart all over again. Seeing her like this—so fragile, so quiet—tears at something deep inside me.

"I'm here," I tell her, squeezing her hand gently. "I'm not going anywhere."

She tries to speak, but her voice is barely above a whisper. "Frankie. Thank you for coming. I'm okay."

I shake my head, my eyes filling with tears. "Of course I came! You don't have to say that. Just rest, okay? You're safe now."

She nods slightly, her eyes closing again, and I can see how much effort it takes for her to even keep them open. I look up, my gaze meeting Hunter's across the bed. He's standing there, watching us with a mixture of concern and genuine care.

As the nurses come in to take Carly to imaging, I reluctantly let go of her hand, stepping back to give them space. Hunter and I follow them out, and once Carly is out of sight, I finally turn to him.

"What happened?" I ask, my voice strained with worry. I didn't want to ask him in front of her.

Hunter's expression is serious, but there's a gentleness in his eyes that surprises me. "She was hit by a car. It was a hit-and-run. I found her right after it happened, and I did what I could to stabilize her until the paramedics arrived. I couldn't just leave her there, so I rode with her in the ambulance to make sure she wasn't alone."

The seriousness of his words sinks in, and a surge of gratitude fills me. He didn't have to do any of this—Carly and Hunter aren't particularly close, and he could have just called for help and moved on. But he didn't. He stayed. He took it upon himself to make sure she was taken care of.

"Thank you," I say, my voice thick with emotion. "Thank you for being there for her, for taking care of her. It means more than you know."

Hunter shakes his head slightly, as if brushing off the praise. "I did what anyone would do."

"No," I insist, taking a step closer. "It wasn't your responsibility to do all of this. You could have just waited for the paramedics, but you didn't stop there. You stayed with her, made sure she wasn't alone. That means something. Thank you, I truly mean it."

He looks at me for a long moment, his expression softening. "I didn't want her to be alone. Waking up in a situation like that, not knowing what's going on, can be super scary. I couldn't let that happen to her."

His words hit me deeply, and I find myself blinking back tears. There's so much more to Hunter than I ever realized, and right now, all I have for this man is gratitude. Gratitude that he was there when Carly needed someone, and gratitude that he called me so I could be here too.

"Thank you," I say again, my voice barely above a whisper.

He nods, a small smile touching his lips. "You don't have to thank me, Frankie. I'm just glad she's going to be okay."

"We are going to have to stop running into each other like this," I say, trying to create some levity. I've now slept with this man, am working with him on my life's work, and now he has seen me cry. The trifecta no other man has had the privilege of experiencing with me.

"We do tend to have a knack for that, don't we?"

As we sit there, the comfortable silence between us starts to settle, my mind inevitably drifting back to the meeting we had earlier today. The trial has been consuming my thoughts for weeks now.

And despite everything that's happened tonight, it's still there, lingering at the edge of my mind.

I glance over at Hunter, wondering if now is the right time to broach the subject. He's been surprisingly open tonight, and more relaxed than I've ever seen him. Maybe that's why I feel the need to ask, to see if there's anything more we can discuss now that we're not in a formal setting.

"So," I start, hesitating for just a moment, "about the trial… I've been thinking about what you said earlier today, about the concerns you had with the data."

Hunter turns his attention fully to me, his expression serious but open. "Yeah? What about it?"

"I've been going over your points in my head," I continue, "and I see where you're coming from. I think there's definitely some room to adjust the parameters we're using, especially in terms of the patient selection criteria. We want to make sure we're targeting the right group for this to be successful."

He nods, considering my words. "I agree. It's not that I don't trust the data, it's just… we can't afford to overlook anything. If this goes to human trials… Let me correct myself, when it goes to human trials, it has to be flawless. We can't take any chances."

His dedication to the project, to ensuring it's as perfect as possible, resonates with me. It's one reason I respect him so much as a surgeon. He's not just driven; he's relentless in his pursuit of excellence.

"I've already started making some adjustments," I tell him, sensing that familiar passion rise within me. "I think if we tweak a few things, we'll not only address your concerns, but we might also improve the overall effectiveness of the pacemaker."

Hunter's eyes light up with interest, and I can tell he's genuinely engaged. "You're already working on it?"

I nod, a small smile playing on my lips. "Of course. This project means everything to me, Hunter. I want to get it right. Of course, we just spoke about it, so it is on paper right now, but yes, I've got some ideas."

He leans back in his chair, a thoughtful expression on his face. "You know, Frankie, I think we make a good team. I know I can be hard on people, but I'm glad to be working with you on this. Thank you for trusting my insight."

His words catch me off guard, and a warmth spreads through my chest. "I'm glad you're on board too. Your input has already made a difference, and I agree, together, we can really make this work."

"Let's keep pushing forward," Hunter says finally, his voice full of quiet determination. "We've got something good here, Frankie. I know it."

"Yeah," I agree, meeting his gaze. "We do."

———

WEDNESDAY, *May 22*

. . .

7:06 *am*

THE FIRST RAYS of morning light filter through the blinds in Carly's hospital room, casting a soft glow over the sterile white walls. I shift slightly on the recliner that served as my makeshift bed for the night, blinking the sleep from my eyes. It wasn't the most comfortable place to sleep, but surprisingly, it wasn't as bad as I'd expected.

Carly stirs in the bed beside me, her eyes fluttering open. I sit up a little straighter, instantly alert, watching as she takes in her surroundings.

"Morning," I say softly, giving her a small smile.

"Morning," she replies, her voice still groggy. She shifts in bed, wincing slightly as the movement reminds her of her injuries. "How are you feeling?" I ask, concern evident in my tone.

"Like I got hit by a car," she jokes, but there's a hint of pain behind her smile. "But seriously, I'm okay. Sore, but okay."

The doctors had gone over her scans late last night, and while the news was reassuring, it had still been a long night. Carly was fortunate—her scans showed no broken bones and her concussion was mild. She stayed the night for observation, but everything else came back clear. The car hadn't been going fast; it had only clipped her leg. The real damage occurred due to the way she had been thrown by the impact and how she had landed.

"You're really lucky," I say, my voice filled with relief. "It could have been so much worse."

"I know," she agrees, her expression softening. "But you didn't have to stay, you know. I'm an ER nurse—I know the drill. Being in the hospital doesn't freak me out like it does most people."

I shake my head, reaching out to take her hand. "I wasn't going to leave you alone, Carly. Not before we knew exactly what we were dealing with. Besides, the recliner wasn't as bad as I thought it would be."

She squeezes my hand, a grateful smile on her lips. "Thanks, Frankie. You're a good friend. As if you don't have enough on your plate."

"Of course," I reply, squeezing back. "You practically live at my house. It's only fitting that I move in with you to your hospital room."

"What did you decide to do about your dad?"

"I met with him, but let's not go into that right now. I'll tell you everything soon, just not now. Change of subject."

"I can appreciate that. When you're ready, let's talk about it."

"Deal."

Carly's smile turns sly, and she tilts her head slightly, her eyes sparkling with mischief. "Okaaaaay. So… Hunter was here last night."

I try to keep my expression neutral, but a flush of hot redness creeps up my neck. "Um, yeah. He was your knight in shining armor."

"More like yours, I'd say. You two seemed pretty cozy," she teases, her voice light despite the discomfort she must be experiencing.

I roll my eyes, trying to brush off her comment. "Carly, we were just waiting together. It's not a big deal."

"Not a big deal?" She raises an eyebrow, clearly unconvinced. "I don't know, Frankie. He was here for me, but he stayed for you."

I open my mouth to protest, but the words don't come. Instead, my mind flashes back to the way Hunter had looked at me last night, the warmth in his eyes, the way he'd made me laugh when I needed it most. He'd been there for Carly, yes, but... had he also been there for me?

Lucky for me, he was still wearing that to-die-for-running attire. I couldn't get enough of stolen glances.

"Don't read too much into it," I finally say, trying to sound dismissive. "He's just...he's a good guy."

Carly doesn't respond right away, but she's watching me closely, a knowing look in her eyes. "Sure," she says after a moment, her tone suggesting she's not entirely convinced. "If you say so."

I turn my attention to the window, trying to push away the thoughts that have been creeping into my mind ever since last night. It's ridiculous, really, to think there could be anything more between Hunter and me. We're colleagues, end of story. Sure, we slept together, but both of us seem to have written that off as a one-off, nothing to it. But even as I try to convince myself of that, I can't help but replay our conversations. The way he'd made me feel so... seen.

"Anyway," Carly says, breaking the silence, "I'm just glad you were both there for me. It made everything a lot less scary. Thank you."

I nod, finally meeting her gaze again. "You know I've got your back, Carly. Always. And it looks like I'm not the only one."

"Yeah," she says with a smile. "I know you do. Hey, you know what really sucks?"

"That you're going to have to eat the shitty hospital breakfast?"

"Well, yes, that. But you know what else? I'm going to miss the fucking gala this weekend. The one thing I was looking forward to. And where am I going to wear that kickass dress?"

"Oh, Carly. I'm so sorry! I wish I could be laid up here in your place and let you go for me. I know you were so looking forward to it."

"Don't worry. Just take copious notes on every detail and fill me in afterwards. God it?"

"Got it."

As the morning continues to brighten the room, a sense of calm settles over me. Carly is going to be okay, and that is what matters most. But even as I focus on my friend, I can't completely shake the thoughts of Hunter—the way he'd been there when I needed someone, the way he'd shown a side of himself I hadn't seen before, not only for me but for someone else.

Maybe there's more there to explore there than I've been willing to admit.

FOURTEEN

Hunter

Thursday, May 23

Hunter's Condo

9:27 pm

I LIE BACK on my sofa and turn on the TV. After the day I've had, I should be unwinding, letting the tension drain away. But I can't. Not with the thoughts of her swirling around in my mind.

Once again, I glance at my phone on the table, the screen dark, my mother's name already pulled up. I've been staring at it for ten minutes, debating whether to make the call. I haven't talked to her for almost a week, avoiding it.

It's only 9:30 here, which means it's 7:30 back in California. She's probably still up, maybe watching one of those crime shows she's always been obsessed with.

With a reluctant sigh, I press the call button and bring the phone to my ear. Each ring makes my stomach tighten, and I almost hang up before she answers.

"Hunter?" Her voice is soft, and I can hear the surprise in it. She's probably been complaining that her surgeon son doesn't care about the fact that she is going through her cancer journey all alone.

"Yeah, Mom. It's me," I reply, trying to keep my tone neutral. "Just wanted to check in, see how you're doing." God, even I can hear the disdain in my words.

"Oh, I'm getting by," she says, the usual small talk beginning. I hear the familiar rattle of the ice in her gin and tonic. "Just had a quiet day. Went to see Dr. Malley for a check-up. You know, the usual."

I nod even though she can't see me, my professional curiosity already kicking in against my better judgement to stay the hell out of it. "How did that go? Anything new?"

She hesitates for a moment, and I can almost see the gears turning in her head. "Well, he mentioned something about trying a new treatment. Something a bit more aggressive. He said it might be necessary given… given the way things are progressing."

My heart skips a beat, and a familiar knot of anxiety tightens in my chest. "What kind of treatment?" I ask, my voice a little sharper than I intended.

"Something about a new combination of drugs," she replies, a hint of uncertainty in her tone. "He explained it, but… you know me, Hunter. I'm not as good with all those medical terms."

I close my eyes, trying to keep my emotions in check. "Mom, do you remember the names of the drugs? Or did he give you anything in writing?"

She pauses, and I hear her rifling through papers. "Let me see... I think I have it here somewhere... Ah, yes. Here it is. Something called brentuximab and... I can't pronounce this one... doxorubicin?"

My grip tightens on the phone, my mind immediately going into overdrive. Brentuximab and doxorubicin—of course, they're talking about more aggressive chemo-therapy. I knew it. I knew this was coming, and yet hearing it makes my stomach do a somersault. I try to keep my voice steady, but the frustration is already bubbling up.

"Those are pretty standard for treating HL," I say, forcing the words out calmly. "It sounds like they're trying to be more proactive, which is good."

There's a silence on the other end of the line, and I can sense her hesitation, the weight of what she's about to ask.

"Hunter... do you think you could... maybe talk to Dr. Malley? You know, just to make sure we're on the right track?"

There it is. The very thing I didn't want to hear. The last thing I wanted to do. I swallow hard, my mind racing. I've been trying to keep my distance, to not get sucked into this, but now she's asking me directly, putting me right in the middle of it.

"I don't know, Mom," I say, my voice tight. "You're already in good hands. Dr. Malley knows what he's doing. You know how doctors get territorial over their patients and protocols."

"I know," she says softly, and I can hear the weariness in her voice. "But I just… I'd feel better if you talked to him. Please, Hunter. I'm scared."

Her words cut through me like a knife, and my anger threatens to overtake my attempt at goodwill—anger at her for putting me in this position, anger at myself for caring so damn much. I already had it in my head at least a dozen times to call him, but stopped myself. Now that she is asking, I might as well at least touch base with him.

Underneath all that, there's something else—something I don't want to acknowledge. Love. As much as I've tried to keep her at arm's length, she's still my mother. And she's scared.

"Okay," I finally say, the word spilling out of me like a reluctant child being pulled away by a parent. "I've got a full schedule but I'll try to reach out at some point over the next few days."

The relief in her voice is palpable. That twists the knife even further. "Thank you, Hunter. I know it's asking a lot, but… thank you." I want to remind her how she felt about my "interference" last time with my father, but that isn't necessary. We both know how that went down.

I resist the urge to just hang up and claim a bad connection. But I know I can't do that. "Yeah. Don't worry about it, Mom."

We exchange a few more words, the conversation winding down, but the tension doesn't leave me. When we finally hang up, I drop the phone onto the table and rub my face with both hands, trying to push back the frustration that's threatening to spill over.

This is not what I want, to be pulled into her care, to be the one who has to make these decisions. But now that she's asked, I can't refuse. It's a phone call. I've got this.

I stand up, the restless energy building in my muscles. I need to get out of here, to do something—anything—to clear my head. Without another thought, I throw on some shorts and a t-shirt, grab my running shoes and head for the door.

The evening air is still and warm, but cooler than the hot late spring day we had. The slight breeze against my skin as I start to run is exactly what I needed.

My feet pound against the pavement as the city lights blur around me. I push myself harder, faster, trying to outrun the thoughts that are chasing me. But no matter how fast I go, they're still there, gnawing at the edges of my mind.

I'm angry—angry at her for asking, angry at myself for caring, angry at the whole damn situation. But more than that, I'm scared. Scared of what it means to be involved, scared of what it will do to me if I let myself get too close.

After my father died a few years ago, I knew that meant I should step up to take care of my mom. But a lifetime of pressure and disappointment from her isn't easy to erase. It's been a delicate balance for me: taking care of a woman that has never made me feel like she took care of me. Providing a roof over my head and food isn't the extent of good parenting.

But I can't run from it. No matter how fast or how far I go, it's still there, waiting for me. And I know, deep down, that I won't be able to stay detached as much as I would like to think I can. Not this time.

As I round the corner, pushing myself to my limits, I finally let the anger out, the frustration spilling over into the pounding of my feet, the burn in my lungs. I run until I can't think anymore until the only thing that exists is the rhythm of my breath and the beat of my heart.

But when I finally stop, doubled over, hands on my knees, gasping for air, I know that nothing has really changed. The dilemma is still there, waiting for me. And no matter how much I want to, I can't run away from her and the fact that she is my mother and I have the tools to help her.

The run was brutal, just what I needed to push everything else out of my mind, even if only for a little while. Hands on my knees, hanging my head, trying to catch my breath, the weight of it all starts creeping back in—until I hear her voice.

"Hunter?"

I look up, my breath still ragged, and there she is. Frankie. The last person I expect to see, yet exactly who I need at this moment. The stress, the anger, the frustration—all of it seems to dissolve the second I see her standing there, illuminated by the streetlights.

She walks up to me, her eyes full of concern, but there's something else there too, something softer that I can't quite put my finger on. "You okay?" she asks, her voice gentle, soothing in a way that nothing else has been tonight.

"Yeah," I manage to say, straightening up, though my heart's still racing—and not just from the run. "Just… needed a good, hard run."

She gives me a small smile, the kind that makes pressure on my chest lighten. "Since we ran into each other at the park,

I've been doing nightly walks. I've been loving it. Never thought I'd be the type to enjoy walking around the city at night, but it's my new thing."

I can't help but smile back, the tension easing out of my muscles just from being near her. "Glad to hear it. You look like you're enjoying yourself." My breathing is slowing enough that I can at least speak in complete sentences.

"I am," she says, then glances at me, her brow furrowing slightly. "But you look like you need to catch your breath," she says with a laugh. "Do you always push yourself that hard? Are you training for something?"

I shake my head, the words coming out automatically, even though my mind is still on that phone call with my mom. "No, sometimes I like to see what I can push my body to do. It's how I clear my head."

She nods, accepting the answer without prying, but I can tell she's curious. It's one of the things I like about Frankie —she knows when to push and when to give space.

"I wish I exercised to clear my head. I go the opposite direction and eat a pint of Ben & Jerry's. Going for a run sounds so much better for me."

"Don't worry, I do that, too. Speaking of, want to grab a beer with me?"

"Now?" She looks at her watch, as if she is Cinderella and she needs to get home.

"Sure. After a run like that," I say, shifting the conversation, "I usually like to grab a frosty one at the Back Forty right here on first. It's my reward. Want to join me?" I want to say that seeing her is my reward, but I resist.

Her eyes light up, and she gives me that smile again, the one that makes everything else fade into the background. "Sure. I'd love to."

———

THE BACK FORTY *Beer Company*

10:52 *pm*

THE DIMLY BAR lighting feels all the softer sitting here with Frankie. Nearby tables occasionally erupt in bursts of laughter, blending with the clink of glasses and the soft hum of conversation.

Frankie and I have been here for a while, mostly making small talk, easing into our out-of-the-office relationship. A pleasant outcome has been the complete unraveling of the tension from earlier. It's easy with her, natural like we're old friends instead of awkward colleagues who slept together once.

I take a sip of my beer, glancing at her over the rim of my glass. She's pensive suddenly, her thoughts clearly elsewhere. I wonder what's on her mind, but it isn't appropriate for me to ask.

"Can I ask you something?" she asks, her voice soft but laced with something, letting me know we have crossed from small talk to a deeper subject.

"Of course," I reply, leaning in slightly, giving her my full attention. Whatever it is, it's clearly important to her.

She hesitates for a moment, her fingers wiping the condensation on the side of her glass. "How much do you know about Hodgkin's lymphoma?"

The question catches me off guard, but I manage to keep my expression neutral. "Quite a bit, actually," I say, trying to gauge where this is coming from. "It's a type of cancer that affects the lymphatic system. Why do you ask?"

She sighs, her eyes dropping to her drink. "Someone close to me… they were recently diagnosed. I've been trying to learn more about it, to understand what they're going through, the prognosis."

I nod slowly, empathizing with her all to well. Of all the things she could have asked about… "I'm sorry to hear that," I say, my voice sincere. "It can be a lot to take in. But the good news is that treatment for Hodgkin's has come a long way. The prognosis can be very positive, especially if it's caught early."

I leave out the fact that there is this newer, more stubborn strain out there. It is rare, and the chances her friend, or loved one, has it are slim. No need to add to her worry.

She looks up at me, her green eyes searching mine, and I can see the concern there, the fear she's trying to hide. "Yeah, that's what I've been reading," she murmurs. "But there are so many variables, you know? I guess I just want to understand as much as I can about it."

I want to tell her about my mom, to let her know that I understand exactly what she's going through. But something holds me back. Maybe it's the part of me that doesn't want to open that door, doesn't want to admit how close to home this hits. So instead, I offer what comfort I can.

"It's normal to get overwhelmed with all of it," I say, keeping my tone even. "But you don't have to have all the answers right away. Just being there for them, supporting them—that's what really matters."

She nods, taking in my words, and for a moment, we just sit there in silence, the noise of the bar fading into the background. I can tell this is weighing heavily on her, and I want to do more, say more, but I don't. We both bask in the comfortable silence instead.

"Thanks," she says quietly, finally looking up at me again. "It helps to talk about it, even if I don't have all the answers."

"Anytime," I reply, meaning it. "And if you ever need to talk more… you know where to find me."

She smiles a small, genuine smile that sends a warmth through me. One that I haven't felt in a long time. For the second time tonight, I have to admit something I have been running from: it feels good.

"Geez," she says suddenly. "I didn't realize how late it was. I probably should get going." With that, she turns up her glass and drains her beer.

Damn. Her hotness level just went up another notch.

FIFTEEN

Frankie

Saturday, May 25

The Florentine

2101 2nd Avenue North

7:12 pm

THE GRAND BALLROOM is everything you'd expect from a high-society gala... right down to the opulent chandeliers sparkling like diamonds swimming above us. The golden glow projected over the sea of elegantly dressed guests ups the fanciness and my anxiety. I don't do these types of events willingly.

The hum of polite conversation mixed with the clink of champagne flutes, and the soft strains of a string quartet playing in the corner is a testament to whoever planned this. Whoever planned this took care of every detail.

It's the kind of event that would make anyone feel under-dressed, no matter how much time she spent getting ready. For me, there's no amount of lipstick that would transform me into the kind of person that fits in here. I stick out like a sore thumb.

I step inside, my heels clicking softly on the polished marble floor, and take a slow breath to steady myself. The dress I'm wearing is beautiful. It's a deep, emerald green gown that Carly insisted would bring out the color of my eyes. It's more like armor than anything else.

Carly sadly swapped her dress for a night on the sofa. She is still too sore from the accident to make it. I wish I could trade with her—I know how much she was looking forward to coming. And, Lord knows, I don't want to be here.

The fact that I'm here without her, my wingman, to woo a potential sponsor for the pacemaker trial doesn't help make it any better. But this is part of my job. So, here goes nothing.

As I scan the room, looking for familiar faces, my eyes land on Hunter. He's standing near the bar, a glass of something amber in his hand, looking both completely at ease and deliciously handsome.

He's dressed in a sharp black tuxedo, the kind that makes every man look good. But on him, it's different. It fits him to a tee. The perfectly tailored fit hugs him in all of the right places.

The usually gruff, intense surgeon seems almost… relaxed. There's still that underlying tension in his posture. I've come to recognize it in our after-hours meetings and discussions about our now-shared project.

He hasn't spotted me yet, so I take a moment to observe him, letting my gaze linger a little longer than I probably should. It's always an unexpected treat seeing him like this, outside of the hospital.

Here, under the soft lights of the gala, he seems more human, less of the driven, borderline-obsessive doctor I'm used to working with. But that's not what surprises me the most.

What surprises me is the stirring in my belly. I've been noticing it more and more lately, when we are together, so it shouldn't surprise me. But with both of us dressed up like this, and the music, the soft lighting—the whole combination intensifies that stirring even more.

I push the thought aside, reminding myself that we're here for a reason. There's no time to get distracted by how good Hunter looks in formalwear. I've got a job to do, and it's a big one.

As I approach him, his gaze finally shifts, and when our eyes meet, something flickers there. It's a recognition, maybe something more, but it's gone before I have to figure out how to respond. He nods slightly, a half-smile tugging at the corner of his lips, and I can't help but smile back.

"You clean up well, Dr. Parrish," I say lightly, coming to stand beside him at the bar.

He raises an eyebrow, taking a sip of his drink. "I could say the same for you, Dr. Renna. That dress might just outshine the chandelier."

I roll my eyes, but I can't hide the smile that tugs at my lips.

"Flattery won't get you out of meeting with Mr. Rich Guy tonight."

He chuckles, the sound low and warm, and it's strange how it makes the butterflies in my stomach flutter even more. "And here I thought you were the one who was going to charm him into funding our project."

"Oh, I'll charm him all right," I reply, my tone playful. "But you're the one with the surgeon's hands. He'll want to hear from you, too."

Oh, those hands. Why can't I stop thinking about them running over me?

Hunter smirks, setting his glass down on the bar. "Theo said Mr. Rich Guy would meet us here. He's probably schmoozing somewhere with the other bigwigs. Ready to go find him?"

"Absolutely," I say, but there's a part of me that's not quite ready for the evening to get underway. For now, I'm content to stand here with Hunter, sharing this light-hearted banter, pretending like we're two people unburdened by the weight of our careers.

As Hunter and I make our way through the glittering crowd, my mind drifts to last week's meeting with my father. It was our second time seeing each other since his unexpected return to my life, and I'm surprised to find myself feeling okay about it.

We met at Shain Park downtown, just as the evening was settling in. The fading sunlight painted everything in soft, warm hues, lending a surreal quality to our encounter. As we strolled along the winding paths, the tension that had defined our first meeting seemed to dissipate slightly.

This time, it felt less like confronting a ghost from my past and more like... getting to know a stranger who happens to share my DNA. We talked about simple things—his work at the car dealership, my research at the hospital. Nothing too deep or painful.

I'm not ready to let him fully into my life yet. A couple of meetings don't erase the years of absence and hurt. But I can't deny that these encounters have been good for me. Good for both of us. It's like slowly draining an old wound I didn't even realize was still festering.

As we walked, I found myself noticing little things—the way he gestures when he talks, how his eyes crinkle at the corners when he smiles. It's strange to see echoes of myself in someone I've spent so long trying to forget.

I shake myself out of my reverie as Hunter and I approach a group of well-dressed individuals. This isn't the time to be lost in thoughts about my complicated family situation. Right now, we have a job to do.

————

10:27 *pm*

THE MUSIC in the background fades as Mr. Remington, the potential sponsor, smiles broadly, extending his hand to both Hunter and me.

"You've convinced me," he says, his voice full of warmth and authority. "I'll have my people draw up the paperwork first thing Monday, but consider your project funded. It's not every day I come across something so innovative, with people as passionate as the two of you behind it."

I'm blown away for a moment and find I can't speak. I know I'm smiling like a dummy. My cheeks hurt from the broadness of it. Years in the making, and Mr. Remington has just committed to bringing this to trial. Finally.

The weight of the world lifts off my shoulders. Hunter and I exchange a look—one of triumph, relief, and maybe even a hint of disbelief. I've been working so hard for this— we've been working so hard. Now, in a moment that is almost surreal, we've actually done it.

"Thank you, Mr. Remington," Hunter says, shaking his hand firmly. "We won't let you down. Now, the real fun begins."

"I'm sure you won't," Mr. Remington replies, then with a final nod, he turns to Theo Bench, who's been standing nearby, grinning like a proud father. The two of them start talking logistics, and Hunter and I step back slightly, taking a moment to breathe.

"That just happened," I whisper, mostly to myself, but in his ear. The reality of it is still sinking in.

"It did," Hunter replies, a slight grin on his face. "We've got it, Frankie. Fuck, yeah. This is happening."

I nod, as a rush of excitement mixed with the over-whelming relief that comes after a long-fought battle envelopes me. Just as I'm about to bask in the victory, something tugs at the back of my mind, a nagging thought about three crucial changes I need to make before we meet on Monday.

"Wait," I say, turning to Hunter. "I need to go back to the lab. The proposal details—there's some data we need to confirm and a file I need to send. We should have it all ready to go first thing on Monday. I don't want anything to hold it up."

Hunter raises an eyebrow, clearly not thrilled about the idea of cutting the celebration short. "Can't it wait until tomorrow?"

I shake my head, the pressure already creeping back in. "No, it's better if I do it tonight. Besides, my work here is done. I want to get it done while everything's fresh in my mind. I'd rather get it done." The truth is, I won't be able to enjoy myself anymore, anyway. I'm too excited about this. I want to go take care of it.

He sighs, glancing around the room as if looking for a way out, too. "Well, if it's gotta be done, you stay here and enjoy yourself, I'll go do it," he says, giving me a playful smirk. "You're not sneaking out early and leaving me to deal with all this."

I raise an eyebrow, crossing my arms. "Oh, no. I'm not letting you off that easy. You don't get to skip out on the rest of this night by volunteering to take care of things. If anyone's leaving, it's me."

He chuckles, shaking his head. "Nice try. I'm doing it."

I narrow my eyes at him, trying to keep a straight face. "We both know you're just looking for an excuse to get out of here, and I am not about to let you have it."

"Sounds like we're at an impasse, then," he says, grinning. "How about we both go? That way, neither of us has to stick around, and we can get it done twice as fast."

I pretend to consider it, tapping my chin. "Fine. We both go. Let's get out of here before Theo or Remington pulls us into another round of schmoozing."

We turn back to Mr. Remington and Theo, offering polite excuses before making our way to the exit. As we step outside, the night air is alive. There is an electricity in the air. The line of cars waiting to take guests home or to their next destination stretches down the driveway, and a sleek black car pulls up just as we approach.

The driver steps out, opening the door for us. Hunter introduces himself and me as he shakes his hand. "Dr. Parrish, Dr. Renna," the driver says with a courteous nod. "Your ride is ready."

I glance at Hunter, who raises an eyebrow, clearly amused. "Fancy service."

"I guess there are some perks to all of this," I reply, sliding into the car. He follows, and as the door closes behind us, the silence inside the vehicle tells me something is different.

The driver pulls away from the gala, heading toward the hospital, and I suddenly realize how close we're sitting, how the space between us seems much smaller than it did before. The tension that's been simmering all night—the excitement, the victory, the unspoken connection—now seems to fill the car, wrapping around us as we move through the quiet streets.

As the city lights blur past the window, I glance at Hunter, and our eyes meet. For a moment, neither of us says anything, but the look we share speaks volumes. Tonight isn't over—not by a long shot.

———

UAB HOSPITAL

. . .

10:59 *pm*

MY FINGERS HOVER over the keyboard, the cursor blinking on the screen as I double-check the last few numbers. I should concentrate on this, making sure everything is perfect before sending the final proposal. Instead, all I can focus on is Hunter standing behind me, close enough that I can almost sense the heat radiating from his body.

"It looks good," Hunter says, his voice low and steady, but there's an undercurrent of something else that's been simmering between us all night.

"Yeah," I reply, my voice sounding far away, even to my own ears. I'm trying to focus, to keep my head in the game, but it's nearly impossible with him this close. "I think we're ready to send it."

I move to click the button, but my hand is trembling slightly, betraying the calm I'm trying to project. Before I can second-guess myself, I hit send, watching as the email disappears into the ether. It's done.

But the weight that should have lifted from my shoulders doesn't disappear. Instead, it's replaced by a different kind of tension, one that's been compounding ever since we left the gala.

The space of the room seems smaller than normal, the air thicker, and I can sense Hunter's gaze on me, more intense than ever.

"Frankie," he says, and there's something in the way he says my name that sends a shiver down my spine. I turn to face him, and the look in his eyes is all the confirmation I need. This isn't about the proposal anymore—it's about us.

His body leans closer, so close that the warmth of his breath on my skin is palpable. My heart is racing, and for a moment, I can't breathe, can't think. I'm caught in the gravitational pull of him, of this, and there's no escape— not that I want one.

Before I can say anything, his hand reaches up and brushes a strand of hair away from my face. His fingers linger ever so slightly against my cheek. The touch is light and tenta- tive, but it sends a jolt of electricity through me, waking up every nerve in my body.

Time seems to slow as he leans in, his gaze locked on mine, searching for any sign of hesitation. But there isn't any. I'm all in. I have been since the moment our eyes met at the gala.

And then he kisses me. It's soft at first, almost questioning, but I answer without words, pressing into him, deepening the kiss. The floodgates open, and suddenly, it's like we can't get close enough, can't touch enough. The intensity of it all overwhelms me but in the best way possible.

It's like riding a bike. Suddenly, that night in this same space comes rushing back, and my body and hands are on autopilot. It's so natural, as if we are picking up where we left off.

I stand, my chair scraping back, and wrap my arms around his neck, pulling him down to me as our lips move together in a frenzy. The edge of the desk digs into the back of my thighs, but I don't care. All I care about is this—about him, about the way he sets my body on fire.

Hunter's hands grip my waist, pulling me closer and lifting me slightly so that our middles are aligned. My fingers tangle in his hair, and it's like every touch, every kiss is erasing the space that's always been between us.

The lab has always been my sanctuary, a place where logic and reason reign supreme and emotion is left outside. But as Hunter's lips crash into mine, all that goes out the window. There's nothing scientific about the way my body responds to his touch, the way my heart hammers against my ribcage, demanding to be let out, to be let free.

His hands are everywhere—on my hips, in my hair, sliding up my thighs, pushing my dress up around my waist. There's an urgency to his movements, a desperation that matches my own. We're past the point of no return, and we both know it.

I pull at his shirt, tugging it free from his pants, needing the heat of his skin against mine, wanting him to fuck me like he did before. He helps me, yanking it over his head and tossing it aside, revealing the sculpted planes of his chest, the tattoos that tell a story I want to dive into and know.

He pulls out his wallet, seemingly rummaging for protection. "I'm on the pill," I whisper. I don't have time for any diversion. I need him now, urgently.

Before I can explore further, he lifts me effortlessly, setting me down on the cool surface of my desk. Papers scatter, files topple, and a pen rolls off the edge, hitting the floor with a soft clatter. Neither of us cares. The only thing that matters is closing the distance between us and having him inside me, where he belongs.

Our lips never break contact as he fumbles with his belt, the metallic rasp of the buckle loud in the otherwise silent lab. I reach down to help him, our fingers tangling together in our haste—zippers being pulled down, buttons being undone, underwear being pushed aside.

And then he's there, filling me completely, stretching me in the most exquisite way. I gasp at the intrusion, at the sudden fullness, but I don't want him to stop. I wrap my legs around his waist, pulling him in deeper, wanting everything he has to give.

Each thrust rocks the desk beneath us. The sound of our bodies colliding echoes off the walls. It's rough and intense, a meeting of two desperate souls, each seeking something in the other. My fingers dig into his back, clutching at his shoulders, holding on for dear life as he drives into me again and again.

The tension is building, a tight coil winding tighter and tighter in the pit of my stomach. I'm close, so close, and from the look on Hunter's face, so is he. He locks his eyes on mine, and the intensity threatens to swallow me whole.

"Hunter," I moan, my voice barely above a whisper, but he hears me.

"Let go, Frankie," he rasps, his voice laced with a need that mirrors my own.

And I do. I let go of everything—my fears, my doubts, my reservations—and surrender to the waves of pleasure that crash over me. "Fuck me, Hunter," I cry out, my body convulsing around his as my orgasm tears through me, leaving me breathless and shaking.

A moment later, Hunter follows me over the edge, his body going rigid before he collapses on top of me, both of us spent and gasping for air. His heart is pounding in sync with mine, a testament to the power of what just happened between us, connecting us.

We stay like that for several minutes, neither of us wanting to break the spell. But as our breathing begins to slow and the reality of our situation starts to sink in, I know that things between us have irrevocably changed. There's no going back to the way things were—not after this.

When we finally break apart, gasping for air, he rests his forehead against mine, and for a moment, we just breathe each other in. The world outside the lab ceases to exist; it's just us, caught in this moment.

"Frankie," he whispers, his voice thick with emotion, with need.

"Come with me," I whisper back, the words spilling out before I can second-guess them. "Come back to my house."

He doesn't hesitate. I pull my dress down and smooth it over my thighs. We gather our things in a blur. Neither of us speaks as we head out of the lab, the cool night air hitting us as we step outside.

The car waiting by the curb seems to materialize out of nowhere, and before I know it, we're inside, the silence between us charged with all the things we're not saying and the endorphins still in overdrive.

I reach for his hand, needing the contact, and to be grounded in this whirlwind. He squeezes back, his thumb brushing over my knuckles in a way that is both comforting and jarring. I'm not thinking about what this means, or even how we will deal with tomorrow. All I can think about is getting him in my bed for round two.

SIXTEEN

Hunter

Frankie's House

11:44 *pm*

I PUSH open the door to Frankie's house, the cool air a welcome sensation to cool the fire that is raging inside me. We're a tangle of limbs before the door even closes behind us, our urgency cutting through the quiet of her home.

Her lips are on mine, fierce and demanding, as I back her into the den. We're all hands and mouths, desperate for the taste of each other's skin. I tug at her dress, unzipping the long zipper that trails down her back. The fabric pools at her feet, leaving her in nothing but a lace thong and heels. The sight of her nearly undoes me. She's a vision of curves and softness, her green eyes dark with desire.

I lift her onto the edge of a nearby table, spreading her legs wide to accommodate me. My fingers find her center, already slick with need, and I stroke her, watching her arch and gasp beneath my touch. "Hunter," she moans, the sound of my name on her lips spurring me on.

I free myself from my pants, the ache in my cock demanding release. With one swift motion, I'm inside her, filling her completely. She cries out, her nails digging into my shoulders as I start to move. Each thrust proclaims and acknowledges that no one can never fully satiate the hunger I now have but her.

Her walls clench around me, the rhythm of our bodies syncopated and frenzied. "You feel so damn good," I growl, capturing her mouth in a deep, searing kiss. She responds by wrapping her legs tighter around my waist, pulling me deeper, harder, until the line between where I end and she begins blurs into oblivion.

We're both teetering on the edge, our breaths ragged and mingling. I know her orgasm is building, the way her body tenses and quivers beneath mine. "Come for me, Frankie," I whisper, and she does, her climax crashing over her in waves that I experience with her, like shocks of electricity throughout my entire body.

Her release triggers my own, and I follow her over the edge, my vision white-hot with pleasure as I empty myself into her. For a moment, we're frozen in time, our bodies locked together in the aftermath of our passion.

Breathless, I scoop her into my arms, carrying her to the bedroom. We collapse onto the bed, a mess of tangled limbs and heated skin. I trail kisses along her jaw, her neck, her collarbone, reveling in the way she squirms and moans beneath me.

"Again," she demands, her eyes shining with a mix of mischief and raw need. "I want to have you inside me again."

Who am I to deny such a request?

I roll her onto her stomach, pulling her hips back toward me. She looks over her shoulder, her gaze smoldering as I position myself at her entrance once more. This time, our lovemaking is slow and deliberate, each thrust a promise, each exhale a vow.

"God, Frankie," I murmur, my hands exploring every inch of her. "You're fucking incredible."

She pushes back against me, meeting my thrusts with equal fervor. "You fuck me so good, Hunter," she pants. "Don't ever stop."

———

WE LIE TANGLED TOGETHER in the sheets, our breathing still heavy, the remnants of our intensity lingering in the air.

The room is quiet except for the sound of our breathing, still labored from what just happened. The sheets stick to my skin, not wanting to release myself from the warmth of her body pressed against mine.

My hand rests on her waist, fingers tracing slow, lazy circles on her back. I don't think I've ever felt this close to someone, not just physically, but emotionally. Our first time was between two strangers who met during a perfect storm. We hardly knew each other, and it was purely physical, the end.

This time, it's… different. And it's terrifying.

She's lying with her head on my chest, her hair fanned out over my skin, and I can hear her breathing start to slow. There's a tenderness around us I haven't felt in a long time, maybe ever, and it makes my chest tighten in a way that's both comforting and unsettling.

I keep my hand moving on her low back, needing that connection, something to ground me. I don't want to break the silence, but at the same time, I have to say something, to let her in a little more. It's been so long since I've let anyone get this close, and it's like a door has opened that beckons me in.

"It's been a long time since I've felt this… connected," I murmur, my voice sounding like it belongs to someone else, but it's the truth. I've been avoiding this, avoiding her, because somehow I instinctively knew she was different.

She lifts her head slightly, looking up at me with those green eyes that always seem to see more than I want them to. "Yeah," she says softly, her voice carrying the same weight as mine. "I know what you mean. I think you and I are cut from the same cloth in that way."

The silence stretches out again, but it's not uncomfortable. It's filled with something unspoken, something that's been building between us for months, and now that we've crossed this line for a second time, I can't pretend it doesn't exist anymore.

"Well, there was that one time in the lab…" She looks up at me with a mischievously devilish smile. I have to give her props for being the first to break the silence on that.

"Good point, there was that one time in the lab."

We both laugh, but neither of us takes it any further. I guess she wanted to address it, so it isn't the elephant in the room anymore. I'm not sure there is anymore to say on the subject. Nothing more than what we just did.

Something I didn't talk about the other night at the bar because I wasn't ready, seems appropriate now, to give her context. But now, with her here, in my arms, it's like a natural opening.

"The other night… when you asked about Hodgkin's…" I start, hesitant but also empowered. Her body tenses slightly against mine, and I know she's listening, waiting, wondering where this is going. "It's been on my mind ever since."

She shifts, her fingers tracing patterns on my chest, and it's like she's instilling in me the strength to keep going. "My mom was diagnosed recently," I finally say, the words heavier than I expected. "With Hodgkin's lymphoma."

Saying it out loud for the first time is a release. Like I don't have to carry it all by myself anymore.

There's a pause, the air between us thick with unspoken emotion. She doesn't say anything right away, just lifts her hand to my face, her touch gentle, grounding me in this moment.

"We aren't especially close, but she is a widow and there is something about her diagnosis, I don't know, it's just weighing on me."

"Oh, Hunter, I'm so sorry."

"You don't have to be sorry at all. I guess I'm just telling you since you brought it up. I told you not to worry, and I mean it. Hodgkins is relatively simple and curable, but it is scary when it is someone you love."

"Yes, it can be scary, you're right." Somehow she always says just enough to comfort me without pushing me or saying too much. It's a true talent.

"I've been trying to stay out of it," I continue, my voice low, "to keep my distance, but… it's not easy. She was always tough on me, pushing me to be better, to do more, and I've spent my whole life trying to live up to that. But now that she needs me, I don't know how to handle it."

Frankie's fingers brush through my hair, and the simple act is enough to make the lump in my throat loosen, just a little. "I'm sorry, Hunter," she whispers, and there's no pity in her voice, just understanding. "That must be so hard."

"It is," I admit, my voice so quiet at this point, my body fighting against itself not to completely lose it. "I'm trying to figure out how to be there for her without getting pulled back into all that old stuff. But it's hard, you know? It's really fucking hard."

"I get it," she murmurs, pressing a soft kiss to my chest, right over my heart. "It's hard watching our parents get sick. I lost my mom, too. It's been years and I'm still grieving her loss. There's something about moms that gets us right in the gut."

"I bet she was a special lady to have raised such an amazing daughter."

"She was pretty amazing. She was a single mom and we grew up together. I wish you could have met her."

"Me, too."

We hold each other, neither of us saying anything for a while. Another thread connecting us, pulling us closer. I've never opened up like this, and with Frankie, something seems so right about it.

I've been carrying this weight for so long, and now that I've let her in, it isn't nearly as heavy. Not with her here.

"Thank you," I say, my baritone thick with emotion I'm not used to sharing. "For listening and letting me tell you a little about my drama. It's nice to talk to someone."

"You don't have to thank me," she replies, resting her head against my chest again. "I'm here for you, Hunter. Whatever you need."

We lie there in the quiet, her hand still moving gently on my skin, and for the first time in a long time, I know I'm not alone in this. Like maybe, just maybe, it's okay to let someone in.

The world outside doesn't matter right now. It's just us, here in this moment, and for once, I'm not scared of what comes next.

———

6:12 *am*

THE LIGHTENING SKY outside nudges me out of my sleep. My body is used to waking early during the week, and doesn't allow me to sleep in even on the weekends.

I lie in Frankie's bed for a moment, staring up at the ceiling. My mind races even though the rest of the world is still asleep. The warmth of Frankie's body is pressed against my side, her breathing deep and even as she sleeps peacefully beside me.

But I'm anything but peaceful.

Our intense union plays on a loop in my mind—the ferocity, the passion, the way we came together like we were the only two people in the world. It's like the first time, the time that almost seemed forgotten, was the preface to what was to come.

It was a test and I failed.

It was a mistake.

The excitement of the evening, the adrenaline from securing a sponsor—I let it cloud my judgment. And now, in the cold light of morning, all I can think about is how reckless it was to let her in like that, to cross that line. Again.

I turn my head slightly, looking at her. Even in sleep, she's beautiful—her dark hair against the white pillow, the rise and fall of her chest steady and calm. There's a part of me that wants to reach out, to touch her, to relive the connection we had just hours ago.

But I know better. This is a slippery slope, one that I can't afford to go down. I don't have the time or the emotional bandwidth for a relationship, especially not with a coworker. Especially not with Frankie.

What the hell was I thinking?

I exhale slowly, trying to ease the rigidness in my body. I can't stay here. I need to get out, clear my head, and put some distance between us before things get any more complicated. It's better this way, for both of us.

Carefully, I shift away from her, moving slowly so I don't wake her. The last thing I need is a conversation right now, especially one where I have to explain why I'm leaving. She deserves better than some half-assed excuse, but I don't have the emotional tools to give her anything else.

As I slide out of bed, I glance over at her one last time. There's a pang of guilt, or is it regret? I push it down, forcing myself to focus on the bigger picture. This isn't about her, or even about last night. This is about me and the bubble I've created for myself to keep from getting too involved with anyone.

I grab my clothes from the floor, quickly pulling them on. My movements are quiet, careful, every sense on high alert in case she stirs. I can't let this turn into something more than what it was—a mistake and something that can never happen again.

Once I'm dressed, I slip out of the bedroom, closing the door behind me as softly as I can. I move through her house quickly, my phone already in my hand as I pull up the Uber app. The sooner I'm out of here, the better.

I step outside, quietly pulling the front door closed. As I wait for the car to arrive, I can't help but acknowledge the gnawing sense of guilt in the pit of my stomach. I shove it aside, reminding myself why I'm doing this. Relationships are messy, complicated as it is. Frankie and I have an important thing we are working on, there is no space for emotion.

I am sitting on her front steps when the car arrives. As I slide into the backseat and give a curt greeting to the driver, I finally breathe.

Her house fading in the distance is the best thing that's happened so far this morning.

———

MONDAY, *May 27*

UAB Hospital

8:32 *am*

"HEY, what's this I hear about you and Dibbins?" Shep doesn't bother to sit down as he stands between my door and desk, hands in the pockets of his white lab coat. I'm seeing clinic patients today, grateful for a break from surgeries.

"Hm?" I'm reading charts and distracted when he makes his appearance.

"Hodgkins lymphoma?"

It takes me another second to process, but realization hits as my mind finally gets past the anxiety that's been building about Frankie. We haven't spoken since I snuck out yesterday morning and I'm in knots about how to deal with it when we inevitably do.

This is precisely why I fucked up when we slept together. For a second time. There is no avoiding her or the awkwardness that is sure to follow when we have to work together.

"I might have mentioned a few cases he would want to

take a look at. Maybe I steered a couple of people his way. What's the big deal?"

"You're a surgeon," Shep says, lowering his chin so he can look at me over his glasses. I don't like when he does this, it seems like he's addressing a minor that's been naughty and needs a talking to. "You just seem obsessed with this lately, that's all. Wondering what the deal is."

Fucker. Why is he pushing me so much? "Yeah, we can help each other around here, right?"

"Why the interest in HL? Fess up, enough with the song and dance."

There's no need to beat around the bush. It's not like some dark secret, anyway. I can be such a weirdo sometimes.

"My mom called me about a month and a half ago about a lump she found under her breast. It turns out she has Hodgkin's lymphoma. So I've been reading up on it. When a patient comes through, I've been sending them to him. Sooner they catch it and come up with a treatment plan, the better the outcome."

Shep seems to take in what I've just shared and thinks about it for a moment. "Is she okay?"

"Yeah, for now," I say after blowing out a sigh, "She's been on my ass about it since she found it. I might not have thought twice about it, but through my reading and research, I've found out there is a rare strain that is defying conventional treatment."

"It wouldn't hurt to talk to Dibbins, you know, instead of sending him a bunch of random cases. Like, really talk to him, I mean. Maybe he can take a look at your mom's case and help her—help you."

Sigh, "Yeah, I could do that." I still haven't called my mom's doctor like I promised. Fuck. Here is the universe again butting its nose in my fate. "I suppose I should talk to Dibbins today."

"I think you should," Shep concedes with a nod. "Hey, the gala was pretty sweet, huh? Where did you disappear to?" I was almost happy for the change in topic until I it was this one.

Dammit, I don't want to go into this, especially since rumors are already flying.

"I'm so glad you were enjoying it. I was working. Bench had me schmoozing a few billionaires. I was able to secure a sponsor for the pacemaker study I've been working on, so we are going to human trials."

I purposefully leave out Frankie's name because I don't want to hear his horseshit about her. I'm sure he is bringing it up to see what I will divulge.

"Your sponsor? Did you close the deal?"

I nod. Shep's smile is genuine as he takes the few steps to reach across my desk and shake my hand as I accept the gesture.

"Congratulations, Hunter. That's a big deal! Way to go! You must have given one hell of a good pitch."

Jill buzzes in, saving me from the awkwardness of having to "aw, shucks" my way through that. "Dr. Parrish, Mrs. Oppenstar is on line one. She insists on speaking to you about a fungus on her toe she thinks is related to surgery."

I roll my eyes and Shep stands. "On that note, I'm outta here."

SEVENTEEN

Frankie
_____

Frankie's House

8:48 am

I'M POURING my first cup of mediocre coffee, trying to wrap my head around everything that happened this weekend, still reeling over the fact that Hunter left without a word and I haven't heard from him since.

I don't have to be at the hospital until 11:30 for my meeting. So I have time to ease into my day, thank goodness, because I need it.

My phone, charging on the stone countertop, buzzes loudly. I reach for it, wondering if it's him. Before I look, though, I already know it's not him. It has to be Carly. She always checks in about this time if she isn't working.

> Good morning, sunshine! How about I bring coffee and bagels? We need to catch up about the gala!

I sigh, the tight knot in my stomach twisting a little more. Carly's not going to let me off the hook. She's going to want every detail, and after the way last night ended... I'm not sure I'm ready to talk about it. But this is Carly. She knows me too well, and there's no way I can avoid this conversation.

> Vanilla skinny latte. I have cream cheese for the bagels. Come on.

I'm happy to pour out this weak ass coffee for something a little stronger—and tastier. Her response is immediate.

> On my way!

I drag myself to the bathroom to change out of my robe and into real clothes. The house is too quiet, too empty after Saturday night. I try not to think about how I woke up alone yesterday, how Hunter was already gone. I can't let myself dwell on it, not with Carly on her way over.

By the time I've set the table and gotten everything ready, I hear the knock on the door. Carly, even nursing her aches and bruises always brings her full energy. I open the door, and there she is, grinning at me with two cups of coffee in hand and a bag of fresh bagels balanced on top.

"Morning!" she chirps, pushing past me into the house. "If I know you, you haven't had a bite to eat yet today." She hands me the coffee, smiling, pleased with herself that she is taking care of me.

"Thanks," I mumble, taking a sip and letting the warmth spread through me. It's a small comfort, but it helps.

"Let's take this outside," Carly suggests, nodding toward the screened-in porch. "It's too nice a morning to stay cooped up in the house." I grab the napkins, butter knife and cream cheese.

I nod, following her out to the porch. The air is fresh. With the ceiling fan, there is the perfect amount of coolness that makes it perfect for sitting outside. We settle into the chairs, and I watch as Carly arranges the bagels on a paper plate in the bag on the table, her movements quick and efficient.

"So," she says, leaning back in her chair and giving me a pointed look. "Let's hear it. I want all the deets."

"First, how are you feeling? I think you made the right decision staying in, by the way. You didn't miss a thing."

Carly sighs dramatically. "Oh, for sure. I hated missing the gala, but there's no way I could've handled it. My head was pounding just from watching TV. Staying in was definitely the right call. And I'm finally starting to feel like a human again. Just in time to go back to work this week. Yippee!"

Her sarcasm is infectious and lets me know she is getting back to her old self.

"Good," I say, genuinely relieved. "I'm glad you're doing better."

"Me too," Carly says, and then her eyes narrow playfully. "But enough about me. I need you to tell me everything about last night. And I mean everything. Best dressed, worst dressed, and all the juicy details in between."

I take a deep breath, trying to steel myself for the barrage of questions I know is coming. Carly doesn't miss a thing, and there's no way I'm going to get out of this without telling her at least some of what happened. But for now, I can keep it light, focusing on the gala itself and not... everything else.

"Well," I begin, trying to sound casual, "the gala was beautiful. They really went all out with the decorations, and the food was amazing. The band was so-so, but full transparency, I wasn't out of the dance floor."

Carly waves her hand, dismissing my attempt to stall. "Please, I don't care about the food or the music. Who had the best dress?"

I can't help but smile at her enthusiasm. "Okay, okay. Let's see…"

Carly's eyes are trained on me, sharp and focused, as I try to keep the conversation light. I'm giving her the rundown of the best and worst dressed at the gala, but I can tell she's not buying it. She knows me too well, and her suspicion is growing with every passing second.

"And then there was Mrs. Pembroke," I say, forcing a smile as I recount the over-the-top feathered dress she wore. "I'm pretty sure she was going for 'glamorous peacock,' but it came off more like 'escaped from a Mardi Gras float.'"

Carly laughs, but her eyes don't leave mine. "Okay, that's a good one," she says, leaning back in her chair. "But enough with the distractions. You're holding something back, Frankie. And don't even try to deny it. How did your 'fuck me' green dress perform?"

A little too well, I should say. But I'm still hoping to avoid that…

I take a long sip of my latte, trying to buy myself a little more time, slurping dramatically. But Carly's not letting up. She's got that look in her eye—the one that says she's not going to stop until she gets the truth out of me.

"What are you talking about?" I ask, attempting to play dumb, but the words come out too quickly, too defensive.

She raises an eyebrow. "Oh, come on. I know you better than that. You're avoiding the biggest news of the night. You guys secured a sponsor, didn't you? That's huge!"

Oh, phew! She was pushing about the news about the sponsor!

"Yes, yes! You're right. How could I forget the biggest news of the night?"

"Hmmm. You've barely mentioned it. So it must be something surrounding that, or, maybe a certain hot doctor, hmmm," she says dramatically, narrowing her eyes and tapping her jaw.

I shrug, trying to keep my tone casual and not taking the bait. "Yeah, we did. It was a big win, but I just—" I pause, struggling to find the right words. "There's a lot on my mind, Carly."

She narrows her eyes at me, clearly not satisfied with my answer. "Uh-huh. And does this 'lot on your mind' have anything to do with aforementioned hot doctor…?"

I bite my lip, as a crawling sensation rises under my skin, prickling with intensity. I should've known she'd go there. Carly can read me like a book, and there's no use trying to hide it any longer.

I sigh, setting my coffee down and meeting her gaze. "Okay, fine. Yes, it does."

Her eyes widen, and she leans forward eagerly. "I knew it! Give it to me, girl. What happened?"

I swallow, trying to keep my voice even, matter-of-fact. "We slept together. After the gala, we both had to go back to the lab to finalize some things, and... one thing led to another."

Carly's mouth drops open for a split second before she recovers. "Wait, you and Hunter Parrish? Slept together? Again?! Oh my god, Frankie! That lab is like an aphrodisiac for you two!"

I nod, forcing a small smile. "It was great, really. But it was just a heat-of-the-moment thing. Same as las time. You know how these things happen—adrenaline, excitement, a few drinks..." I leave out that we came back to my house for rounds two, three, four and five.

Carly's expression shifts from shock to something more concerned. "And what happened after?"

Shit.

I hesitate, then finally admit the part that's been bothering me the most. "He came back here. And then left early Sunday morning before I woke up. He didn't say goodbye. And he hasn't called or texted since."

Carly's face softens, and she reaches across the table, placing a hand on mine. "Frankie, I hate to say 'I told you so,' but... I kinda told you so. Hunter's got a reputation, you know? He's not exactly the settling-down type. But you got a little fun out of it. You can never expect too much with him."

I nod, trying to keep my emotions in check. "Yeah, I know. And honestly, that's fine. I don't have time for a relationship, and I definitely don't want to get involved with a coworker. It was just a little jarring there for a minute yesterday, that's all."

Carly's eyes search mine, looking for any sign that I might be lying. "Are you sure? Because it sounds like maybe you were hoping for something more."

I force a laugh, shaking my head. "No, really. I enjoyed it, but that's all it was. A one-time thing. I'm not looking for anything more, and I'm certainly not going to get my hopes up about someone like Hunter."

But even as I say the words, a small part of me knows they're not entirely true. There's a sliver of disappointment, of hurt, that I can't quite shake. I thought maybe I was different to him. There was a part of me that thought there was something growing between us. Then I remind myself how foolish that thought is.

I give Carly a reassuring smile, trying to convince her— and myself—that I'm fine. "Really, Carly. I'm okay. It was just a little action, nothing more. Let's just focus on the fact that we secured the sponsor and move on."

Carly looks at me for a long moment, then nods slowly. "Alright, if you say so. But if you ever need to talk about it… you know I'm here."

"Thanks," I say softly, squeezing her hand. "I know."

———

UAB HOSPITAL

11:13 *am*

· · ·

188

THE HOSPITAL IS BUSTLING with activity for a late morning on a Monday. It seems unusually lively, but maybe Mondays always are.

It's strange being here in the middle of the day when I'm usually working from home. I try not to come until later in later in the day if I need to for any reason. My visits to the hospital are rare and often brief, but today is different. Today is a big day.

I make my way to the admin office, where the sponsor's representative is waiting for me to sign off on some paperwork.

This is it—the moment we've been working toward for months, years, really. The FDA approval is just a signature away, and once it's done, the real work begins. There's still so much to do—recruiting hospitals, finalizing protocols, getting everything ready for the human trials. But this... this was the hardest hurdle to overcome. Without the money, nothing else can happen.

As I step into the office, the rep greets me with a smile, and we exchange a few pleasantries before getting down to business. The stack of paperwork in front of me is daunting, but I'm used to it.

I've been through this process before, and I know the drill. Still, as I start signing page after page, there's a heaviness in my chest that I can't shake. Maybe it's the weight of the responsibility, or maybe it's everything else that's been piling up lately.

I try to focus, pushing everything else to the back of my mind. I can't afford to be distracted right now. Not when something I have been dreaming about for so long is about to come to reality.

After signing the last page, I hand the papers back to the rep, who smiles warmly. "Congratulations, Dr. Renna. This is a huge step forward. We look forward to working with you and to a successful clinical trial."

I nod, offering a small smile in return. "Thank you. I'm just glad we've made it this far."

The smarter people who deal with the money and the financial side will handle all of those mundane details. My work has nothing to do with that part of it, but capitalism pays my salary and makes it all work, so it is an important element, too. It is all symbiotic.

The rep leaves, taking the signed paperwork with him, and I'm left alone in the small office. I should accept the sense of accomplishment, relief even, but only a gnawing anxiety in the pit of my stomach remains.

There's still so much to do, and now, on top of everything, I'm going to have to work with Hunter more closely than ever to finalize the protocol. The thought of spending more time with him, especially after what happened, is unsettling, to say the least.

This is why you don't sleep with your coworkers, no matter how hot and irresistible they might seem. Why do I keep making this mistake with him?

My phone buzzes on the desk, pulling me out of my thoughts. I glance at the screen and Bill, my father's name, flashes up. Talking to him could be the straw that will break my back.

We are making good progress, but I can't talk to him right now. Last we spoke he told me he would call to update me on his latest labs. I can't take any bad news right now, and I don't think I can be positive enough for good news.

So I send it to voicemail, the screen flashing one last time before it goes dark. I release a breath I didn't realize I was holding, but the relief is short-lived. The anxiety is rising, pressing down on me from all sides. The trial, Hunter, my father—it's all too much, all at once.

I stand up, pacing the conference room, trying to shake the feeling of being overwhelmed. This is turning out to be a very bad Monday. The kind of Monday where everything that could go wrong threatens to, just waiting for the right moment to come crashing down.

Taking a deep breath, I force myself to sit back down. There's no time to dwell on this now. There's work to be done, and I have to keep moving forward, no matter how heavy everything seems.

But as I open my laptop and try to focus on the protocol, my mind keeps drifting back to the inevitability of losing my father before I even have him, to Hunter and whatever the fuck is going on there, to the pressure of making sure everything is perfect for this trial. Everything is piling up.

This is going to be one hell of a week. There's no way around it, so I've just got to get through it.

———

1:51 *pm*

I'M HUNCHED over my desk, the soft glow of my laptop screen casting a blue tint on my face as I work on the protocol draft. My fingers fly over the keys, trying to put together something coherent that we can start with, but my mind keeps wandering back to the voicemail I'm avoiding and the mess that is my life right now.

A light knock on the doorframe pulls me out of my thoughts, and I look up, my heart sinking as soon as I see who it is.

Hunter. Fuck. "Hello."

I offer a weak smile instead of speaking.

He's standing there, looking as composed as ever, but there's something in his eyes that makes my pulse quicken. I curse myself for not going home when I had the chance.

"Is this a good time?" he asks, his voice smooth, but there's an edge to it, like he's not sure how this conversation is going to go.

I take a deep breath, pushing aside the anxiety that's been gnawing at me all day. "Sure," I say, gesturing to the chair across from my desk. "Come on in."

He steps into the office, his movements measured, and takes a seat. The air between us is tense, thick with the things we're not saying. Neither of us addresses the other night or the next morning, and I'm grateful for that, even if it leaves the omission a little suffocating.

"I heard you signed the paperwork with the sponsor earlier," Hunter says, breaking the silence. His tone is professional, but there's an underlying tension I can't ignore.

"Yeah," I reply, forcing a smile. "It's official. Now we just have to get everything ready for the trial."

He nods, his eyes scanning the papers scattered across my desk. "You're working on the protocol?"

"Just a first draft," I say, trying to keep my voice steady. "I figured I'd get started on it. But, of course, I'll ultimately defer to you. You've got the experience with pacemakers."

Hunter leans back in his chair. His gaze focused on me, making it hard to breathe. "We'll need to make sure the protocol is solid, of course. Everything has to be precise, every control exact. We'll have to outline the specific patient criteria—age range, severity of heart failure, and any co-morbidities that could affect the outcomes."

I nod, jotting down a few notes as he talks. "Right, of course. And we'll need to define the endpoints clearly. Whether we're measuring improvement in ejection fraction, reduction in hospitalization rates, or overall survival."

He leans forward slightly, his eyes narrowing as he considers the details. "We should also think about incorporating some novel features into the pacemaker itself. Maybe something like real-time telemetry for remote monitoring. If we can show that it not only improves patient outcomes but also reduces the need for in-person follow-ups, that could be a game-changer."

"That's a great idea," I say, genuinely impressed. "We could also consider looking at how the pacemaker interacts with other implanted devices, like defibrillators, to make sure there's no interference."

Discussing work, and the excitement of this all becoming a reality, is certainly making this interaction easier. Just like the last time, each work meeting will get easier, until there is no more tension.

Until we both find ourselves in the lab and fuck each other's brains out.

Hunter nods again, his focus intense. "We'll need to work closely with the engineers on that, make sure everything's seamless."

There's a pause as I finish typing up my notes, as the tension continues to shift, becoming something more palpable, more personal. I know his eyes are on me, and when I look up, there's something in his expression that makes my breath catch.

"Well," Hunter says, standing up, his tone casual but his eyes still locked on mine. "I should let you get back to it. Once you're finished, I can go over it with a fine-toothed comb and offer my thoughts."

I nod, swallowing hard. "Of course. Thanks for stopping by."

He hesitates for just a second, then adds, "Hey, I was wondering if you might be up for dinner tonight."

The question catches me off guard, and I blink at him, not really sure what to make of it. My heart does a little flip, but my brain is already racing, trying to figure out how to respond. Is this about the trial? Or… something else?

Before I can think myself out of it, the word is out of my mouth. "Sure."

Hunter's eyebrows raise slightly, surprised, perhaps. Maybe he expected me to say no. "I was planning to grab some tapas and a beer at The Southern Kitchen & Bar downtown around seven. Would you be up for joining me? I can pick you up so we both don't have to find parking."

The directness of his approach throws me off balance, but I recover quickly, shaking my head. "I'll meet you there," I say, my voice steadier than I feel. I'm not sure what this is about, but staying independent allows me to roll with it easier and gives me an out.

"Alright," he says, a small, almost imperceptible smile playing on his lips. "See you then."

He turns and walks out of my office, leaving me staring after him, my mind a whirl of conflicting emotions. I should have said no—clearly, decisively, no. But, I didn't And now I'm going to dinner with Hunter Parrish tonight.

―――――

5:16 *pm*

I GATHER MY THINGS, shoving my laptop into my bag and trying to ignore the sense of impending doom that seems to surround me. It's been a long day, and the thought of going home to shower and get ready for dinner with Hunter seems more like an obligation than a treat at this point.

I know I should check Bill's message. I'm sure part of it is worrying about what it contains, not wanting to get more bad news I won't know how to process.

My finger hovers over the screen, hesitating for a moment. I don't want to listen to it, but I also know I won't stop thinking about it until I know what the update is. Taking a deep breath, I tap on the notification and bring the phone to my ear.

"Hey, Frankie. It's Dad." It still gets me every time he refers to himself as that. I haven't used any such title to his face, because calling him "Dad" is so disingenuous.

"I just wanted to let you know that I got my labs back today, and… well, it looks like the latest treatment is working. It's still early to tell for sure, but the good news is, things aren't getting worse. And best-case scenario, it might actually be improving."

There's a pause, and I can hear him take a breath, as if he's unsure of what to say next. I follow suit and fill my lungs with a relieved breath.

"I'll be getting labs again in two weeks, so we'll know more then. But I just wanted to share the positive news with you. I hope you're having a good Monday."

The voicemail ends, and I'm left standing in the middle of the office, the phone still pressed to my ear, the importance of his words resonating with me. I lower the phone slowly and stare at the screen.

The name "Bill" taunts me as if somehow, miraculously, something will pop up, giving me direction on what to do next.

I exhale the full breath slowly, trying to push aside the confusion and the tangled mess of emotions that always seem to surface whenever he's involved. He's still the man who walked away, the man who left my mother and me to fend for ourselves. But he's also the man who's now fighting a battle I can't ignore.

And maybe I don't want to ignore it anymore.

I tuck my phone into my bag and sling it over my shoulder,

grateful for some good news. At least some of the weight on my shoulders is a little lighter.

EIGHTEEN

Hunter

The Southern Kitchen & Bar

6:55 pm

I ARRIVE at the restaurant a few minutes early, scanning the space for a good spot. It's a casual, trendy place. The lighting is dim and there's a bit of indie music playing in the background. It's a mix of people chatting over drinks and appetizers, the perfect place for us to meet without feeling like we're on display.

I find a couple of open seats at the bar and take one, ordering a whiskey neat while I wait for Frankie.

My mind's still on the protocol we discussed earlier today, but more than that, I keep replaying Saturday night—or rather, yesterday morning—in my head. Leaving her house before she woke felt like the right call.

I couldn't afford to complicate things more than they already are. But now, sitting here, waiting to see her again,

I can't shake this feeling that I'm about to bulldoze all the good I did by leaving.

Soon I thankfully spot Frankie walking in. Her eyes scan the room before they land on me. She's dressed casually, in a light sweater and jeans, but she looks ridiculously beautiful, like she always does. She spots me and heads over, offering a small smile that I can't quite read.

"Hey," she says, sliding onto the stool next to mine. God, she has effortlessly cool down to a science. I want to be like Frankie when I grow up.

"Hey, you," I reply, nodding to the bartender who comes over to take her drink order. She asks for a gin and tonic, and I watch as she settles in, her posture relaxed, but there's something guarded in her eyes.

"I opted for a whiskey instead of a beer. Feels more like a Monday-appropriate decision."

"Excellent choice. Cheers. This place is nice. I haven't been here before."

"Yeah, it's got a good vibe," I say, taking a sip. "Figured it would be better than some stuffy restaurant."

She nods, and we lapse into a bit of small talk about the menu, the food, the kind of things you say when you're trying to avoid the real conversation. The unspoken words between us are almost unavoidable, but I'm not ready to go there yet. Not here, not now.

Probably not ever, if I can avoid it.

As we order a couple of appetizers to share, I decide to address the obvious. "About yesterday," I start, keeping my tone light. "I'm sorry for leaving like that. I didn't want to wake you. It was early and I needed to get a few things done."

She glances at me, her expression unreadable. "It's fine," she says, but there's a slight edge to her voice. "No worries at all, I get it"

I nod, relieved that she's not pushing the issue."Thanks," I say, finishing my drink. "I just didn't want things to get weird, you know?"

"Right," she replies, her tone still cool. "No need to complicate this trial. Our schedule is jam-packed for the foreseeable future.

As a moment of silence ensues, the food arrives just in time to relieve the tension. We both dig in, focusing on the Cajun Angels and pimento cheese dip, but I am completely aware it is all a fragile shroud that keeps us both safe from going there.

After a few bites, she speaks up again, her voice softer. " Actually, I got some good news today. The person I mentioned the other night—the one with Hodgkin's—he got his labs back, and it looks like the treatment might be working."

I glance at her, surprised by the shift in conversation. "Yeah? That's great news." She said "he." Unexpectedly jealousy rises up at the idea she is seeing someone else.

She nods, her eyes flicking to mine briefly before she looks back down at her drink. "I mean, it's still early, but he said things aren't getting worse. And there's a chance it could be improving. What do you think?"

I lean back slightly, considering her words.

"That's definitely a good sign. Hodgkin's is often very curable, especially if the treatment's showing results early on. The fact that it's not getting worse is a win in itself. If he keeps responding well, there's a good chance he'll beat it."

She looks relieved, and I can see the tension in her shoulders ease a little. But as I say the words, I can't help but think about my mom. She's got a long road ahead, and while I've been trying to keep my distance, this conversation brings it all back to the surface.

I should be doing more—calling her doctor, checking on her treatment plan—but every time I think about it, that familiar resistance, that wall I've built to keep her at arm's length, and I always find a reason why I can't in that moment, keeps me at bay.

Frankie's voice pulls me back to the present. "That's good to hear. I was worried, but… this gives me hope."

I nod, not trusting myself to say more. My thoughts are too all over the place about what I should be doing, what I've been avoiding, and what it all means. The last thing I need is to let my guard down again, especially after this weekend.

Opening up to her was a fleeting moment of bad judgement. That, and the sex, of course.

We continue to eat, the conversation shifting back to work—discussing the trial, the next steps, and keeping things as professional as possible. But the tension lingers, like a current running beneath the surface.

As the night winds down, I realize I'm not ready to walk

away from this—whatever "this" is. But I also know I'm not ready to face it head-on.

Not yet.

Frankie catches my eye as we finish the last of our drinks, and there's something unspoken there, something that tells me I'm not the only one. "Hey, you up for a walk tonight? It's a nice night."

"That would be nice."

———

9:19 *pm*

THE EVENING AIR IS CRISP, a slight breeze rustling through the trees as our enjoyable walk is coming to a natural end. We are back at the entrance near the restaurant, where both of our cars are parked.

We've been talking, mostly about work and about the trial, but we've come to an end, and the conversation has slowed. The sudden silence between us is startling with everything we've left unspoken. Luckily, we can each go our separate ways.

I glance over at Frankie, her face softened by the glow of the streetlights. There's something about the way she moves, the way her hair catches the light, that makes it hard to look away. I've been trying to keep it professional, to stay focused on the work, but the more time I spend with her, the harder it gets to maintain that distance.

We stop at a crosswalk, waiting for the light to change, and there is a palpable force in the cool night air. I can't stop thinking about how easy it was to talk to her tonight, how comfortable it felt—like we were on the same wavelength, even when we weren't talking about anything important.

As the light changes and we cross the street, Frankie's hand brushes against mine, just for a second, and my body turns into a sensory-seeking missile. The touch is so fleeting, so light, that it could have been an accident. But it sends an electric current through me, something that bypasses my brain entirely and goes straight to instinct.

Before I even realize what I'm doing, I reach out and gently grab her hand, stopping her in her tracks just as we reach the sidewalk. She turns to look at me, her eyes wide with surprise, but there's something else there too—something that mirrors the pull I've been trying to resist.

"Frankie," I say, my voice low, rougher than I intended. I don't know what I'm about to say next, if I'm about to say anything at all, because suddenly, the words don't seem important anymore.

It's as if my body has a mind of its own, and before I can stop myself, I'm stepping closer, my free hand coming up to cup her cheek. She doesn't pull away; instead, she leans into my touch, her eyes searching mine, as if she's waiting for me to make the next move.

And then, without thinking, I do. I lean down and press my lips to hers, the kiss soft at first, tentative, like I'm testing the waters. But the moment our lips meet, it's like something snaps inside me—a floodgate opening, releasing everything I've been holding back.

Frankie responds almost immediately, her hands sliding up to rest against my chest, grasping my shirt into two fistfuls, pulling me closer. The kiss deepens, becomes more urgent, more intense. I can't help the low groan that escapes from the back of my throat. It's like I've been starving for this, for her, and now that I've had a taste, I don't want to stop.

The world around us blurs, fades away, until it's just the two of us, standing in the middle of the city street, lost in each other. The kiss is sensual, almost too much, but it's everything my instinct knew it would be. It's like my body is finally being honest, doing what I've been too afraid to admit I wanted.

When we finally break apart, we're both breathing hard, our foreheads resting against each other. The air between us crackles with tension, with something new, something we've been trying to avoid but can't anymore.

"I... I didn't mean for that to happen," I murmur, my voice rough, still out of breath. But even as I say it, I know it's a lie. I meant every second of it to happen.

Frankie's eyes meet mine, and I can see the same confusion, the same conflict swirling there. But there's something else too, telling me she's as into this as I am, even if neither of us knows what the hell to do about it.

My mind is spinning, trying to come up with something appropriate to say while also assessing what that meant. I want to follow her lead since she is so self-assured and measured, but I can tell she is waiting to see what I say, what I do.

The reality of whatever this is, both together with work, and this blossoming "thing," whatever it is, after work, we can't just pretend that didn't happen. We also can't dive headfirst into something that neither of us is sure what it is.

Frankie shifts slightly, her hand still resting on my lower back after loosening the hug. I can see the conflict in her eyes—like, what the fuck.

"I… I should probably head home," she finally says, her voice soft but steady. She takes a small step back, her hand slipping away from my body. The loss of her touch is immediate and sharp.

"Yeah," I agree, though the word is like sandpaper in my throat. "We have a busy day tomorrow. I have two surgeries early before our meeting with Bench."

Her eyes flicker with something. I'm not sure if it is disappointment or relief. Maybe both. She nods slowly, her gaze dropping to the ground for a moment before she looks back up at me. "Thank you for tonight. This was a delightful change to my boring schedule."

There's so much more I want to say, but the words get tangled up in my head, stuck somewhere between what I feel and what I'm afraid to admit. Instead, I just nod, the silence stretching out between us like a chasm.

"I guess I'll see you tomorrow," she says, taking another step back, putting more distance between us. Her voice is quiet, almost tentative, like she's testing the waters of whatever this is between us now.

"Yeah," I reply, trying to muster up a smile that doesn't quite reach my eyes. "Tomorrow."

She hesitates for just a second like she might say something else, but then she turns and starts walking away. I watch her go, my chest tight, every instinct in me screaming to call her back, to close the gap between us again. But I stay rooted in place, knowing that this is how it has to be. For now.

As she disappears around the corner, I let out my breath, the night suddenly a lot more dreary than it did a few minutes ago.

We're both in too deep already, and if we're going to make anything of this—whatever "this" is—we have to take it one step at a time. Rushing in will only make everything more complicated and confusing.

We both seem to be aware that if we hadn't already, we've crossed a line, and there's no going back. And finally, for the first time since all of this started months ago, I don't want to.

———

TUESDAY, *May 28*

UAB Hospital

9:32 am

THE OR IS QUIET, the only sounds coming from the steady beeping of the monitors and the soft murmurs of my surgical team. We've been at this one since six this morning, and we are making good time.

I'm in my element, finishing up a routine coronary artery bypass grafting, a CABG, as my team and I call it. My hands move swiftly, suturing the graft into place, making sure the blood flow is restored to the heart. It's a familiar rhythm, one I've done countless times before, and yet today, my mind keeps drifting away from the task at hand.

I should be focused solely on this patient, on making sure everything goes perfectly, but I can't stop thinking about what's coming later today—the meeting with Theo Bench and Frankie, the next steps for our pacemaker trial. And, if I'm being honest, the memory of last night keeps sneaking in, unbidden and unwelcome.

"Dr. Parrish, all vitals are stable," one of the nurses says, snapping me back to the present.

"Good," I reply, my voice steady even as my mind continues to race. I glance at the monitors, confirming the readings for myself before turning my attention back to the sutures. The graft is secure, the heart is beating strong, and we're almost done here.

As I carefully close the incision, I can't help but replay last night's walk with Frankie, the way her lips felt against mine as our time was coming to an end. My dick twitches a bit at the memory of the way her arms felt wrapped around me.

I should be thinking about the trial, about what we're going to discuss this afternoon. Theo's been pushing hard to get everything ready for the next phase, and today's meeting is critical. We need to finalize the protocol, ensure we're all on the same page before we present it to the FDA for approval. It's a huge step forward, and I can't lose my focus.

Instead, I'm thinking about how I'm going to face Frankie after everything that happened between us. Last night was different, and it's gnawing at me. I've been able to chalk up the two times in the lab as a product of extenuating circumstances. But last night was an unforced error, and there is nothing I can pin it on except what is going on inside of me regarding my growing affection for her.

"Almost done," I murmur, more to myself than to anyone else, as I finish the final stitches. The surgery went smoothly—textbook, really—but I can't shake the feeling that I'm off my game today.

I step back, letting the nurse take over the closing, and strip off my gloves, the cool air hitting my bare hands. Normally, I'd be relieved at the end of a successful surgery, but today there's no satisfaction. Just a gnawing anxiety about the meeting this afternoon, about seeing Frankie again.

"Dr. Parrish," one resident says, pulling me out of my thoughts. "Everything looks good. Should we proceed with post-op protocols?"

"Yes," I reply, giving a quick nod. "Make sure the patient is monitored closely for any signs of complications. I'll check in on her later."

As I walk out of the OR, I push the thoughts of Frankie and the trial to the back of my mind, at least for a few more hours. But it's no use. They're there, just beneath the surface, making it impossible to focus on anything else.

Today is another full one. I've got a meeting with Dibbins in between surgeries and then a few hours before the meeting with Bench, so I need to get my head straight. I can't afford to be distracted, not with so much riding on this project.

———

2:12 pm

I'M PEELING off my surgical gown, the material sticky with sweat from the protective layers, when I hear the door to the locker room swing open. I glance over my shoulder to see Shep Duncan walking in, looking as worn out as I am. He's already pulling off his gloves, his face set in that focused expression he always wears after a tough case.

"What's up, Duncan?" I greet him, tossing my gown into the bin and reaching for my scrub top.

"Hunter," Shep nods, his voice a little gravelly, probably from hours of talking his team through the intricacies of brain surgery. He starts removing his own gear, and I can see the fatigue in his movements, the kind that comes after a particularly grueling procedure.

"How'd your case go?" I ask, more out of habit than anything. Shep's a damn good neurosurgeon, and his cases are often far more complex than mine.

"Complicated," Shep admits, pulling off his mask. "Had to navigate through some seriously delicate tissue. Took longer than expected, but the patient pulled through. It's a glioblastoma, so it's a tough one. I think we bought him some significant time. Touch and go for a while, though."

I nod, knowing how those kinds of surgeries can drain you, both physically and emotionally. "Glad to hear it, man. Mine was routine, my second CABG today. Quick and clean, no surprises."

He grunts in acknowledgment, hanging up his gown and reaching for his scrub shirt. "I'd take that."

As we both start washing up, Shep glances at me sideways, a look I've come to recognize. He's got something on his mind. "So, did you ever get a chance to talk with Dibbins about your mom's Hodgkin's?"

I pause, letting the warm water run over my hands as I think back to earlier today. "Yeah, actually, I did. Spoke with him this morning in between surgeries."

Shep raises an eyebrow, clearly interested. "And?"

I take a deep breath, as a strange mix of relief and tension consume me. "He's going to review her chart notes and treatment plan, see if there's anything we're missing or if there's a better approach we haven't considered."

Shep nods, his expression serious. "Good. I'm glad you talked to him. Dibbins knows his shit, and it's important you're on top of it, especially with it being your mom."

I glance at Shep, grateful for his friendship. "Yeah. Thanks for pushing me on that. I needed to get over myself and actually do something."

Shep gives me a small, understanding smile. "It's never easy dealing with this stuff when it's personal. But you know as well as I do that getting another set of eyes on it can make all the difference."

"Exactly," I agree, drying my hands off and finding myself a little more settled. "Its weird being on this side of things —trying to be the concerned son and the objective doctor at the same time."

"Can't say I envy you," Shep replies, slinging his towel over his shoulder. "But you've got good instincts, Hunter. Trust them."

I give him a nod of appreciation. "Thanks, dude. I'll see what Dibbins comes up with."

"Keep me posted," Shep says, his tone lightening as he finishes washing up. "And if you need to talk it out or just grab a beer, you know where to find me."

I chuckle, as my tight muscles seem to release ever so slightly. "I might take you up on that."

We finish getting dressed, the conversation drifting to lighter topics as we head out of the locker room. Before I leave for my next stop, I thank him again for encouraging me to talk to Dibbins. I guess I needed that extra nudge to do the right thing from time-to-time.

I'm starting to realize I need that in more areas than just with dealing with my complicated relationship with my mom and dealing with her diagnosis.

NINETEEN

Frankie
___

3:03 pm

SITTING across from Bench as we go over the details of the trial, as my body seems to be intimately aware that Hunter will walk in any minute. My pits are sweaty, and another area is more wet than usual. Focus, Frankie.

The table in front of us is cluttered with papers—protocol drafts, charts, and research summaries. We've been at it for about twenty minutes, fine-tuning the specifics before Hunter arrives. I've been trying to focus on the work, but my mind keeps wandering to last night, to the kiss that's still sitting on my lips, taunting me.

"Now, Frankie," Theo says, snapping me back to the present. "About the patient selection criteria, you're confident that the inclusion parameters are set correctly?"

"Yes," I reply, nodding as I push aside the thoughts of Hunter. "We've narrowed it down to patients with a specific profile: those with advanced heart failure who have not responded well to existing pacemaker technology. We're also focusing on a subset with concurrent arrhythmias that aren't well managed with medication alone. The goal is to target those who would benefit the most from the new pacing algorithms we are testing."

Theo nods thoughtfully, tapping his pen against the table. "Good. And the exclusion criteria?"

"We're excluding patients with a history of severe ventricular arrhythmias that aren't controlled by ICDs or antiarrhythmic drugs, as well as those with significant comorbidities that could interfere with the trial results. We want to ensure we're testing this in a controlled population to get the most accurate data possible."

Theo seems satisfied with that, but before he can respond, the door opens and Hunter steps in. My heart skips a beat as he walks into the room, looking every bit the fucking cover model for a *Vogue* hottest surgeons in America issue.

"Sorry I'm late," Hunter says, sliding into the chair across from Theo and beside me. "Just finished up in surgery. We got a little later start than we planned, so everything got pushed back a little."

"No worries, Dr. Parrish," Theo replies, shifting a stack of papers toward him. "We were just discussing the patient selection criteria and the final steps before we submit the protocol for FDA approval."

Hunter nods, picking up the papers and scanning them quickly. "I've looked over the draft. The criteria look solid, but I had a few concerns about the pacing algorithms. Specifically, how we're going to handle patients who develop new arrhythmias during the trial. Are we set up to monitor those in real-time?"

The tension in the room rises as Hunter shifts into surgeon mode, his tone all business.

He bites his bottom lip as he thinks, a mannerism I've come to adore. It's a subtle reminder of what happened between us last night. I force myself to stay focused, to keep my voice steady.

"We've accounted for that," I say, leaning slightly forward to meet his gaze. "The devices will be equipped with real-time monitoring capabilities, and we've arranged for continuous telemetry for the first forty-eight hours post-implantation. Any new arrhythmias will trigger an automatic alert, and the patients will be brought in for immediate evaluation."

Hunter nods, seeming satisfied with my response, but he doesn't break eye contact. "Good. That's critical. We can't afford to have any surprises once we're in the thick of it."

Theo jumps in, sensing the intensity between us and perhaps trying to steer the conversation back to safer ground. "Hunter, your surgical expertise will be invaluable during the implantation phase. We've identified the top five centers that will participate in the trial. We'll need you to coordinate with the surgical teams at each site to ensure they're fully trained on the new device and procedures."

"I'm on it," Hunter says, turning his attention to Theo. "I'll set up training sessions with each team, making sure they're comfortable with the protocol and the device specifics. We'll also need to train my team here so they can assist. I want this to be a well-oiled machine before it goes out."

Theo nods, clearly pleased. "Exactly. And Frankie, I'll rely on you to oversee the data collection and ensure we're capturing everything we need. This trial has the potential to be a fundamental change, but a lot of that will depend on how we roll this out and conduct the trials. They have to be beyond reproach."

"Absolutely," I agree, though I can't shake the awareness of Hunter sitting so close beside me. "We'll be setting up a centralized database where all the trial data will be stored and monitored. I'll be coordinating with the statisticians to make sure we're analyzing the data in real-time, so we can adjust when necessary."

The conversation continues, a back-and-forth of technical details, logistical planning, and strategic decision-making. But underneath it all, there's an unmistakable tension between Hunter and me. At least for me. I can't help but wonder if he is experiencing it, too.

As the meeting wraps up, Theo leans forward, his elbows resting on the table. He looks between the two of us. "This is going to be a tough trial, but I'm confident we've got the right team to pull it off. Let's meet again next week to finalize the submission."

Hunter and I both nod, and Theo gathers his papers, leaving the room with a quick word of encouragement. The door closes behind him, and suddenly, it's just the two of us, the silence thick with everything we're not saying.

I glance over at Hunter, unsure of how to break the tension. But before I can figure it out, he stands up, gathering his things. "I'll be in touch with the surgical centers," he says, his dry affect leaves me reeling.

And then he's gone. Suddenly, I find myself all alone with my thoughts, realizing that whatever is happening is limited to the after hours.

Good, that's where it belongs.

————

4:28 *pm*

I DECIDE to stop by and see Carly on the OR floor before heading out. I shoot her a quick text to make sure she's at the desk and not with a patient. When she confirms she's free, I let her know I'm on my way up to say hi.

As I step off the elevator, I spot Carly's vibrant blond locks behind the nurses' station. She looks up and breaks into a wide smile as I approach.

"Hey, stranger!" she calls out, her eyes twinkling.

I lean against the counter, returning her smile. "How are you doing? First day back and all?"

Carly stretches her arms above her head, wincing slightly. "A little sore still, but it's good to be back in the swing of things. I was going stir-crazy at home."

"I bet," I chuckle. "How's the pace been today? Not too overwhelming, I hope?"

She shakes her head. "Nah, it's been pretty steady. Nothing I can't handle. Though I have to admit, I'm moving slower than usual."

I nod sympathetically. "That's to be expected. Just don't push yourself too hard, okay? It's only your first day back."

"Yes, Nurse Ratched," Carly rolls her eyes playfully. "But seriously, thanks for checking in. It means a lot."

"Of course," I reply, reaching out to squeeze her hand. "That's what friends are for."

We chat for a few more minutes about her recovery and the latest hospital gossip. As I'm about to leave, Carly leans in conspiratorially.

"So, any updates on the Hunter situation?" she whispers, eyebrows raised.

My cheeks flush and I quickly glance around to make sure no one's within earshot. "Not now, Carly. God, you're impossible. I'll fill you in later, I promise."

She grins, clearly enjoying my discomfort. "I'll hold you to that! I'm off at seven. Can I stop by your place on the way home?"

"Duh. Of course, you can. I would think something was wrong if you didn't!"

———

4:42 pm

WALKING through the hospital parking lot, I pull out my phone, my fingers hesitant to call Bill, but it is hanging over me. It's been a full twenty-four hours since he called with news that his labs were promising, and I still haven't returned his call.

It's been sitting in the back of my mind, lingering. There is no doubt I've been avoiding it, avoiding him, unsure of how to handle the slow rebuilding of a relationship I never really had.

I take a deep breath and swipe to call him, holding the phone to my ear as I unlock my car. The line rings a few times before I hear his voice on the other end.

"Frankie," he answers, sounding surprised but pleased. "Hey, there."

"Hi," I reply, sliding into the driver's seat of my VW Passat and shutting the door behind me. "I got your message yesterday. Sorry I didn't call back sooner—things have been hectic. But, I was so happy to get your voicemail."

"No worries," he says, and I can almost hear the smile in his voice. "I just wanted to share the good news. The labs are looking better. The treatment might actually be doing something. It seemed that the doctors were pleased."

"That's great to hear," I say, meaning it. "I'm always glad for good news."

"Yeah," he agrees, but there's a hesitation in his voice, like he's not sure what to say next. "I know it's still early, but I'm hopeful. And I wanted to make sure you were kept informed, you know?"

I nod, thinking of all the implications of what the healing could mean. "I appreciate that, Dad."

There's a brief silence. The awkwardness and normalness of what I just said sits there on display for both of us. It's the first time I've called him anything, let alone the intimate moniker.

Neither of us says anything, and he clears his throat. Maybe he is as emotional as I am about it.

"Anyway," he says after a moment, "I don't want to keep you. I know you're busy."

"I am, but... I'm glad to catch you," I say, surprising myself with how much I mean it. "Maybe we can meet again for coffee this week. I mean, if you're up for it."

"That would be amazing," he replies, almost a little too energetically. "I'll make myself available any time that works for you."

"How about we touch base later in the week?" I say, my voice quieter now, and I'm not sure if I'm talking to him or myself. "I have a big project I'm working on that is trying to get off the ground in the short term. But I'll know more as the week goes on."

"That sounds good. You know how to find me. I would really enjoy that."

"Okay," I say, smiling a little. "Take care."

I hang up and sit in the quiet of my car for a moment, letting the conversation sink in. It wasn't much, just a quick call, but it's progress. Slow, but steady. Like we're both trying to figure out how to navigate this, one step at a time.

As I start the car and head home, I can't help but think about how everything in my life seems like it's on the edge of something—my relationship with my father, this trial with Hunter, and especially whatever it is that's happening between Hunter and me on a personal level.

It's all so tenuous, so fragile, but for the first time in a long time, I think things might actually be moving in the right direction, somewhere toward happiness.

And that's enough for now.

FRANKIE'S HOUSE

7:46 pm

CARLY ARRIVES at my place not long after I get home. I had to run by the grocery store and then I picked up Chinese for us. I know Carly well enough to know she hasn't eaten a proper meal all day.

She's still in her scrubs, of course, looking tired but cheerful as she steps inside. I'm sure being on her feet for twelve hours for the first time since the accident was hard, but somehow she always manages to show up like she is on top of the world. If I could have just a smidge of that optimism and eternal happiness I would get good to go.

"Hey, you," she says, giving me a quick hug before dropping her bag and collapsing on the sofa. "I smell Chinese, don't I?"

"I was starving," I admit, heading to the kitchen to prepare our dinner. "I got you your favorite."

"General Tso's," she finishes the sentence for me.

"Yes!" I grab plates and chopsticks and set them down on the coffee table. "I could definitely use some comfort food."

Carly digs in, wasting no time. I'm about to do the same when she glances over at me, her eyes narrowing slightly.

"So," she starts, her mouth full but probing, regardless. "When I ran into you at the hospital earlier, you looked like you had something on your mind. Or rather, someone. Who could that be, hmmm?"

My face immediately goes hot and turns a bright crimson, I'm sure. Of course she knows exactly who she's referring to. "It's nothing," I say, trying to brush it off, but Carly just raises an eyebrow, clearly not buying it.

"Frankie, come on," she says, her voice a mix of amusement and concern. "We both know there's some 'there-there' with you and Hunter. So quit playing dumb with me."

I sigh, knowing there's no point in trying to deny it any longer. Carly is like a dog with a bone when it comes to this stuff. "Okay, fine. There's... something. I've resigned myself to the notion that it isn't, or wasn't, just a one time thing."

Carly leans in, her eyes gleaming with curiosity. "Something? That's it? I need details, girl. What's happened since we spoke yesterday morning?"

I take a deep breath, thinking back to everything that's happened since then. Shit, has it only been since yesterday? "Well, after you and I spoke, I met with Hunter at the hospital. It was... awkward, to say the least. As you know, he didn't call at all on Sunday."

Carly nods, urging me to continue. "And?"

"And," I say, rolling my eyes a little. "It was weird seeing him after that. Neither of us acknowledged it at first."

"True," Carly agrees, "but to be fair, you didn't call him either, so it's not like it's all on him. This isn't the 1950's, you know. The woman can call the man, too."

"Yeah, I know," I admit, feeling a little sheepish. "Anyway, after that, he invited me to join him for a drink that night. It was casual, nothing formal. And it just… it felt natural, easy. We talked, we laughed, and then we went for a walk."

"A walk? How romantic."

I happen to agree, but I don't let her taunt ruffle me. Or, at least I don't show it.

"And?" Carly prompts, her eyes widening in anticipation.

"And then he kissed me," I say, the words coming out faster than I intend. Just saying it aloud makes my heart skip a beat, reliving the moment in my mind. "It was intense. But in a good way. Right there on First Avenue."

Carly's eyebrows shoot up. "Whoa, okay. That's big. Like, right there in the open, in downtown Birmingham? So, what now?"

"Yup. That's the thing," I say, picking at my fried rice with my chopsticks. "I don't know. We both acted like nothing happened when we met today for our meeting with Dr. Bench. We were completely professional, but I couldn't stop thinking about it. About him."

Carly leans back, crossing her arms as she studies me. "Frankie, you've got it bad."

"I know," I admit, letting out a sigh, admitting it for the first time to myself and out loud. "But it doesn't seem like just a fling. I'm not sure what it is, but there's something brewing between us. Something real. And I'm kind of excited to see where it goes, you know?"

"Yeah, real sex. You know Hunter's reputation, right? Please remember my warning."

"I know. I know. That's why before now I didn't think much of it. But, I don't know, Car. It know he's feeling it, too."

"That's what all the ladies say, I'm sure."

"You know I'm not like that. I'm not one to get all googly-eyed over a man. I wasn't looking for anything when we slept together. This is progressing contrary to an attempt to keep it at bay."

Carly gives me a skeptical look, but there's a softness in her eyes that tells me she's happy for me, even if she's worried. "I never thought I'd see the day when you'd be giddy over a guy, especially one like Hunter Parrish. But you seem different. Happier, I guess."

"I am," I say, a small smile tug at my lips forming involuntarily. "I really am. And I'm starting to think that maybe we can figure out a way to do the work thing and the more thing."

Carly's expression shifts to one of cautious optimism. "Well, I won't say I'm not worried. Hunter doesn't do the commitment thing, and you know that. But it's nice to see you like this. I just don't want you to get your heart broken."

We continue eating, talking and laughing until our bellies hurt. Carly doesn't let up with the questions. It's freeing to let it all out, to admit to someone else finally that I might actually be falling for Hunter. For the first time, I'm not just thinking about the risks—I'm thinking about the possibilities.

And that's a pretty big step for me.

———

8:59 *pm*

AFTER CARLY LEAVES, I pace in my living room, her words echoing in my mind. She's right—I could have texted Hunter too. Maybe he's holding back, waiting to see if I'm interested. The thought makes my stomach flutter.

Before I can talk myself out of it, I grab my phone and open our text thread. My thumbs go to quick work, crafting the perfect message. Keep it casual, Frankie. Nothing too forward.

I type out a message, then delete it. Too formal. I try again, erasing that one, too. Too flirty. Finally, I settle on something simple:

> Hey, up for an evening walk?

My heart races as I hit send. The message shows as delivered, and I hold my breath, waiting. One minute passes. Then two. I set my phone down, trying not to stare at it.

Just as I'm about to give up and distract myself with some work, my phone buzzes. I snatch it up, fumbling in my haste to read his response.

> Actually, I'm about to throw a filet on the grill. I bought a two-pack. Would hate for it to go to waste. Join me?

Shit. I'm stuffed from my fried rice and General Tso's, but I don't know if I can pass this up. Fuck it.

Perfect. Send me your addy.

I rush to my bedroom, rummaging through my closet for something cute but casual. I settle on a pair of fitted yoga pants and a soft, oversized linen shirt. As I'm lacing up my sneakers, I catch sight of myself in the mirror. My cheeks are flushed, and there's a sparkle in my eyes I haven't seen in a long time.

This is crazy, I think to myself. But for once, I'm not over-thinking it. I'm just going with it, and it's empowering.

TWENTY

Hunter

9:25 pm

I'M STANDING on the balcony, the warm evening air brushing against my skin as I look out over the city. From the 20th floor, Birmingham sprawls out beneath me, a mix of twinkling lights and the quiet hum of the night. I never get tired of the view. There's something about seeing the city from up here that helps me clear my head, especially after a long day.

The grill beside me sizzles softly, the steaks nearly done, their smoky aroma mixing with the distinct scent of the city air.

I'm lost in thought when I hear the soft buzz from the intercom inside. It's Frankie. She texted me a little while ago, and on a whim, I invited her over for dinner. I had two steaks already on the grill and figured, why not? But now, with her about to walk through the door, I am suddenly and surprisingly nervous.

I push the anxiety aside, wiping my hands on a towel before heading inside to the door. The condo is dimly lit, the only genuine light coming from the kitchen and the few candles I've set out, their warm glow reflecting off the clean, minimalist surfaces.

Whatever this is with Frankie is anything but my normal preference of orderly and organized, like I keep my place. But I'm still drawn to her.

When I open the door, Frankie is standing there, looking as effortlessly beautiful as ever. Her auburn hair catches the low light, and she smiles warmly, but I sense she is a little uncertain about things, too. There's also something else—a natural ease between us that's hard to ignore, even with everything that's happened.

"Hey," I say, stepping aside to let her in. "Come on in to my humble abode."

"Hello to you," she replies, stepping through the door and looking around. "This place is… wow. This view is insane, Hunter."

I close the door behind her, a slight awkwardness lingering between us as she takes in the space. "Thanks. The space is small but I bought it for the view."

She glances around, her eyes tracing the sleek lines of the furniture, the carefully chosen artwork on the walls. "It's really nice. Very you."

I chuckle, leading her further inside. "What, you mean controlling and type-A?"

She laughs softly, a sound that eases the last bit of tension in the air. "Something like that."

We walk through the living area, and I give her a quick tour. The space is efficient—everything has its place, from the state-of-the-art kitchen with its quartz countertops to the plush leather couch that faces the fireplace and a massive flat-screen TV mounted on the wall. A few abstract paintings bring some color, but overall, the space maintains a muted ambiance with cool tones and clean lines.

"Very nice. So different from my pre-World War II house with its creaky floors and old windows."

"I like your place," I say genuinely. She's right, it is different, but it is inviting and warm. It feels like home.

"And this is the gym," I say, opening the door. This is my pride and joy of my house and I'm sure she can see by how well-appointed it is.

Frankie steps inside, and I can see her eyes widen as she takes in the view. The gym is small but fully equipped—weights, a treadmill, a stationary bike, and a few other essentials. But the real showstopper is the floor-to-ceiling windows that look out over the city, the skyline stretching out before us like something out of a movie.

"Wow," she breathes, walking over to the windows. "This is incredible. I can see why the view sold you."

"Yeah, it's not bad," I say, watching her as she looks out at the city. "Helps keep me motivated to work out when I've got a view like this."

She turns back to me, her expression softening. "You've got a really great place, Hunter."

"Thanks," I reply, as a little of that nervousness eases away. "It's home."

We stand there for a moment, the city lights twinkling outside as the last bit of awkwardness dissipates. I can see the candlelight flickering in the living room, the low lighting casting everything in a warm, inviting glow. It feels ordinary, somehow, to have her here, in this space that's usually just mine.

"Shit," I say, breaking the silence. "I need to get the steaks off."

As I turn off the gas and close the grill I nod toward the kitchen letting her know I'm done. "I roasted a couple of potatoes and some asparagus. Nothing like a good 'ol hearty meat and two sides, huh?"

"My mouth is watering just thinking about it. Thank you for having me over."

She follows walks toward the balcony, and I notice how we've slipped back into that easy company we've always kept, even with everything that's happened. I walk inside with my masterpieces, adding the rest to the plate and setting them down on the kitchen island.

"Red or white?"

"Honestly, I love them both. Chef's suggestion."

"Red, it is." I uncork the wine and pour each of us a glass.

We sit down to eat, and as we start talking—about the trial, about the day, about anything and everything. It's only a few minutes before I realize how much this is lacking in my life. Not just the conversation but the connection. The ease.

And even though there's still that undercurrent of something more between us, something we haven't quite figured out yet, maybe we don't need to figure it out right now. Maybe it's enough just to be here, together, in this moment.

As we eat, I relax more and more. The conversation flows naturally and the awkwardness from earlier is completely gone. By the time we're finishing up, the candles have burned low, and the city outside is quiet with the stars just starting to peek out from behind the clouds.

Frankie leans back in her chair, a contented smile on her face. "This was really delicious, Hunter. Thanks for this unexpected treat. This was much better than a walk. Food, any day of the week."

I smile back at her, my pulse quickening. She is talking like this time is coming to an end, but I'm desperate not to let that be true. "Anytime, Frankie. One more glass of wine?"

When I return with the wine, I suggest, "Why don't we take these out to the balcony? The city looks great from up here at night."

"That sounds nice," she says, following me as I lead the way.

Out on the balcony, the air is cooler now. The faint sounds of the city below add to the serene atmosphere from on top. We take our seats, side by side, and for a while, we just talk—about the city, the trial, random things that come to mind. It's easy, like slipping into an old routine, and it reminds me of why I enjoy being around her.

As the night deepens, the city lights start to dim, the energy below winding down, leaving us in a quiet bubble above it all. Our conversation naturally tapers off, and we sit there in a comfortable silence, both of us just enjoying the view.

After a while, I catch myself staring at her again, the soft glow from the balcony lights casting a gentle shadow across her face. There's something about this moment—something about her—that makes it impossible to look away. She looks so peaceful, so content, and I want to be closer to her.

I reach out, almost without thinking, and brush a stray strand of hair away from her face. The touch is small, barely anything, but it sends a jolt through me. Our eyes meet, and for a moment, its like everything else fades away. It's just us here in this quiet, perfect moment.

"The city's beautiful tonight," I say, my voice low, almost a whisper. I'm not even sure why I say it, but it seems appropriate since what I want to tell her is that she looks beautiful tonight.

"It really is," she replies, her gaze still locked on mine. There's a softness in her expression, a look that makes my heart beat a little faster.

The silence stretches between us, the air thick with something unspoken. There's a pull, an urge to close the distance between us, to kiss her like I've wanted to since the moment she walked into my place. I've been holding back, trying to keep things professional, but right now, all I can think about is how much I want her.

Without really thinking it through, I lean in slightly, my hand still resting on the back of her chair. "I've wanted to do this all night," I murmur, the words slipping out before I can stop them as my lips brush the side of her cheek.

She turns her head to look at me, and the proximity, her lips just inches from mine, makes it impossible to hold back any longer. I close the gap, pressing my lips to hers in a slow, deliberate kiss. It starts soft and tentative, but it doesn't take long for it to deepen, the intensity building between us.

She kisses me back with the same urgency, her hand finding its way to my chest as I pull her closer. The taste of the wine on her lips, the warmth of her body against mine —it's all-consuming, and for a moment, nothing else exists but this.

I've been fighting this pull all night, trying to maintain some semblance of control, but the way she looks at me with those fiery green eyes is like a match to gasoline. I can't resist her any longer.

I scoop Frankie up into my arms, and her legs instinctively wrap around my waist as I carry her inside. Our lips never part. I press her against the cool glass of the floor-to-ceiling window overlooking the city. Her back arches as the coolness seeps through her clothes, a stark contrast to the heat radiating between us.

Her fingers tangle in my hair, pulling me closer, as if she's trying to fuse us together.

I can't get enough of her—the taste of her lips, the velvety smoothness of her skin on mine, the soft moans escaping her throat. My hands roam her body, tracing the curves of her hips, the small of her back, the swell of her breasts. I want to explore every inch of her and memorize the sounds she makes when I touch her just right.

Breaking our kiss for a brief moment, I pull her yoga pants down, my fingers grazing her silky skin. She's panting, her chest heaving against mine as I fumble with my belt, letting my jeans drop to the floor.

She watches me with hooded eyes as I roll the condom on my cock, her gaze filled with raw, unbridled desire. It's all the encouragement I need. I press against her again, the length of my body aligning with hers, and the world falls away.

I enter her with one swift thrust, burying myself to the hilt as I fuck her against the clear glass window, the city night alive behind her. She gasps, her nails digging into my shoulders, and I still for a moment, savoring the tight, wet heat of her surrounding me. It's exquisite—better than anything I've ever felt before.

We find our rhythm quickly, our bodies moving in sync. Each thrust is deeper, harder, and more frenzied than the last. The sound of our ragged breathing and the slick slide of our bodies fills the room, punctuated by the occasional moan or whispered curse.

I reach between us, my fingers finding her most sensitive spot, and she shatters around me. Her internal muscles pulse in waves as I drive into her one last time, reaching my climax with a guttural groan.

Our bodies are slick with sweat, our hearts pounding in sync as we come back down to earth. I bury my face in her neck, inhaling the scent of her, a mix of her perfume and the musk of our lovemaking. I never want to let her go.

As our breathing slowly returns to normal, I pull back just enough to look into her eyes. There's a vulnerability there that I haven't seen before, a connection that goes beyond the physical. It scares the hell out of me, but at the same time, I want more of it, of her.

I withdraw from her, both of us wincing slightly at the loss of contact, and deal with the condom before pulling her back into my arms.

We stand there for a moment, her head resting against my chest, the steady rhythm of my heartbeat filling the silence. The remnants of her essence leave a mark on the window, an homage to this beautiful woman and our intense lovemaking.

I know I should be careful and guard my heart, but as I hold her close, I can't find it in me to care. For the first time in a long time, I am alive, and it's all because of her.

———

WEDNESDAY, *May 29*

5:21 am

THE ROOM IS DARK, the only light coming from the faint glow of the city outside the window. Frankie is curled up beside me, her breathing steady and soft, her warmth a comforting presence against the cool sheets. I'm half-asleep, drifting in that space between dreams and reality, when the buzzing of my phone on the nightstand jolts me awake.

I groan softly, reaching for the phone, trying not to disturb Frankie as I glance at the screen. It's an urgent text from the hospital's answering service. My eyes narrow as I read the message:

> Nurse Grace—heart attack on the floor.
> Need you in ASAP.

Shit. Grace. Big Mama. The thought of her down with a heart attack hits me like a punch to the gut. It's not like this came out of nowhere with her incident a few months ago. Still, she is so stoic and so damn stubborn that I guess I let it outside of my radar.

Fuck.

Even though Wednesdays are usually my clinic days with no surgeries scheduled, I have no doubt—I'm going in for Grace. She's always been there for us, and now it's my turn to be there for her.

I turn my head to look at Frankie, still fast asleep beside me. Frankie's auburn hair spreads out over the pillow and her face remains peaceful, even in sleep. I take a moment to appreciate her beauty, stunning, so at ease. The fact that she's here, in my bed, after everything finally gives me peace instead of angst. It's hard to pull myself away, to leave this warmth and comfort, but duty calls.

Gently, I place my hand on her shoulder, giving her a soft shake. "Frankie," I whisper, my voice low so as not to startle her. "Frankie, I need to go."

She stirs, her eyes fluttering open, still heavy with sleep. "Hunter?" she murmurs, her voice drowsy.

"There's been an emergency at the hospital," I explain, brushing a strand of hair away from her face. "Grace had a heart attack while working. They need me to come in."

Her eyes widen slightly, and she sits up a little, concern flashing across her face. "Oh no... is she going to be okay?"

"I don't know any details," I say, fully aware of the gravity of the situation. "But I need to get there. I hate to leave you like this, but it's an emergency."

She nods, fully awake now, her hand resting on my arm. "Of course, you have to go. I understand. I can get up quickly."

"No, stay in bed. There is nothing you can do there right now." I lean down and kiss her gently, savoring the softness of her lips against mine, the warmth of her body radiating out of the bundled covers wrapped around her. "Stay as long as you want," I tell her, pulling back just enough to look into her eyes. "Sleep in, help yourself to anything. The door will lock behind you, so just pull it closed when you leave."

"Okay," she whispers, her voice full of understanding. "Go take care of her. Keep me posted and give Grace my love."

I give her one last look, hating the fact that I have to leave her, but knowing there's no other choice. "I'll see you later," I promise, kissing her forehead one last time before standing up.

As I get dressed, pulling on scrubs that I keep in the closet for emergencies like this, I can't help but glance back at Frankie. She's already lying back down, but her eyes follow me, a soft smile on her lips despite the situation.

"Be safe," she says, her voice filled with a quiet strength that I've come to admire.

"I will," I reply, giving her a small nod before heading out the door.

TWENTY-ONE

Frankie

7:41 am

I WAKE UP SLOWLY, the warmth of the sheets wrapping around me like a cocoon. For a moment, I'm disoriented, not entirely sure where I am, until I bury my face in the pillow beside me and breathe in his scent.

Hunter.

I'm in his bed. The realization washes over me, and I let out a soft sigh, snuggling deeper into it.

It's surreal, being here in his place without him. The room is filled with his presence, even though he's not here—his scent lingering in the sheets, the faint hum of the city outside his window. I feel a little out of place, like I'm intruding on something private, even though he invited me to stay.

But there's no time to linger. I know I need to get up and get home to shower before my midmorning meeting with

Theo. As much as I'd love to stay here, wrapped up in this moment, in the essence of him, reality is calling.

I stretch out, my hand brushing across the empty side of the bed where Hunter should be. I remember the way he woke me up, his voice soft but urgent as he explained what had happened. I appreciate that he did verses just leaving like he did before.

Poor Grace. I hope she is going to be okay. I don't know her well, but I've heard enough about her to know she's a fixture on the OR floor, someone everyone respects and relies on. The thought of her being down with something so serious sends a pang of concern through me for her family and everyone that works with her.

I reach for my phone on the nightstand, checking the time, and see that I missed a text from Carly. She must have sent it when she went in for her shift at seven. I open it, reading quickly.

> Going in now. Grace had a heart attack on the floor early this morning. Sounds like it is a shitshow at the hospital. See you later?

I make a mental note to get to the hospital early enough to stop by and see Carly, to get an update on how Grace is doing. I can't shake the worry that's settled in my chest, even though I barely know the woman. But I know what it's like to be surrounded by people who care about you, who rely on you. The thought of someone like that being taken down is unsettling.

With a sigh, I force myself to sit up, running a hand through my hair as I glance around Hunter's bedroom. The space is neat and orderly, just like the rest of his condo. It's strange to think that just a few hours ago, we were here together, wrapped up in each other, and now he's at the hospital, doing what he does best.

I pull myself out of bed, knowing that I need to get moving if I'm going to make it to the hospital on time. But before I go, I take one last look around the room, letting the reality of everything sink in.

Oh, my God. I need to brush my teeth. I can't imagine that I will have to get all the way home in this state. I need to start traveling with a toothbrush in my bag if we're going to be having these impromptu spend the night parties.

Being here with Hunter, waking up in his bed—it's like we've crossed some invisible line, like things are starting to shift between us in ways I'm not entirely sure I'm ready for.

But for now, I push those thoughts aside. There's too much to do, too much to focus on. I gather my things, dressing quickly and quietly as I prepare to leave. The condo is quiet, almost too quiet without Hunter here, and it's a little lonely, even though I know it's ridiculous.

As I step out of the bedroom, I make sure everything is in place, just as he left it. I'm about to head out the door when I catch sight of the kitchen, the remains of our dinner still on the counter.

I make a quick decision to clean the kitchen. I don't want him to come home to this mess. A small gesture, but it's nice to be able to do something for him. Something about the act itself is somehow turning me on.

When I pull the door closed behind me, the lock clicks into place with such finality that it makes my heart flutter just a little. Something about this entire morning, and the night that proceeded it, is like a fairytale.

As I head down the hallway, I shoot a quick text back to Carly, letting her know I'll be in soon and that I'll stop by to see her. I need to know how Grace is doing, and I need to see my friend. She's going to lose her shit when I tell her I just sent that text from Hunter's.

9:57 *am*

PULLING into the hospital I get a text back from Carly after I asking for an update on Grace. I let her know I was on the way to the hospital.

> Come see me!

I park my car in the hospital garage, my mind still replaying the events of last night against the cold glass window with Hunter as I make my way to the OR floor.

There's about thirty minutes until my meeting, so I'll stop by and see if there's any news about Grace.

I step off the elevator and walk toward the OR, the sterile smell of antiseptic and the busy bustle of hospital activity fill the air. I pick up my pace, eager to find out how Grace is doing.

Turning the corner, I spot Carly down the hall, standing outside a patient room, talking to a couple of nurses. I'm about to turn around and head up to my office when I see

Hunter walking by, completely covered in his surgical outfit —scrubs, mask, cap, the works.

My heart skips a beat, and my stomach flutters at the sight of him. He looks so different, so focused, and I'm struck by how commanding he seems in this setting, how in his element. His quiet confidence and power enhances his handsome face and incredible body. The body that was all over mine just a few hours ago.

He's moving quickly, clearly on his way somewhere, but when he spots me, he slows down just enough to walk over. There's a moment of hesitation, but then his eyes soften, and he gives me a quick smile behind the mask.

"Hey," he says, his voice muffled by the mask but still warm. Then he pulls it down, leaving it to rest on his chin.

"Hey, you," I reply, breathless. "How's Grace?"

He glances around, making sure no one is urgently calling him, and then looks back at me. "She's stable. It was a close call, but we got to her in time. She's in the ICU now, and they're monitoring her closely. I'm heading back in to check on her. I just assisted Hughes on a surgery, unplanned. He's still in there but I was able to slip out so I can peek in on Grace before my next patient."

Relief floods through me, and I nod, grateful for the update. "That's good to hear. I'm glad she's going to be okay."

Hunter nods, his eyes lingering on mine for a second longer than necessary. "I'll keep you in the know."

"Thanks," I say, a rush of warmth fills me seeing his concern.

"I trust you found everything you needed at my place? I hated to leave you." Everything except a spare toothbrush.

"Oh, yes, I was fine. Thank you. Only one thing missing," I flirt, the words coming out before I can think better of it. He smiles warmly and then puts his hand on my arm.

"I hate to run again, but I have a patient in ten minutes and want to stop in and check Grace's chart. Can I text you later?"

"Of course. Please, go. Let's talk later."

He gives me a quick nod before heading off down the hall, and I watch him go, my heart still racing. There's something about seeing him like this, so focused, so dedicated, that makes me admire him even more.

As I turn back to Carly, who's now watching me with an amused expression, I know I'm not hiding anything from her. She grins as I approach, her eyes twinkling with mischief.

"Oh my freaking hell, Frankie," she says, barely holding back a laugh. "I've never seen you or Hunter, for that matter, with such googly eyes. You're in trouble, girl."

I can't help but laugh, rolling my eyes at her teasing. "You don't even know the half of it," I whisper, leaning in closer. "I spent the night at Hunter's last night."

Carly's eyes widen, and she nearly loses it, laughing so hard she has to hold on to the wall for support. "Oh, Frankie, this is too good! You dirty dog!"

I shake my head, unable to keep the smile off my face. "I'll tell you more later. Gotta run upstairs."

"Oh, yes you will, Missy," Carly says, still chuckling. Her expression softens, and she glances toward the ICU doors. "My heart is literally in shreds about Grace—she had a pretty severe heart attack, but they got her stabilized. She's in the ICU now, resting. She's a tough old bird. If anyone can pull through this, it's that little woman in there. But, damn, seeing her like that gets you right in the gut."

I nod, feeling a mixture of relief and concern. I know how close she and Carly are. "I'm glad she's okay, now. Thank God it happened here. It sounds like it was touch and go for a bit according to Hunter."

"Yeah, it was," Carly agrees, her tone more serious now. "But she's in excellent hands, and everyone's pulling for her. Hunter jumped in, once again, like a hero. I'm starting to see him in a new light."

"Good," I say, prideful at hearing her say that. "I'll check in on y'all later."

Carly nods, then gives me a sly grin. "But first, you better get ready to spill all the details about Hunter. I'm not letting you off the hook, you know, just because we have a personal medical emergency down here."

I laugh, shaking my head. "Wouldn't dream of it. I've got to meet with Theo first."

———

11:59 *am*

AFTER OUR MEETING WRAPS UP, I gather my things and head out of the hospital. The weight of the day's events presses on me, but there's also a sense of accomplishment. I need to get back to my joggers and my home office. I can't imagine why I would be so exhausted.

The meeting went well, and we're moving forward with the trial. Still, there's a lot to do, and I know I'll need to buckle down and get some work done as soon as I get home.

As I step out into the warm sunlight, I remember I told Bill, er, my dad, that I would reach out later in the week. I pull out my phone and scroll through my recent calls until I find his number. I hit the call button and hold the phone to my ear, listening to the ring as I make my way to the parking garage.

I notice the dread and anxiousness aren't there when I make the call like they have been in the past. It's a nice but subtle change.

It takes a few rings, but eventually, he picks up.

"Hello?"

"Hey, it's me," I say, trying to keep my tone light. "I was just checking in, seeing how you're doing."

"I'm doing good. Feeling pretty good, actually. How is your project going?"

"Busy," I admit with a small laugh as I slide into the driver's seat. "We had a big meeting today about the trial I'm working on, so there's a lot to do. But, you know, it's good. Just trying to keep up with everything."

"I bet," he says, a note of pride in his voice. "You're a hard worker. Just like your mom."

The mention of my mom sends a pang through my chest, but I push it aside. Part of me wants to tell him he doesn't have the right to bring her up. But I know he means well and is giving me a compliment, so I leave it at that.

"Yeah, well, I guess I got that from her. Listen, I was thinking. I've got a lot of work to do this afternoon, but I'm probably going to need a break later. Do you want to meet for coffee? Maybe around four?"

"Yeah, I'd like that. Coffee sounds wonderful. Where do you want to meet?"

I think for a moment, then suggest the café that's not too far from my place, making it more convenient for me. "How about the same place as last time? Frothy Monkey. It's close to where I live, and they've got great coffee."

"Frothy Monkey is perfect," he agrees, and I can hear the relief in his voice. "I'll see you there at four."

"Great," I say, a sense of accomplishment and, dare I say, excitement. "I'll see you then, Dad." It's starting to get easier, letting myself think of him as my dad.

"Looking forward to it, Frankie," he says softly before we hang up.

As I end the call, I take a deep breath, a mix of emotions swirling inside me. It's still hard to believe that I'm making plans with my dad. Everything outside of my comfort level seems to be coming at me at once, and it is giving me a little extra pep in my step.

––––––––

FRANKIE'S HOUSE

. . .

7:11 *pm*

I'M WRAPPING up my work for the day when my phone buzzes on the desk beside me. I pick it up and see a text from Carly. Just like clockwork. I swear, I could know what time it is when she has a shift based on her calls, texts and stopovers.

> Finishing up my shift. Is it cool if I stop by? I can grab takeout on the way.

I smile at her offer and quickly type out a reply.

> Absolutely. Takeout sounds perfect. How about Thai tonight?

> Done. See you in a bit!

With that settled, I close my laptop and start tidying up, grateful for the break. It's been a long day, and the idea of a quiet evening with Carly sounds like just what I need. I'm looking forward to catching up with her, especially after everything that's happened in the last 24 hours.

"Delivery for the lady of the house!" Carly announces herself as she lets herself inside.

I laugh, walking to the door to greet her. She walks in with bags of food and her usual bright smile. "You're the best," I say, taking one of the bags from her.

"I know," she grins, stepping inside. "And you better believe I'm here for all the details from last night. Deets, girl."

We move into the kitchen, setting the food down on the counter. I grab some plates and utensils, and we start dishing out the food, the aroma of Thai spices filling the air. Carly's eyes are practically sparkling with curiosity. Usually, it's me living vicariously through her, but I think the roles have reversed lately.

"So," she starts, leaning against the counter with her arms crossed, "I left your place after eight last night—how did you end up in his bed this morning?"

A blush climbs up my neck as I think about last night, the events still fresh in my mind. "Well," I begin, trying to sound casual, "I took some of your unintended advice and texted him to see if he wanted to go for a walk last night after you left. He invited me over for steak, instead."

Carly raises an eyebrow. "Um, you ate dinner with me. Did you eat twice?"

"A girl can never have too much protein. Especially when she's doing all of this working out she isn't used to." I waggle my eyebrows with this last part, hoping the salaciousness of the suggestion is enough to satisfy her hunger for the juice.

Her eyes widen, and she lets out a low whistle. "And then you two had a slumber party after?"

I nod, my cheeks flushing again. "Yeah, something like that."

Carly's grin turns mischievous. "I will say you have a glow about you. And I saw how he looked at you at the hospital. I've never seen him look at another woman like that before. And he's had plenty of admirers."

"Anyway," I say, changing the subject, "have you heard any more about Grace?"

Carly shakes her head, her expression turning serious. "Not much new. She's stable, but they're keeping a close eye on her. It's still touch and go, but she's got the best team on her side. She's our rock, even when she's down."

"That's good to hear," I say, relieved that she's holding on. "I hope she pulls through. I know how much she means to all of you."

"She will," Carly says with confidence. "Big Mama isn't going down without a fight."

We fall into a comfortable silence for a few moments, eating and reflecting on everything that's been going on. Even though Carly doesn't ask, I find myself wanting to share something else with her.

"I had coffee with my dad today," I say, almost casually.

Carly's head snaps up, surprise written all over her face. "Really? How'd that go?"

"It was… good, actually," I admit, surprised at how true that statement is. "We've been talking more since we reconnected, and today was the first time we really sat down and just… talked. I'm not saying everything's perfect, but it's a start. He's trying, and I'm trying to give him a chance."

Carly nods, a supportive smile on her face. "I'm glad to hear that, Frankie. I know it's not easy, but it sounds like you're doing the right thing. It's never too late to try and make things better."

"Yeah," I say, a weight lifting off my shoulders. "I think so, too. It's interesting how sickness and thoughts of leaving this earth can soften the heart. Now that he's doing better it was a catalyst, but gratefully we don't have to deal with the sadness of it. It's given us a second chance."

We spend the rest of the evening chatting about lighter topics, the comfort of our friendship a welcome balm to the full day. As Carly heads out later, I am extra grateful for the people in my life—the ones who've always been there and the ones who are starting to be.

TWENTY-TWO

Hunter

Thursday, May 30

UAB Hospital

6:34 *am*

WALKING INTO THE OR, the surgical team is already preparing for the procedure and ready for me. I try to shake off the thoughts swirling in my mind. The patient on the table depends on me, and I need to be fully focused on the task at hand. But pushing everything aside is hard, especially when the weight of the world presses down on my shoulders.

I can't stop thinking about Frankie and how much I regret not being able to meet up with her last night. After the day I had, dealing with everything around Grace and then that damn phone call with my mother's doctor, I just didn't have the energy.

The truth is, that phone call with Dibbins about my mother knocked the wind out of me. Her Hodgkin's lymphoma isn't responding to the treatments, and the latest labs suggest she's got that rare, resistant strain I've been reading about. The one with a prognosis that makes my stomach twist just thinking about it.

My mother, who's been battling this disease all alone, doesn't understand what it all means. I don't think her doctor there does, either.

It's heavy, and I don't know how I'm supposed to deal with it. Should I move her out here, closer to me, so I can keep a better eye on her care? Even thinking about that—about uprooting her life, about the strain it would put on both of us—it makes my head spin.

I glance at the clock, mentally preparing myself for the surgery ahead, but my thoughts keep circling back to the same place.

I've always been the one who's in control, who handles everything with a steady hand and a clear mind. But this... this is different.

Right now, I have a patient to focus on. I can't afford to let my mind wander, not when there's a life on the line. I take a deep breath, trying to clear my head as I step into the OR, the surgical lights bright overhead.

It's time to do what I do best—focus on the task at hand and save a life. The rest... I'll have to deal with that later.

———

11:39 *am*

. . .

AFTER FINISHING THE SURGERY, I scrub out, my mind already drifting back to the heavy thoughts I've been trying to push away all morning. I dry my hands and check my phone, noticing a missed call and a text from Jonah. The message is short and direct.

> Call me as soon as you get this. It's about Grace.

My heart sinks, and a wave of dread washes over me. Grace has weighed on me since the heart attack. I'm not her doctor of record, but I've been consulting with her cardiologist to make sure she gets everything she needs.

Her stats have been stable, but she is very sick. I know Dr. Calloway, her doctor, has been exploring different options for her, but she can't do anything until she gets her strength up. I hope things haven't taken a turn for the worse.

The fact that Jonah is calling me about her isn't a good sign. He is her de facto son. As a general surgeon, there isn't much he can do for her, except advocate for her care. I quickly dial his number and head toward my office, already mentally preparing for the worst.

Jonah picks up on the first ring. "Hunter, meet me at your office. We need to talk about Grace."

"I'm on my way," I say, my voice tight as I pick up the pace.

As I walk through the hallway, I see Shep Duncan heading toward me with a dumb fucking grin on his face. It's nice to know someone around here doesn't have the world crumbling all around him.

"Hey, Parrish!" Shep calls out as we approach each other. "Heard the good news about Mrs. Falworth?"

I shake my head, distracted, but slow down just enough to give him a moment. "No, what's up?"

Shep doesn't stop walking, but he turns back as we pass each other. "She finally quit smoking! Can you believe it?"

Mrs. Falworth, our stubborn, chain-smoking patient, finally quit? I never thought I'd see the day.

"That's incredible," I call back, a genuine smile pulling at the corners of my mouth despite the anxiety gnawing at me. "Thanks for letting me know."

Shep nods and continues down the hall, leaving me with a rare burst of happiness in an otherwise shitty morning. It's a small victory, but right now, I'll take it. It's proof that sometimes, no matter how stubborn or set in their ways people might be, change is possible.

I push forward, that small glimmer of hope fueling me as I head to my office. When I get there, Jonah is already waiting, leaning against the door frame, his expression serious.

"Jonah," I say, nodding as I unlock the door and push it open, gesturing for him to come in. "What's going on with Grace? Is she okay?"

He follows me inside, and the tension in the air. We both take a seat, and I can tell by the look on his face that whatever he's about to say isn't good.

"It's not good, Hunter," Jonah begins, running a hand through his hair. "The damage from the heart attack is worse than we initially thought. Dr. Calloway has considered every option for her, but it's clear now that she's not

going to be able to manage without some kind of intervention."

My stomach tightens. "What's he thinking?"

Jonah takes a deep breath. "She needs a pacemaker, but
she's not a candidate for the traditional ones. Her condition, her age, the damage, the complications... it's too
risky."

I nod slowly, already seeing where this is going. "So what
are you suggesting?"

Jonah leans forward, his eyes locking onto mine. "What
about the pacemaker you've been working on? The one for
the trial. It's designed for patients like her, right? Those
who can't handle the traditional devices?"

My mind races, weighing the options, the risks, the possibilities. "Jonah, we haven't even started the trial yet. We've
got the FDA approval, and we've secured funding, but
there is still so much that has to be done before we can
start. The hospital board hasn't even met to review our
protocol that isn't even completed. It's just not there yet,
man, I'm sorry."

"I know that," Jonah says, his voice urgent. "But we're
talking about Grace's life here. She's not going to make it
without some kind of intervention, and soon. You've got
the approval, you've got the device—there has to be a way
you can use it to save her. She is important to all of us, we
have to come through for her."

I lean back in my chair, running a hand over my face. "It's
not that simple, Jonah," I say frustrated. I'm pissed he is
putting this one me, like I'm the one who will make or
break this. "There are protocols, regulations, a system."

"I get it," Jonah cuts in, "but we both know that sometimes, you have to bend the rules a little to save a life. You've got the important stuff: the FDA approval, the money. If anyone can make it happen, I know it's you."

I stare at him for a long moment, the enormity of it all swallowing me. We've never done a human trial, we don't even have all of the fucking protocols in place.

Goddammit. Grace's life depends on this, and I know it.

"I'll look into it," I finally say, my voice firm. "I'll see what I can do. But I can't make any promises. It's likely the hospital wouldn't even agree to it if I figured out how to pull it off. They would have to be on board."

Jonah nods, relief flooding his features. "Thanks, Hunter. Just try. I know it's a lot to ask, but she's got no other options."

As Jonah leaves, I sit back, my mind already spinning with the possibilities. There's a way to do this—I just need to figure out how. The compassionate use program is designed for situations like this, where a patient needs access to an experimental treatment outside of a clinical trial.

The board will have to agree. It's almost easier to get an act through congress than it is to get them all on the same page.

I get up from my chair, pacing the room as I think through the logistics. I'll need to talk to Theo and get his okay, and then together, we would have to put in an emergency request with the IRB and the Ethics Board.

But more than that, I need to make sure this is the right move for Grace. She deserves the best care possible, and if this pacemaker is her best shot, then I'll have to figure out how to make it happen.

I open my laptop and fingers start flying over the keyboard as I draft an email to Frankie and Theo about the compassionate use request for Grace Petit. I've got to start somewhere, and nothing will happen without their blessing.

The words are coming quickly—too quickly, maybe—but the urgency of the situation is overriding everything else in my mind. I need to get this message out, to start the process, to figure out how to make this work. Grace doesn't have time to wait.

Subject: Compassionate Use- Grace Petit

Frankie, Theo—

Just as I'm about to dive into the specifics, Jill pops her head into my office, her voice cutting through my concentration like a knife.

"Dr. Parrish, your patient is prepped and on the table, ready for surgery."

I freeze, my body and mind are in two different places as her words sink in. Shit. I completely forgot.

I glance at the clock on my computer screen, cursing under my breath. How the hell did I lose track of time like that?

"Shit, Jill, I—" I start, but she's already nodding, understanding written all over her face.

"You have a lot on your mind, Dr. Parrish. Just get in there."

I slam my laptop shut, pushing back from my desk and practically leaping to my feet. All thoughts of compassionate use and Grace Petit are shoved to the back of my mind as I rush out of the office, Jill already moving ahead of me to make sure everything's in place.

This is what I'm here for, after all—surgery. The catastrophes I'm expected to thwart will have to wait a little while longer.

———

SHAIN *Park*

7:08 *pm*

THE EARLY EVENING air is cooler than I expected as I walk down the quiet street, the sun dipping low on the horizon. After the day I've had, I needed this—needed to get out of the hospital, away from the blank walls and endless responsibilities. But more than that, I need to see Frankie.

I reach for my phone, hesitation prickling at the back of my mind. It's been a long day and I can't shake the urge to hear her voice, to see her. So I send her a quick text, asking if she's up for a walk and maybe grabbing something to eat. I'm relieved when her reply comes back almost immediately.

> Sure. I could use a break. Meet you at the park in 20?

The familiar sight of Frankie waiting by the fountain

brings a small sense of calm to my otherwise chaotic mind. Seeing her long, toned legs in her athletic shorts and a tank top almost makes me forget about the shitshow of a day I've had. She smiles when she sees me, and inside I melt.

"Hey," I say as I approach, that familiar flutter in my chest when she's near.

"Hey, yourself," she replies, falling into step beside me as we start walking down the path. "Bad day?"

"You could say that," I admit, rubbing the back of my neck. "How about you?"

She nods, her expression thoughtful. "Yeah. Busy. Got your email about the compassionate use for Grace."

I glance at her, trying to gauge her reaction. I know this is a big ask—maybe even too big—but Grace doesn't have much time. "What do you think?"

She takes a deep breath, clearly choosing her words carefully. "Hunter, you know how much I care about this trial. I've spent years working on this device, even before our official research at UAB started, perfecting the science behind it. If we approve compassionate use for Grace, it's outside the trial, and anything that goes wrong could jeopardize the entire study. It could even put an end to it."

I can hear the concern in her voice, and I get it. This trial, this device, it's her life's work. She's put everything into it, and the stakes are incredibly high.

"I know, Frankie. And I respect that, more than you know. But Grace, she's not just another patient. She's been at that hospital since before I went to med school. She's the glue that holds that OR floor together. Without this pacemaker, she won't make it. It's not just about data and numbers and reports, it's about saving her life."

Frankie stops walking, turning to face me. Her deep emerald green eyes search mine, looking for something.

"Hunter, I understand where you're coming from. I do. But we have to be responsible. We have to consider the risks, not just for Grace, but for the future of this device, for all the other patients who could benefit from it down the line."

I take a deep breath, the heaviness of her words, the truth in them. But I can't shake the image of Grace lying in that hospital bed, clinging to life.

"I know the risks, Frankie. I do. But I also know the promise of it. Grace doesn't have a future at all if we don't at least try. This device was designed for patients like her, who don't have any other options. I just can't stand by and do nothing when I know the solution is within my reach."

She looks down at the ground, her shoulders tense. "I just don't want to lose everything we've worked for because we rushed into something."

Her words seem more poignant than ever. Not just about the trial and Grace, but every storm swirling around me.

I step closer, gently tilting her chin up so she has to meet my gaze. "We're not rushing into anything. We would be making a calculated decision."

She searches my eyes for a long moment, and I can see the conflict written all over her face. But slowly, she nods. "Okay. Let's put it before the IRB and see what they say. Theo said ultimately the decision was up to me. We can't cut corners."

"We won't," I promise. "We're in this together."

We stand there for a moment, the park quiet around us. There is a swell of gratitude for this woman standing in front of me. She's smart, determined, and fiercely protective of her work. But more than that, she's compassionate, and that's what makes her so damn hot.

The short athletic shorts and tight ass don't hurt.

"Thank you, Frankie," I say quietly.

She nods, a small smile playing at the corners of her mouth. "What do you say about grabbing a pizza and taking it back to my place?"

"I can't think of a better idea," I respond a little too eagerly. Suddenly the sky seems to open just a little. With Frankie's blessing and willingness, if we can solve at least one thing hanging over me, I will call that a win.

Now, for pizza. And, more importantly, dessert…

TWENTY-THREE

Frankie

_8:34 pm_

THE STRING LIGHTS CAST A WARM, inviting light over the screened-in porch as Hunter and I settle into the cushioned chairs, each holding a glass of wine. The night air is warm, but the gentle breeze created by the ceiling fan creates the perfect temperature. It's peaceful here, and for the first time today, I can actually relax.

The quiet sounds of the night settle in around us as my mind races with memories of my mom. All of this has stirred up so much of that painful time.

I think about those final days, watching her wither away, her heart betraying her, and the helplessness that consumed me. If there had been anything that could have given her a little more time, a few more months, even a year, I would have fought tooth and nail to get it for her.

Unfortunately, by the time the doctors identified the problem, there wasn't. We didn't have options back then. The resources weren't there. I was barely an adult, watching the strongest person I'd ever known, my best friend, slip away because her heart couldn't keep up.

Now, sitting here with Hunter, knowing Grace's life is hanging in the balance, I know helping Grace is the right thing to do. She's someone's mother, someone's friend, an institution at the hospital, and I have the chance to help.

It's true, the trial isn't ready, and there are risks to doing this. But how could I look at Grace, or anyone else, and say I didn't try when I had this device that could change everything? It's personal. If this were my mom, dying before my eyes, I wouldn't have hesitated for a second. I won't let Grace go like that if I can help it.

I glance at Hunter and know I have to make the call. For the first time, I know it's the right one. I won't let Grace's story end like my mom's. Not if there's a chance this device could save her.

The pizza is long gone, both of us hungry after our full and busy day, and now, with the food cleared away and the wine flowing, everything's just... easy. Uncomplicated. Like this is exactly where we're supposed to be.

I marvel at Hunter, taking in the way the ambient light plays across his features. His normal, intense expression is softer at night when we are together like this. He looks content, almost at ease, which I never see at the hospital. It pleases me to know he's let his guard down, even if it's only fleeting.

"Thanks for the pizza," I say, breaking the comfortable silence. "It hit the spot."

He chuckles, his gaze meeting mine. "It was a good call. Sometimes you just need something simple."

"Simple but perfect," I agree, taking a sip of my wine. The rich, fruity flavor rolls over my tongue, and I savor it, savor this moment.

We fall back into silence, but it's not the awkward kind. It's the kind of silence that sneaks up on you when you least expect it, where words aren't necessary. The warmth of the wine spreads through me. Being here with Hunter, just like this, is perfection.

The comfortable tranquility stretches between us as we find some things to laugh about together. For once, we don't talk about the trial or cancer or heart disease.

The night settles in around us like a warm blanket. The wine has done its job, loosening the knots of tension that continue to battle within me, and I'm content.

"I should probably get going," Hunter finally says, his voice soft, almost reluctant. "It's been a long day. I know you probably want to get some rest, too."

"Yeah," I agree, though part of me wishes we could just stay here a little longer. Suddenly, I'm a child again, not wanting the night to end, for my easy friend to abandon me. But I'm not bold enough to say so. "I'm pretty wiped too."

As we move inside, I grab our empty wine glasses and head to the sink. Hunter lingers by the door, pulling out his phone to check it. I rinse the glasses, the sound of the running water filling the space between us, and I can't help but feel like this moment is slipping away too quickly.

I dry my hands on a towel, turning to find Hunter still glued to his phone, his expression distant, as if he's already halfway out the door. He's focused, almost too focused, on leaving, and it stings a little more than I'd like to admit.

"Everything okay?"

"Oh, yes. Sorry. I had a few texts and a missed call from my mom."

Oh, how I'd love to have a missed call from my mom. The thought leaves a lump in my throat.

His hand reaches for the door knob when he turns to say something. Maybe he wants to stay?

"Thanks, again, for a great night. I really enjoy spending time with you."

"Same," I simply say. I hope my disappointment isn't evident that he instead didn't say something along the lines of, "I really enjoy spending time with you, therefore I can't leave. You complete me." Okay, too cheesy. But, I'm disappointed none the less.

Then Carly's words echo in my mind: *It doesn't always have to be him calling the shots.*

Before I can think twice, I take a step toward him, my heart pounding in my chest.

"Hunter," I say, my voice catching slightly in my throat. He pauses, turning back to me, his brow furrowing in question. I reach out, grabbing his hand before I lose my nerve. "Stay."

It's a simple word, but it almost seems like I'm asking him for the world. For a moment, he just looks at me, the surprise clear in his eyes. I can see the battle waging inside him, the conflict between what he wants and what he thinks he should do.

"Frankie…" he starts, but I can hear the hesitation, the doubt, in his voice.

"Please," I whisper, my grip on his hand tightening. "Just stay."

Something shifts in his expression, the tension easing as he looks at me, really looks at me, and I can see it—the same desire, the same longing that's been eating away at me for weeks. Slowly, almost as if he's afraid to move too quickly, he steps closer, our bodies nearly touching.

Then, without another word, he pulls me into him, his lips crashing against mine in a kiss that's as desperate as it is passionate. It's as if all the tension, all the uncertainty we're both living under lately, is being poured into this one moment, and I can't help but respond with the same intensity, the same need.

His arms wrap around me, pulling me closer, and I lose myself in him, in the friction of his body against mine, in the way his hands grip me like he's afraid I'll slip away if he lets go.

When we finally pull back, both of us breathless, he rests his forehead against mine, his breath warm against my skin. "Frankie," he murmurs, his voice rough with emotion.

I don't respond, my heart still racing, my thoughts a whirl-wind of what this means, what comes next. But right now, in this moment, all that matters is that he's here, with me, and that he chose to stay.

The world outside my living room fades into the background as Hunter's lips claim mine with a fervor that sends shivers through my entire body. His hands, strong and sure, tangle in my hair, pulling me closer as our bodies press together with an urgency that is both thrilling and terrifying.

He bends me over the back of the sofa and jerks my pants down. I hear his buckle clank metal-on-metal as his pants fall to the floor. He spreads my legs and positions himself at my opening and shoves himself into me.

I cry out in pleasure, appreciating the girth of his massive cock as he goes in and out, in and out. It's fast and furious and deliberate.

When I come and collapse forward out of pure exhaustion and pleasure, he picks me up and turns me back to face him. He holds me tenderly for a moment and then asks if we can go to my bedroom. I don't answer with words, grabbing his hand instead and leading him down the hall.

Our breathing is still ragged as we stumble toward the bedroom, shedding the rest of our clothes along the way. His shirt falls to the floor just as I toss mine along with my bra.

The back of my knees hit the edge of the bed, and we collapse onto the mattress in a tangle of sheets and need. Hunter's body covers mine, the weight of him both comforting and exhilarating. His lips trail a path of fire down my neck, his teeth nipping at my skin, making me gasp with pleasure.

I arch into him, my body aching for more. Our eyes meet, and in his gaze, I see a reflection of my own desperate longing. "Hunter," I whisper, my voice trembling with anticipation. I'm tender down there, but not done. I'm swollen and desperate to have him inside of me again.

"I want you, Frankie," he growls, his words sending a thrill through me. "I need you."

I don't have time to respond before his mouth is on mine again, his hands exploring my body with a hunger that is primal. I can feel him, hard and insistent against my thigh, and I can't hold back the moan that escapes my lips.

He enters me with a single, powerful thrust that steals my breath away. Our bodies move together in a rhythm that is both wild and beautiful, each stroke driving me higher and higher. I cling to him, my fingers gripping his back as I meet him thrust for thrust, our bodies slick with sweat and passion.

The sounds of our lovemaking fill the room—the rhythmic creaking of the bed, the wet slap of our bodies coming together, our cries of pleasure mingling in the air. It's raw and real and more intense than any other time with him before.

"You are so good," Hunter groans, his voice strained with the effort of holding back. "So perfect."

A fierce energy gathers inside me, brimming just below the surface, threatening to break free. My body is on fire, every nerve ending alive with sensation. And then, with a final, powerful thrust, the world shatters around me, and I'm falling, falling, falling into a sea of ecstasy.

As the waves of pleasure slowly ebb away, I'm cradled in Hunter's arms, our bodies still intimately connected. He presses a gentle kiss to my forehead, his breathing slower now.

For a long moment, we lie in silence, listening to the sound of our hearts beating in sync. And in that moment, I realize that something has shifted between us, something profound and irreversible.

I turn to look at Hunter, my eyes searching his for some sign of what he's thinking, how he perceives this. But his expression is unreadable, his eyes guarded.

"Don't overthink it, Frankie," he finally says, his voice soft but firm. It's almost as if he is reading my mind. "Let's just enjoy this... whatever it is."

I nod, choosing to take his advice. After all, I've spent so much of my life worrying about the future, about being strong and standing on my own without anyone else. For once, I want to let my heart depend on someone else, to embrace the uncertainty and see where it leads.

———

FRIDAY, *May 31*

6:14 am

THE SOFT GRAY light of early morning filters into the room, casting a delicate glow over everything it touches. I blink awake, surprised that I'm up this early—especially after last night. Normally, I'm the last one to rise, but something stirred me, something that tells me it's more than just the remnants of a dream.

I turn over, and my breath catches in my throat. Hunter is still asleep beside me, his face softened in the quiet serenity of slumber. The lines of worry and determination ever present along his brow are gone, leaving him looking almost boyish in the soft dawn light. I smile involuntarily at how handsome and peaceful he looks.

And he's in my bed.

My gaze drifts over his features, taking in the sharp angles of his jaw, the strong curve of his cheekbones, the way his lips are slightly parted as he breathes deeply, rhythmically. Even in sleep, there's a quiet power about him, a kind of strength that seems to radiate from within.

And then my eyes are drawn to the tattoos that cover his arms and chest, peeking out from under the sheets. The ink is dark against his skin, swirling patterns and intricate designs that tell stories I've yet to learn.

I've never been with a man who has this much ink, and I can't deny how incredibly sexy I find it. The tattoos give him an edge, a hint of danger that contrasts sharply with the kindness and empathy I've come to know in him. And it suits him.

As the daylight begins to spill more fully into the room, it highlights the details of the ink, the way it contours to his muscles, enhancing the natural lines of his body. He looks like something out of a fantasy—bad boy on the outside, but now I know better. Beneath the tattoos and the gruff exterior, Hunter is one of the most caring, compassionate people I've ever known.

My heart aches a little as I watch him, a mix of fear and longing swirling in my chest. I'm falling for him, hard, and that scares the shit out of me. I didn't plan for this, didn't want this, but now that it's happening, I don't know how to stop it. And maybe, deep down, I don't want to.

I just hope I'm another victim to think she will be different. My mom always told me, when a man tells you who he is, believe him. He's said from the beginning he didn't want anything.

In fairness, so did I. Intentions change. Feelings grow. I can only follow my heart and trust that it wouldn't lead me astray.

I reach out tentatively, tracing the edge of one of the tattoos on his arm with my fingertips. His skin is warm and smooth under my touch. He shifts slightly in his sleep, mumbling something incoherent, but doesn't wake. I let my hand linger a moment longer, soaking in the aura of him, before pulling back.

The room is slowly brightening, and I know he'll wake soon. This rare, stolen moment of pure voyeurism is fleeting, I know. I want to soak up as much of him like this that I can.

His eyes flutter open, those deep blues locking onto mine, and he smiles—a little sheepish, a little sleepy, and a lot sexy. It's the kind of smile that could power the whole city, and for a moment, it's like the only woman in the world who's been lucky enough to receive it.

"Good morning," he murmurs, his voice a low rumble that sends a shiver through me.

I don't trust myself to speak, so instead, I let my actions do the talking. My hand slips beneath the sheets, finding the firm planes of his stomach, tracing the contours of his muscles until I reach the prize I'm seeking. I wrap my fingers around his growing erection, feeling it swell and harden in my grasp.

Hunter's breath hitches as I begin to stroke him, his gaze never leaving my face. There's a hunger there, a raw need that mirrors my own, and it spurs me on.

With a swift, fluid motion, I straddle him, my hair falling in a curtain around us as I lean down to capture his lips in a searing kiss. His hands find my hips, gripping me tightly as I rock against him, the friction sending sparks of pleasure radiating through my core.

I savor the pressure, hard and insistent, urgent against my entrance, and I don't waste any time. I rise up, positioning him at my center, and then I sink down, taking him in fully with one swift motion. We both gasp at the suddenness of the connection, the exquisite fullness of it.

Our rhythm is fast and frenzied, driven by the urgency of our impending separation. He thrusts up to meet me, each stroke sending waves of ecstasy crashing over us both. Our bodies move together as if they were made for this dance, each motion more intense than the last.

Hunter's hands wander, exploring the curves of my body with an urgency that speaks of unspoken desires and the bittersweet knowledge that this moment can't last. He palms my breasts, teasing my nipples into tight buds, and the sensation shoots straight to my core, intensifying the building pressure.

I throw my head back, my movements becoming more erratic as I ride the edge of release. Hunter sits up, wrapping his arms around me, and captures my nipple in his mouth. The added sensation sends me tumbling over the edge, and I cry out as my orgasm crashes over me in relentless waves.

Hunter isn't far behind, his own release following swiftly on the heels of mine. He buries his face in the crook of my neck, muffling his groan as he finds his release, his body shuddering beneath mine with the force of it.

We stay like that for a moment, our ragged breaths gradually syncing up with the steady beat of our hearts. Then reality starts to intrude, and with a reluctant sigh, Hunter gently disentangles himself from me.

"I have to go," he says, his voice tinged with regret. "Surgery waits for no one."

I nod, understanding the demands of our professions all too well. As he gets up and starts to dress, I can't help but watch him, memorizing every line and curve of his body, every detail of his tattoos.

He catches me looking and flashes me that smile again, the one that seems to hold a promise of more to come. And despite the early hour and the swift departure upon us, I can't help but bask in a sense of contentment.

Morning sex has a way of setting the tone for the day, and this passion, connection, the raw honesty of it, is definitely something I could get used to.

———

2:49 pm

THE LATE AFTERNOON sun filters through the trees, casting dappled shadows on the ground as I walk along the familiar path in the park. It's quieter than usual today, the typical hum of joggers and dog walkers replaced by a gentle breeze rustling the leaves.

I asked my dad to meet me here. This park has become our place over the past couple of meetings, a neutral ground where we've been slowly getting to know each other.

As I round the bend, I see him sitting on the same bench where we we've met before, his hands clasped in his lap, head slightly bowed. He looks up as I approach, and his face breaks into a small, tentative smile. There's something different in his expression today—something heavier.

"Hi, Dad," I say, the word still foreign on my tongue, but less so than it did weeks ago.

"Hi, Frankie," he replies, standing up as I reach him. He hesitates for a moment, then gestures to the bench. "Shall we sit?"

I nod, wishing we could walk to take away some of the awkwardness of sitting here together with nothing to occupy us but our words, or lack thereof. Perhaps he isn't feeling well today and needs the rest. He appears a little more pale than the last time I saw him.

Quickly I sink onto the bench beside him, the warmth of the late afternoon sun on my back. There's a tension in the air, unspoken things hanging between us, and I can tell this time is different. He isn't his usual overcompensating self.

We sit in silence for a few moments, just listening to the sounds of the park, and then he takes a deep breath, turning to face me. "Frankie, there's something I need to tell you. Something I've been holding back because I wasn't sure how to say it. But I think it's time."

A tight knot forms in my stomach, pulling tighter as I meet his gaze, the seriousness in his eyes telling me that whatever he's about to say, it's important. "Okay," I say quietly, bracing myself.

He looks down at his hands, taking a moment to collect his thoughts before he begins. "When your mother and I were together, I wasn't… I wasn't the man I should have been. I had a problem, Frankie. An addiction. I was spending money we didn't have on things we, as a family, didn't need, and I wasn't being the husband or the father that you and your mom deserved."

His voice is steady, but there's a tremor beneath it, a raw honesty that I haven't heard from him before. I swallow hard, the weight of his words settling over me. "Addiction?"

He nods, his eyes still fixed on his hands. "I was an alcoholic and I had a gambling problem. I tried to stop, for your mom, for you, but the grip it had on me was too strong. I kept relapsing, kept making the same mistakes. Your mother gave me so many chances, more than I deserved. But in the end, she made the right decision for both of you. She asked me to leave."

My heart pounds in my chest causing a mixture of emotions to swirl inside me—anger, sadness, confusion. "She didn't tell me," I whisper, more to myself than to him.

"She didn't want you to know," he says softly. "She was trying to protect you and your idea of me. I understand that now. But back then it felt like the end of everything. I tried to get clean, but I couldn't do it on my own. By the time I finally did, years had passed, and by then I didn't know how to find y'all."

His voice breaks slightly, and I can see the pain in his eyes, the regret etched into every line of his face. "Once I finally tracked down an address, I sent cards, letters, I called. But everything was sent back, and the phone numbers were blocked. I don't know if you remember, but when you were thirteen I came by, but your mom said it was best if I leave. By that point, it wasn't my place to argue with her. When you moved, I didn't know where you were. I wanted to be in your life, Frankie, but I didn't know how."

Tears well up in my eyes, and I blink them back, trying to process everything he's telling me. "I thought... I thought you didn't care," I say, my voice trembling. "I thought you just left."

"I never stopped caring," he says urgently, reaching for my hand. "Not for a single day. I never forgot about you, Frankie. But I was a coward, and I didn't fight hard enough to be in your life. And that's something I'll regret for eternity."

I look down at our joined hands, his grip warm and steady, and for the first time, I see him—not just as the man who wasn't there, but as a man who made mistakes, who's spent years trying to atone for them. "I saw you on those commercials. You had a wife and children. It felt like you left us for a better life."

He swallows, his Adam's apple bobbing as he fights back tears of his own. "I did remarry, and God blessed me with two other children. But none of them were a replacement for you. My sons are grown now, and I'm still married to a

275

patient woman, but I never stopped loving your mom or you. I threw away my life without even realizing it."

A tear slips down my cheek, and I don't bother wiping it away. "I wasn't," I whisper. "I needed you. I needed my dad."

"I'm so sorry, Frankie," he says, his voice breaking completely now. "I'm so sorry I wasn't there for you. That's why I made it a mission to find you. When I was diagnosed with cancer it hit me that I might never get the chance to make things right, to tell you how much I love you, how much I've always loved you."

I can't hold back the tears anymore, and they flow freely down my face. The pain of all those years of feeling abandoned, of thinking I wasn't enough, crashes over me, but with it comes a strange sense of relief. Because now I know —it wasn't that he didn't care. It was that he didn't know how to be the father I needed in time.

Without thinking, I reach out and pull him into a hug, my arms wrapping around him tightly. He stiffens for a moment, surprised, but then he hugs me back, his embrace strong and trembling at the same time.

We sit like that for a long time, both of us crying, both of us healing, as the sun hides behind some clouds, giving a rare reprieve in the heat.

And for the first time in my life, I'm finally beginning to understand, to forgive, and to let go.

TWENTY-FOUR

Hunter
_____

UAB Hospital

3:19 *pm*

"YOU, too, Mrs. Oppenstar. You keep getting healthier and you'll be running circles around Dr. Duncan and me."

It's amazing when you get to see with your own eyes a patient actually taking the hard steps to better herself. It's unbelievable how much better she is doing now that she has hung up that disgusting habit.

My phone in my breast pocket vibrates. I pull it out to see it's my mother. Shit.

"Hello, Mom," I say wearily, closing my eyes after pushing the button to accept the call. I'm literally about to head out to work out, but I know if I don't take this call I'll put off calling her back. What's another five minutes?

"Hunter…"

I sit up a bit, frowning. I did expect a tirade right off the bat, but the tone of her voice in that one word says a lot. Of course, it could be a trick.

"Mom. What's wrong? I mean, has something happened?"

"I know you've spoken with Dr. Momford, my oncologist. He told me he consulted with you and a doctor colleague of yours there. Thank you for putting that together."

"Yes, I have." I'm not sure if her quiet tone is because she is unhappy with something I did or because I didn't do it sooner. Either way, I'm sure I did something wrong in her eyes.

"He told me that my cancer will not respond to treatment."

There it is. Before I was involved, she had hope. Now, she is aware her cancer is especially dangerous and very likely aggressive. Fuck. I knew I should have stayed out of it.

"I'm sorry, Mom. That was my worry when you told me bits and pieces of your diagnosis. That is why I called Dr. Dibbins and he offered to call your doctor. The good news is there are a few trials happening that you can participate in. This isn't a death sentence, Mom."

"Son, was I hard on you?"

"What?" That's kind of an odd question and one I didn't expect to hear from her, especially in the context of this topic.

"Did I push you too hard? Your father," I can hear her pursing her lips in the pause, "he and I only wanted the best for you. We saw your potential."

Good lord, I want to shout at her that she was on my ass all the time to do better, to accomplish everything, to be the fucking best at everything. But I don't unload that baggage right now, I don't need to.

"You wanted the best for me, Mom, I get it."

"Then why did you rebel so much? Why did you always seem so angry?"

This conversation is getting weirder by the minute. My parents and I don't talk like this, open up, share feelings.

Staring death in the face does the strangest things to people. I do not really want to have this discussion with my mother. That ship has sailed. There is no need to rehash the last thirty-two years.

But I do need to make sure that she's okay, and it seems like this is something she wants to get off her chest. Despite the bitterness I've held onto, she's still the woman who gave birth to me, and I am trying to find something that can save her life.

Inhaling through my nose, I reply, "You and Dad did push me, Mom, and I started to resent it early on. Nothing I ever did felt like it was good enough. Even when I got straight A's in school, you didn't let up. I wanted to please you, but…"

"But, what? Tell me, son."

"I felt like no matter what I did, how good I was, how perfect it was, nothing pleased you."

"You've always pleased me, Son. I'm sorry we made you believe otherwise. I've never been so proud of anyone or anything my whole life."

Who is this person? Did she start early on her gin and tonics? My mother has never said anything remotely close to this. The word "proud" was not in their lexicon. I'm starting to get worried. "Mom, are you okay? Do you need help?"

"No, I'm perfectly fine," she says, sounding almost happy. "I just wanted to know, that's all."

Her words are slurred and now her breathing sounds labored.

"Mom, I'm going to call an ambulance and Dr. Momford. Are you home? I need to know you're safe and secure, okay?"

My body is going into complete panic mode. I buzz Jill while I'm still on my cell phone with Mom and ask her to call 911 and direct them to my mother's house in California. She has the address. I'm keeping my mom on the phone until they arrive.

"Don't," she breathes into the phone. "I just need a rest, that's all. I'll let you go, I just wanted you to know."

What the fuck?

"Mom?! Mom, are you still there?"

"One more thing. I've written you a letter. Please…know… that I do, love….you."

"Mom?! Mom!"

The line goes dead. I'm shaking as I stare at the phone in my hand. Blinking several times, I try to focus as I search for the contact number for her oncologist. Right now, though, it's all I can do to keep my fingers around the phone.

3:27 pm

I HANG up the phone with Dr. Momford and sit there, staring at the phone. I told him that we already had an ambulance sent to her house. He said that my mother seemed to take the news fairly well when they met first thing this morning and that she seemed otherwise healthy, considering.

Well, she isn't okay now. I don't know if she took too much Valium or hit the bottle early, but something is wrong. He assured me he would call me as soon as he knows more. He already put a call into the hospital about her coming in and they will alert him of her condition as soon as she arrives.

I can't do anything from two thousand miles away. Now, more than ever, I know I need to move her here. All I can do is stay on top of the clinical trials, make sure she is taking her meds properly, and make sure she is comfortable.

But I meant what I said to her. I don't think this has to be a death sentence. Obviously, her doctor there isn't up on the latest with this cancer. She needs to be here. If she is closer, I can make sure we do everything we can to beat this beast.

4:58 pm

. . .

I SLAM the weights back onto the rack with a grunt, the metallic clang echoing in the stillness of my home gym. My muscles are burning, my breath coming in short, ragged gasps, but it's not enough. It's never enough. No matter how hard I push, how much I sweat, I need to push harder, do more reps.

I stand there, dripping sweat, staring blankly at the cars below starting to stack up for the afternoon commute. The view usually calms me, but this afternoon, it's just adding to my anxiety. My heart is pounding, and my mind is racing, chasing down every possible scenario, every worst-case outcome.

When I called 911, they said they'd dispatch someone immediately. But waiting for news? It's killing me. I called her house several times on my ride home but no one answered. I'm here, thousands of miles away, helpless.

The phone vibrates on the bench beside me, and I grab it, my hand slick with sweat. It's Dr. Momford.

"Dr. Momford," I answer, my voice hoarse, not from the workout but from the fear clawing at my throat.

"Dr. Parrish," his voice is calm, too calm. It makes my heart plummet.

"Please, call me Hunter."

"Hunter. I'm afraid I have bad news. The emergency responders arrived at your mother's home. I'm so sorry to have to tell you over the phone, Hunter… she was pronounced dead at the scene."

For a moment, I don't say anything. The words don't register, not fully. Dead? How? My mom was just on the phone with me, slurring her words, sure, but alive. She was breathing. Talking. And now she's gone?

"How?" I finally manage to choke out, my voice breaking. I'm certain they don't have definitive answers so quickly, but surely they must have an idea. I don't care about being strong right now. I just need to know.

"From what the EMTs described, it sounds like she may have suffered a pulmonary embolism, likely caused by a blood clot," Dr. Momford explains gently. "Given her condition, it's not uncommon, especially with the strain her body was under from the lymphoma and the treatments. The slurred speech... could have been an indication of a cerebral hemorrhage. It seems everything happened very quickly."

I nod, even though he can't see me. It makes sense medically. Hell, I've seen it a hundred times in patients. But hearing it applied to my own mother is like a punch to the gut. My knees buckle, and I sink down onto the bench, my head in my hands.

"I know I didn't do enough," I trail off. I don't know Dr. Momford. He doesn't want to hear me babble on about my mother. I've been in his shoes a hundred times, delivering this news.

"She knew, Hunter," Dr. Momford says softly. "She knew you cared. That's why she called. It sounds like she wanted you to hear her say those things, to have some closure."

"I should have done more," I whisper, more to myself than to him. "I should have... I should have been there. I should have insisted she come here."

"You did what you could," he says, and I can tell he means it, but it doesn't make the guilt any easier to bear. "She was just saying to me this morning at our appointment, before we went over everything, how proud she was of you. I could tell how much it meant to her that you had someone call me about her care."

Those words hit me like a ton of bricks. Proud of me. It's all I ever wanted to hear from her, from either of my parents, but it comes too late. The tears that I've been holding back finally break free, hot and angry, mixing with the sweat still dripping down my face.

"I'm sorry, Hunter," Dr. Momford says, and I can hear the genuine sympathy in his voice. "Please call me if you have any questions. The hospital will be in touch about how to proceed from here. But please don't hesitate to call me any time."

I murmur something that might be a thanks before the line goes dead. I'm left sitting here in the silence of my gym. The surrounding air, the muffled sounds of the city below, the cool AC blowing on my damp shirt—all of these sensations are like a dream.

She's gone. Just like that. All the distance, all the walls I put up between us are more like a prison now keeping all of the pain in instead of keeping it out. I spent so much time being angry, being resentful, all that's left is this crushing grief, this sense that I failed her. That I failed us both.

I drop the phone beside me, burying my face in my hands as the tears come harder and faster until I'm sobbing. The weight of everything crashes down around me. And for the first time in a long, long time, I let myself feel it all.

_7:10 pm_

I DON'T KNOW how long I've been driving, but the city lights blur past, the steady hum of the engine the only thing grounding me.

Getting out and getting some fresh air to clear my head was all I could think about. Anything that doesn't involve sitting alone in my apartment and drowning in thoughts of what I should have done differently.

Without really thinking about it, I text Frankie. She seems like a life raft at this point, something to keep me from slipping under.

> Hey. You up for a walk?

This has somehow become our thing we do together. And it is good for me. I need it now.

It's impulsive, but I can't be alone right now, not after everything that's happened. Walking is something I can manage, something that's controlled, a way to keep my emotions at bay.

Her response comes quickly.

> Sure, but I dropped my car off for service today. I can't pick it up until tomorrow. Wanna pick me up?

I don't hesitate to reply.

> I'm close by. Be there in a sec.

I stick my head in through the cracked door and call out. "Hello? Frankie? I'm here."

"I'll be right out," she yells from the back of the house. "Make yourself at home.

I pause, suddenly overcome with the emotions I thought I had tucked back away in the dark caverns of my psyche. All of them are threatening to surface. The idea of walking seemed like a good way to avoid confronting them, but now, standing here in her living room, everything seems front and center again. Something about being here, about seeing her.

I sink onto the couch, the cushions soft beneath me. Frankie joins me only seconds later. "Hey, you. Looks like you already had your workout. You saved the warm down for me. You know me so well!"

"Yeah, I got in some weights earlier. Sorry if I'm stinky."

"You're not at all. I could just tell you've already been to hell and back."

If only you knew, I want to say.

For a few moments, we just sit there, the quiet of her home wrapping around us as she fiddles with the zipper on her lightweight hoodie.

"I got a call this afternoon," I start, my voice rough but something driving me to share with her, to seek comfort. "From my mom."

Frankie turns to face me, her expression gentle, encouraging me to continue.

"Oh? Is everything okay?"

"It was strange," I say, rubbing a hand over my face. "Her words were slurred, and she she apologized for some things that happened years ago. And then the call just ended." Suddenly, I regret bringing this up right now. Clearly, I wasn't thinking.

I'm having a hard time forming cohesive sentences. There are some things I know if I say them I will completely lose my shit and I do not want to do that. But the words keep spilling out.

Frankie grabs my hand. She must see that I'm struggling. She doesn't say anything, which I appreciate. I didn't realize how much I needed that touch until now.

"I called 911, and then I called her oncologist," I continue, my voice trembling. "They found her at her house. She was... she was already gone by the time they got there. I didn't do enough," I continue, my voice breaking. "I should have been there. I should have... I don't know. I should have done something."

"You couldn't have known, Hunter," Frankie says softly. "You did everything you could. You've been doing everything you can."

I shake my head, the tears I've been holding back finally slipping free. "She told me she was proud of me, for the first time in my life, and now she's gone. I didn't even get to tell her..."

My voice falters, and I can't finish the sentence. Frankie shifts closer, wrapping her arms around me in a hug that's warm and steady. The kind of hug that holds you together when everything feels like it is falling apart all around you.

"I'm so sorry, Hunter," she whispers, her voice thick with emotion. "I'm so sorry."

I let myself cry. Dr. Momford is the only person until now that has heard me cry since I was a boy. It's a strange but freeing sensation, letting myself be vulnerable like this with her.

The tears come and I let them, let the grief pour out of me. And Frankie is there, holding me, not saying anything, just allowing me to get it out. And somehow, that's enough. More than enough.

After what seems like an eternity, I pull back and wipe my eyes. "I didn't mean to unload all of this on you," I say, my voice still shaky. "I had every intention of completely avoiding even talking about it. That's how I typically deal with shit like this."

"You never have to apologize," Frankie says, her eyes locked on mine, full of understanding. "You don't have to go through this alone, Hunter. I'm here."

Her words hit me deep, cutting through the pain. For the first time since I got that call, I feel like maybe I'm not drowning. Maybe, with her help, I can keep my head above water.

I reach out, take her hand, and squeeze. The connection between us is stronger than ever. "Thank you," I manage to say, my voice still rough around the edges.

She just nods, her thumb brushing lightly over my knuckles, a silent reassurance that she's here and not going anywhere. We sit there for a while longer, just holding on to each other, the quiet filling the space between us.

"I have an idea. Do you like ramen?"

I nod, not sure where this is going, but I appreciate her taking the reins.

"Whenever I feel crummy, I call Uber Eats and order ramen and Jeni's Ice Cream. My favorite is Brown Butter Almond Brittle, and I sit in front of the TV and eat until I'll burst. What do you say?"

I nod as a wave of gratitude washes over me. "That sounds perfect," I say, my voice still a tad hoarse from crying.

Frankie smiles softly and reaches for her phone. "Any preferences? I usually go for the Tonkotsu ramen, but they've got a great miso option, too."

"Tonkotsu sounds good," I reply, realizing I haven't eaten since... I can't even remember.

As Frankie places the order, I lean back into the couch, completely drained but somehow lighter. The significance of everything that's happened today still presses down on me, but it's more manageable being here with her, knowing I'm not alone.

"Alright, food's on the way," Frankie announces, setting her phone down. "Now, let's find something mindless to watch."

She grabs the remote and starts scrolling through Netflix. I watch her, struck by how effortlessly she's created this bubble of comfort around us. There's no pressure to talk, no expectation for me to be anything other than what I am right now - a mess of grief and exhaustion.

"How about this?" she asks, highlighting some action movie I've never heard of.

"Sure," I nod, not really caring what we watch.

As the movie starts, Frankie settles back next to me, close enough that her warmth radiates through her clothes and onto me. We sit in comfortable silence, the movie's dialogue a distant hum in the background.

TWENTY-FIVE

Frankie

11:34 pm

I WAKE up to the soft glow of the television as the credits
of something, I'm not sure what, roll silently across the
screen. My body is curled into the warmth of Hunter's, his
arm draped protectively around my waist.

The steady rise and fall of his chest against my back is
soothing. Beneath that, the firm evidence of his arousal
presses into me. He's asleep, lost in dreams, and I can't
help but wonder if those dreams involve me.

Slowly, I reach my hand around, my fingers brushing
against the fabric of his boxers, absorbing the heat he puts
off even through the soft, thin cotton.

I trace the outline of his erection, a surge of desire
coursing through me as it twitches in response to my touch.
I'm turning myself on while stroking his pleasure, the

sensation of his hardness growing under my caress too tempting to ignore.

As I continue to explore him, his breathing changes, becoming shallower, and I realize he's waking up. His hand finds mine, guiding it more firmly against him, and when I look back over my shoulder, I see the smoldering look in his eyes.

"Frankie," he murmurs, my name a soft pleading on his lips.

Without a word, I roll over to face him, our mouths meeting in a kiss that's equal parts hunger and tenderness. Our hands are everywhere, pulling at clothing, seeking skin. He slips his fingers under the waistband of my pajama shorts, finding me already slick and ready for him.

Our movements are impatient and frenzied as we are both suddenly desperate for each other. He pulls my shorts down just enough to free me from them, and I push his boxers down, aligning our bodies as they were meant to be.

He enters me with a single, fluid thrust that draws a gasp from my lips. The couch isn't wide enough, isn't comfortable enough for what we need, but we're beyond caring. We're driven by a need that's as primal as it is profound.

The slap of skin against skin, the sofa as it pounds against the wood floor, our ragged breathing, and the occasional moan or whimper as we chase our pleasure are the only sounds. We're lost in each other, the world outside our little bubble ceasing to exist.

We move to the floor, removing our shorts along the way. The change in position allows for a deeper connection. I'm straddling him now, my hands braced against his chest, pressed against the ripple of his muscles as he thrusts up into me. The new angle sends waves of pleasure crashing over me, each one more intense than the last.

I throw my head back, my hair cascading down my back as I ride him harder, faster. The tension builds within me, gathering low in my belly, and I know I'm close, so close.

"Hunter," I gasp, and he knows I'm coming.

He sits up, wrapping his arms around me, holding me close as he drives into me with renewed vigor. I cry out as my orgasm rips through me, my inner muscles clenching around him.

He follows me over the precipice, his body shuddering beneath mine as he finds his own release, his name a whisper on my lips as we both come down from the high.

The other times have been good, but lying next to each other, naked on my floor, makes this time even better. Initially, we don't say anything. Panting is the only noise we make. I dare to press myself against him, hoping I haven't overextended my welcome on this precarious night after he lost his mom.

"You doing okay?" I ask him, keeping my gaze on the distinct lines that trace his pecs. I continue to rest my cheek on his inked chest. His left arm is cradling me and I sense a mild hint of tension as I ask this question. I can tell he isn't used to talking about his feelings.

"I'm doing better now that I'm with you."

I didn't expect this, nor did I think he would ever be so forthcoming with affection for me. But I'll take it, even if it is just a moment of weakness.

"I'm sorry, Hunter. That was a shitty way to have to say goodbye your mom."

He doesn't move either, but he does continue speaking. I listen because I figure that's the best thing to do right now. What I hear as he continues to talk about his family is far different than what I heard during our first night together. He kept it short and sweet.

At some point, I even find myself ready to cry as he reveals what he was put through. I can imagine now, knowing him, the kind of pressure on him. But hearing the pain as he describes it makes me want to hold him and never let him go.

"My mother barely spoke to me at my father's funeral," he says, his voice distant and emotionless. "We weren't really talking because after he got sick, I recommended a doctor they ended up not agreeing with. Somehow, everything that went wrong was my fault. When they switched doctors, they stopped taking my calls. He went downhill fast, and it turns out my recommendation was the way to go. Anyway, that is why I was so reluctant to help with my mom."

"That's awful. The end should not be like that."

All I do is hold him tighter. He definitely suffered some emotional abuse from his parents. I guess we all do to some degree. My mom did what she thought was right by keeping my father away. But in reality, believing he chose to stay away was more painful than anything she was protecting me from.

I don't resent my mom because we had a different kind of relationship than Hunter had with his mom. But I understand how our parents have the ability to cut us deeper and hurt us more than anyone else on this planet.

Although I know I can't do anything to take away the pain, hopefully, my being here with him gives him some comfort as he comes to terms with all of this.

I decide to do something I rarely do. I open up even more than usual, and share what I've been going through with Bill and my family dynamic. It seems like the timing is appropriate, not to mention it's a way to connect with him and to seek some comfort.

"My father wasn't in my life at all. I saw him a handful of times as a kid," I start. I pause, before finishing, "I thought he traded us for a new family."

"Frankie, I'm so sorry."

"No, you don't have to say that. I guess since we are opening up, I thought I would share what has been going on in my life with my parents. He has been contacting me," I say softly. "He's the one I was referring to when I asked you about Hodgkins."

"Oh, my goodness," he says sincerely. "Last you told me he was doing well, right?"

"Yes, it seems so. Although I saw him today and he looked frail to me."

"It's probably just his body going through the treatment. It's hard on the body."

I decide to leave it that for now. Tonight is his night to grieve. I just wanted him to know he can trust me, by showing that I trust him. Even if it is just a little bit, that feels good. It feels right.

———

SATURDAY, *June 1*

8:14 am

THE FIRST THING I notice is the warmth of Hunter's hand on my arm. The morning light is peeking through the curtains, but I'm awake now, acutely aware he is kneeling beside my bed.

"I've got to get some of this restless energy out," he whispers, his tender voice the best wake-up I've ever had. "I'm going to the gym, and then I have a few errands, but I want to see you later."

I nod, not trusting my voice yet, and feel him stand. But before he can move away completely, I grab his hand and pull him back down to me. I turn to face him, our noses almost touching in the dim light.

"Text me when you get up?" he asks, his eyes searching mine.

"Of course," I whisper, my voice still heavy with sleep. But before he can pull away again, I slide my hand to the back of his neck and pull him down for a kiss.

It's not the light, quick kiss he was expecting; it's deeper, more urgent, the kind that leaves no room for doubt about how much I want him to stay.

He responds instantly, his hand tangling in my hair, his body pressing against mine in a way that makes me never want to let him go. He climbs in the bed beside me, staying on top of the covers.

"I have an idea for how to get some of that restless energy out," I whisper, my hand sliding down his chest, tracing the curves of ink on his skin that I can barely see in the almost nonexistent light. "See what you think."

He groans softly as I find the waistband of his shorts, his resolve melts away with every touch. "Frankie," he protests halfheartedly, but I can feel him hardening against me, and I know I've won. Again.

I push him onto his back and straddle him, my hair falling around us like a curtain. I lean down and capture his lips in a searing kiss, my tongue sliding against his as I grind against him, his erection fully intact against me now.

His hands are on my hips, pulling me closer, his fingers digging into my skin as he bucks his hips up to meet mine. I break the kiss and sit up, rolling my hips as I ride him, the sound of our bodies moving together filling the room.

He reaches up and cups my breasts, his thumbs stroking over my nipples, making me gasp and arch my back. The tension builds inside me, a spring winding tighter and tighter with each movement.

"Fuck, Frankie," he growls, his voice strained as he fights to maintain control. But I don't want him to hold back. I want him let go, to lose himself in me the way I'm losing myself in him.

I lean down and nip at his bottom lip, then soothe the sting with my tongue. "Let go, Hunter," I whisper, and he does.

He flips us over in one swift motion, pinning me beneath him as he drives into me with a fierce intensity that makes me cry out. He pulls my legs up, my heels digging into his ass as he thrusts deeper and deeper, each stroke sending waves of pleasure coursing through me.

The room is filled with the sounds of our passion—moans and gasps and the wet slap of skin on skin. As my orgasm builds, a tide of sensations threaten to overwhelm me, until I'm there, clinging to Hunter as I fall apart beneath him.

He follows me, spilling his seed in me, burying his face in my neck as he groans out his release. We lie there in the aftermath, our bodies slick with sweat and tangled in the sheets, our breathing slowly returning to normal.

Finally, he lifts his head and looks at me, his eyes filled with a warmth that has nothing to do with the heat of our love-making. "You were right. That was the best way to burn off some energy," he says, a note of amusement in his voice.

I smile and press a kiss to his lips. "Glad you are pleased."

———

9:49 *am*

I'M FLOATING SOMEWHERE between sleep and wakefulness, the warmth of the bed and the lingering scent of Hunter on the sheets wrapping around me like a swaddling blanket.

I could easily sleep for another few hours, letting the events of the night before drift through my mind. But then, I hear it—Carly's voice calling out from the front door.

"Rise and shine, sleepyhead!"

I groan and bury my face in the pillow, cursing myself for ever thinking it was a good idea to give Carly a key. She's the best friend anyone could ask for, but her timing... not so much. Reluctantly, I throw off the covers and reach for my robe, tying it loosely around my waist, and run to the bathroom to brush my teeth.

When I walk into the living room, Carly is already making herself at home with a wide grin on her face. "Good morning, sunshine! What took you so long to drag your lazy bones out of bed?"

I rub my eyes and manage a sleepy smile. "Ah, I had to brush my teeth. It's early morning on a Saturday. What in the hell are you doing here?"

"That's right. You can't do anything before your beloved morning ritual. Just thought I'd check on my favorite gal on my way home from my night shift. Plus, I brought you a latte. Figured you could use the pick-me-up."

She holds up a to-go cup like it's a peace offering, and I can't help but smile as I take it from her. "You're lucky you're cute. Otherwise, I'd be tempted to throw you out. After I take the latte, of course."

"Love you too, babe," she says, flopping down onto the couch. "So, how's my favorite friend doing this fine morning? Besides being sleepy."

I smile to myself remembering to myself what happened on that very sofa just a few hours ago. And then the floor below it... And then the bed I just peeled myself out of... I digress.

I take a sip of the warm amazingness in a cup, savoring it as it travels through my body. "Not bad. Just tired."

"Poor baby, who calls her own hours and works from home," Carly says, smiling like the smart-ass she can be. "I had another overnight shift. It was pretty quiet, though, thank God. Grace is still the same—no real status change. The docs are trying to figure out a long-term solution for her. She's really sick, Frankie. It's so hard to see her like that."

I nod, a pang of concern for Grace forms as a lump in my throat, but I decide not to mention the possibility of the pacemaker. It's too soon to get anyone's hopes up, and we don't even know if it's feasible yet.

"How are you doing, really?" Carly asks, her tone shifting to something softer, more concerned. "I was giving you a hard time, but seriously, are you okay?"

I sigh and sink into the armchair across from her. "Yeah, life's been busy and full, for sure."

"Talk to me," she says, leaning forward. "What's going on? Now that you have a boy toy, I don't get to see you as much."

I take a deep breath, trying to figure out where to start. "I had a really intense conversation with my dad yesterday."

Carly raises an eyebrow. "Bill? That dad?"

"Yes, Carly. That dad. Only got one."

"What happened?"

I tell her everything—about the history with my dad, the truth he revealed about why he wasn't in my life, and how he's been trying to make amends now that he's sick. As I speak, I can see the sympathy in Carly's eyes, the way she listens without judgment.

"Wow, Frankie… that's a lot to process," she says when I finish. "How are you doing with all of it?"

"I don't know," I admit, running a finger over the rim of the plastic cup top. "Part of me is relieved to finally understand what happened, but another part of me is just… exhausted. I'm sad we lost all that time."

Carly nods, her expression thoughtful. "It's going to take time. But I'm glad you're talking to him. It sounds like you're starting to heal."

"I guess the bright side is, we have the future. In some good news, his treatment seems to be working for his cancer."

"Yes, I like that perspective."

"Hmm," I think to myself softly. "And then, on top of that, Hunter's mom passed away yesterday."

Carly's eyes widen. "Oh my God, Frankie. You did have a busy day!"

"Yeah," I say with a wry smile. "It's been overwhelming. Hunter was really vulnerable last night and opened up to me about everything. In a weird way, it brought us closer, I think."

Carly's expression softens, and she reaches over to squeeze my hand. "I'm really happy for you, Frankie. I know this is a lot you have on your plate, but it sounds like you're handling it really well. Like always, a badass bitch."

I laugh at that notion. I'm a lot of things, but a badass bitch is not one that comes to top of mind. "You're a nerd. I don't know what I'd do without you."

"You'd probably sleep a lot more," she says with a grin, making me laugh despite everything.

"True," I admit. "But then who would bring me lattes and listen to my life's drama?"

"Exactly," Carly says, leaning back into the couch. "So, what's next? How are you going to deal with everything?"

I shrug, taking another sip of my coffee. "One step at a time, I guess. I've got the trial to focus on, and… well, Hunter and I will see where things go, I suppose. Still keeping my expectations low, don't worry."

Carly gives me a knowing look. "Sounds like a plan. Just remember, I'm here if you need anything. Even if it's just to vent. Or, drink coffee."

I nod, grateful for her as a sounding board. She gives me pause. "I know. And I appreciate it."

"Alright, enough heavy stuff," Carly says, suddenly brightening. "What's for breakfast? I'm starving."

I laugh, as the tension slides off my shoulders. "What does this look like, Waffle House?"

———

4:36 *pm*

I'M deep into the third draft of the protocol when I hear a knock on the door. It's firm but not urgent, the kind of knock that makes my stomach flip with a sense of unease. I know it isn't Hunter, I know his sound now. And Carly wouldn't knock, she barges in like she owns the place.

I set my laptop down and head for the door, stretching as I walk. I didn't realize how long I've been sitting until I got up and everything is tight.

When I open it, a woman is standing there, probably in her early fifties, with kind eyes and a face that shows the lines of life lived fully. She is strangely, vaguely familiar, but I can't place how.

"Hello," she says, her voice soft. "Are you Frankie Renna?"

I nod, unsure where this is going. "Yes, that's me. Can I help you?"

She hesitates, clearly uncomfortable with what she's about to say. "I'm sorry to intrude, but I'm Janice Renna. Bill Renna was my husband."

As soon as she says it realize I recognize her from the commercials of my father's dealership years ago. She is older now, but the resemblance is unmistakable.

The world tilts for a moment. My heart stops, and I stare at her, trying to process what she just said. "Bill Renna?" I echo, my voice barely above a whisper.

"Yes," she says, a hint of sadness in her eyes. "May I come in? There's something I need to talk to you about."

I step aside, still in shock, and gesture for her to enter. She walks in slowly, taking in the space around her as if trying to get a sense of me through my home. I lead her to the kitchen table and offer her a seat.

"Can I get you something to drink?" I ask, my voice sounding far away even to my own ears.

She shakes her head. "No, thank you."

I sit down across from her, worried my legs might give out at any moment. I'm not sure if I want to hear what she has to say, but I know I have to. She wouldn't have come here if it weren't important.

Janice looks at me with those kind eyes and takes a deep breath. "Bill specifically asked me to deliver the news to you in person. I'm so sorry to have to tell you this, but... your father passed away last night. Peacefully."

The words hit me like a punch to the gut. My eyebrows involuntarily raise and I blink rapidly as my breath catches in my throat. Tears prick at the corners of my eyes while the room spins around me. "He's... he's gone?"

She nods, her expression full of sympathy. "Yes. He didn't want you to know how sick he was. He wanted to spend what little time he had left with you focused on healing, not on his illness."

I can't speak, can't move. The room seems to spin and close in around me as the reality of what she's saying sinks in. We still had so much left to do, to say.

Janice continues, filling in the blanks my father never mentioned. "Bill's Hodgkin's had been present for a while. It was an aggressive form, but he was in a clinical trial that seemed to be working—until the last several months. When the doctors told him there was likely nothing else they could do, he made it his mission to find you. He wanted to apologize in person before he died. That was all he wanted."

Through trembling voice, I manage to say, "He didn't tell me. He said nothing."

"He didn't want you to worry," she explains gently. "Only when he knew time was running out did he truly dedicate himself to locating you, after years of trying. Yesterday, he didn't feel well, but none of us thought it would be the day. He took a turn for the worse in the late afternoon, and by the time we got him to the hospital he was in organ failure. There wasn't much time."

Tears spill over, and I can't stop them. "I didn't know. I didn't know he was that sick."

"He didn't want you to," she says, reaching across the table to take my hand. "He wanted you to remember the good, to focus on the time you had together. He was so happy to have found you."

I nod, trying to steady myself, as an overwhelming wave of grief, regret, and anger falls over me all at once. Janice continues, her voice gentle but firm. It's not her fault, but her presence is intrusive right now and I suddenly want her gone.

"I also wanted to let you know Bill wanted his estate divided equally among his three children—you, and the two sons we shared. For the last twenty years, he built a considerable fortune through his used car business. He has several dealerships all around the Southeast. There are twenty-five Bill's Bargains across Alabama, Georgia, South Carolina, and North Florida. I'll be retaining ownership of three of the Alabama dealerships and the house. But he secured a buyer for twenty-two of them before he died and the proceeds will go to you kids. He wanted to make sure you knew how much he loved you."

I stare at her, unable to process the magnitude of what she's saying. "He did all that?"

She nods. "He did. And he wanted to make sure you were taken care of."

I'm speechless, the tears still falling as I try to absorb everything she's telling me. My father, the man who had been a ghost in my life, spent his final days trying to make amends, to leave something behind for me.

Janice squeezes my hand again, then slowly stands up. "I should go. I know this is a lot to take in. But if you ever need anything, or if you want to talk more, please don't hesitate to reach out."

I nod, unable to find the words. As she heads to the door, I follow her in a daze, my mind spinning with everything I've just learned.

She turns back to me before she leaves. "He really did love you, Frankie. He never stopped. Losing you broke a piece of his heart that was never whole again."

And with that, she's gone, leaving me alone with my thoughts, my grief, and the overwhelming sense of loss. I stand there for a long moment, unable to move, unsure of what to do next.

The first person I want to call is Hunter. I need his steady presence, his calm, his understanding. But even as I reach for my phone, I hesitate, not wanting to burden him with more after what he's just gone through with his own mother.

With trembling fingers, I type out a message, asking if he can come over.

TWENTY-SIX

Hunter

_____

City Walk BHAM

4:59 pm

I SLAM the ball over the net, aiming for the corner of the kitchen. Shep lunges, his paddle outstretched, but the ball whizzes past him. Game point.

"Damn it!" Shep curses, wiping sweat from his brow. "That was a killer dink shot."

I can't help but grin. "Thanks. Your third shot drop almost had me earlier."

We shake hands at the net, both of us breathing hard. The late afternoon sun beats down on the court, gluing my shirt to my back.

"Good game, man," Shep says, clapping me on the shoulder. "But I demand a rematch next week."

"You're on," I laugh. "Maybe by then you'll learn how to handle my backhand drive."

We grab our water bottles and head to the bench. As we cool down, Shep asks, "How's that pacemaker trial going? Heard you got some big-shot sponsor on board."

"Yeah, it's moving along. Still a lot of red tape to cut through, but we're making progress."

"And how's working with Dr. Renna? I've heard she's brilliant."

I nod, trying to keep my face neutral. "She is. We make a good team."

As I reach for my phone to check the time, I notice a missed text from Frankie. My stomach drops when I read it.

> Hunter, can you call me when you get a chance? It's important.

Something about this message, now, when she knows I'm playing pickleball, sets off alarm bells. I quickly start packing up my gear.

"Everything okay?" Shep asks, noticing my sudden change in demeanor.

"Not sure," I reply. "I've gotta run. I'll catch you later, alright?"

He nods, concern evident on his face. "Sure thing. Let me know if you need anything."

I hurry to my car, my mind racing. What could be wrong? Is it about the trial? Or something more personal? I need to call Frankie and find out.

The cryptic nature of the message leaves too much to the imagination. Did she find out something from the IRB? Surely it's too soon to know already.

I hit the call button, my heart pounding as hard as it was during my run. She answers on the second ring, and I can hear the tension in her voice immediately.

"Hunter…"

"Frankie, what's going on? Are you okay?"

There's a pause, and then she exhales softly. "I just… I really need to see you. If you're not busy."

"I just finished my game," I tell her, already in the parking lot. "I can be there in ten."

"Okay. Thank you."

Her voice is quiet, fragile, and it tugs at something deep inside me. I don't waste any time and jog the rest of the way to my car. My mind is racing with possibilities. I know she's been dealing with a lot, between her father and the pressure of the trial, and now I'm worried it's all catching up with her.

If it had been something with the trial, she would have told me, right?

As I drive, a sense of urgency quickly replaced the adrenaline from our game. Whatever's going on, she reached out to me, and that means she trusts me enough to let me in. I won't let her down.

That's not something I take lightly.

———

FRANKIE'S HOUSE

5:22 pm

WHEN I PULL up to her place, I see her standing in the doorway, waiting for me. Her face is pale, her eyes red-rimmed, and it's clear she's been crying. I'm out of the car and up the steps in seconds, not even bothering to shut the door behind me.

"Frankie, what happened?" I ask, my voice low, trying to keep the panic out of it.

She steps aside, letting me in, and then closes the door behind us. "It's my dad… he… he passed away last night."

The words hit me like a punch to the gut, and I immediately pull her into my arms, holding her tight. She trembles against me, her tears soaking into my shirt. I don't say anything right away. What can I say? I let her cry, let her release the pain that's clearly been building up inside her.

When she finally pulls back, I keep my hands on her shoulders, searching her face. "I'm so sorry, Frankie. This is unbelievable."

She shakes her head, wiping at her eyes. "He didn't tell me how sick he was. He didn't want me to worry. And now he's gone."

The helplessness in her voice cuts through me, and I have an overwhelming desire to take her pain away, to make it better somehow, even though I know I can't. "I'm here, okay? Whatever you need, I'm here."

She nods, and for a moment, we just stand there, taking comfort in each other's presence.

Finally, she speaks again, her voice steadier this time. "Thank you for coming. I didn't want to call anyone else. I'm kind of blown away that we both lost a parent to the same disease on the same day."

"I can't even wrap my head around it. All I know right now is you're not alone. I'm here and I'm not going anywhere."

I gently guide her to the couch, sitting beside her, close enough that our knees touch. She leans into me, resting her head on my shoulder, and I wrap an arm around her, holding her close. We don't need to say anything else. Just being here, together, is enough for now.

Frankie shifts slightly, pulling back just enough to look up at me. Her eyes are still wet, but there's something else in them too—something that makes my heart skip a beat. I can't quite place it, but it's there, and it's powerful.

"Thank you for being here," she whispers, her voice barely audible. "I feel better already."

I nod, my throat tight. "I wouldn't want to be anywhere else."

For a moment, we hold each other's gaze, the air between us heavy with unspoken things. Her hand is still resting on my chest, and without thinking, I cover it with mine. Her skin is soft and warm, even with the slight tremble in her fingers.

"I don't know what I'd do in this moment without you," she says, her voice trembling slightly.

Something in me shifts at her words, a deep, primal need to protect her, to be there for her in every way I can. Without really thinking about it, I lean down, brushing a strand of hair away from her face, my fingers lingering on her cheek.

Her eyes flutter closed at my touch, and when she opens them again, there's no mistaking what's there. It's a look I've seen before, but never like this. It's a look that says she needs me, not just for comfort, but for something more.

I lean in slowly, giving her a chance to pull away if she wants to. But she doesn't. Instead, she closes the gap between us, her lips meeting mine in a kiss that's soft and tentative at first, but quickly deepens. It's a kiss that's full of emotion, of need, of everything we've both been holding back.

And in that kiss, I lose myself. I completely surrender to her lips against mine as she melts into me. It's like nothing else matters in this moment, just the two of us, finding solace in each other.

When we finally pull away from each other, both of us are breathing hard, our foreheads resting against each other. There's a moment of silence, where everything hangs in the balance, and then I pull her closer, pressing a kiss to her forehead, her temple, her cheek.

"Frankie…" I start, but she shakes her head, silencing me with another kiss, this one softer, more tender.

"It's okay," she whispers against my lips. "I want this. I want you."

I respond by kissing her again, this time with more intent, more purpose. I let my hands roam, tracing the curves of her body, the warmth of her skin. She responds in kind, her hands sliding up my chest, around my neck, pulling me closer.

And then, as if by unspoken agreement, we both stand, our hands never leaving each other. We move together, towards her bedroom, the air between us charged with anticipation, with need. But it's not just about the physical —it's about everything we've both been through, everything we've shared.

When we reach her bed, I stop, taking a moment to look at her, to really see her. She's beautiful, inside and out, and I can't believe how lucky I am to have her in my life, whatever that means for the future.

I glance down at Frankie, her eyes a vivid, shimmering green in the soft light of her bedroom. There's a vulnerability in her gaze that tugs at something deep within me.

"Are you sure about this?" I ask, my voice barely above a whisper. I need to hear her say it, to affirm that this is what she wants, what we both need.

She nods, her fingers tracing the contours of my face. "I've never been more sure," she replies, her voice steady and sure.

I lean in, capturing her lips in a kiss that's tender and full of promise. Our clothes seem to melt away, each piece discarded with a reverence that speaks to the sacredness of the moment. I take a moment to drink in the sight of her, the soft swell of her breasts, the gentle curve of her hips— she's a masterpiece, and I'm humbled by the trust she's placing in me.

As we lower ourselves onto the bed, our limbs entwine, fitting together as if we were made for each other. My hands explore her body with a gentle touch, mapping out every inch of her skin, every dip and curve. She sighs softly beneath me, her body arching to meet mine.

I enter her slowly, conscious of every sensation, every nuance of her response. The connection between us is electric, a current that hums through our veins, binding us together in this singular moment of vulnerability and trust.

Our movements are slow, deliberate, as if we're moving to the rhythm of our own heartbeats. I watch her face, her expressions guiding me, telling me what she needs. When her eyes meet mine, there's a silent exchange of emotions, a wordless dialogue that speaks volumes.

I gently, softly unbutton her shirt, removing it one arm at a time. She lays there, still, peaceful. I watch her as I rub my hand down her chest, resting on the middle clasp of her bra. I unclip it with one hand, quite proud of my skills.

As I remove her bra, she arches her back ever so slightly, letting me know she is completely in tune with the slow, sensual tenor of the moment.

I shimmy my pants down, never taking my eyes off of her and then position myself over her. She closes her eyes and slowly runs her tongue over her beautiful, full lips.

With my hand, I lightly brush the head of my cock over her wet opening. The sensation of her on the one million sensitive receptors almost makes me come right there, but I hold it back. I want to drive her absolutely fucking crazy before she explodes.

I enter her slowly, watching her back arch and her head fall back. She never opens her eyes, only moans quietly. I've never taken the time to go so slowly and purposefully and realize I have been missing out. The act itself is orgasmic, never mind the intense sensation of her clenched tightly around my shaft as she swallows me whole.

Her muscles narrow around me as her entire body responds to mine. There's no rush, no urgency—just the two of us, lost in each other, lost in a moment that is both timeless and fleeting.

"Hunter," she whispers, her voice laced with emotion as she finally speaks. It's a plea, a benediction, and I respond by increasing the tempo ever so slightly, my body moving in sync with hers.

We climb higher, our breaths mingling, our hearts beating in unison. And when we finally reach the precipice, we leap together, our cries of release echoing through the room.

After the zealous orgasm, we both fall limp. It was more intense than anything I ever remember experiencing before. I am closer to her now than ever.

I lie in Frankie's bed, her warm body curled against mine, our limbs intertwined. The bedside lamp casts a gentle light across her face, highlighting the curve of her cheek, the slope of her nose. I trace my fingers along her arm, marveling at how right this is, how natural.

"You okay?" I whisper, pressing a soft kiss to her forehead.

She nods, her hand resting on my chest. "Yeah. I am okay. I've never felt so safe and I'm so grateful that we've forged this, whatever it is, so that I'm not alone right now."

I feel the same way. It's almost as if we came into each other's life right at the right time, to be there for each other while we each go through some shitty, heavy stuff.

Frankie shifts, propping herself up on one elbow to look at me. Her eyes, usually so bright and full of life, are tinged with sadness, but there's a warmth there too, a depth of emotion that takes my breath away.

"It's strange," she says softly. "I barely knew my father, and yet he was a part of me. It…."

"It still hurts," I finish for her. She nods, and I pull her closer, savoring the steady, light thump of her heartbeat against my chest. "Loss is loss. It doesn't matter how well you knew someone. The potential of what could have been... that's what hurts."

She's quiet for a moment, her fingers tracing patterns on my skin. "Tell me more about your mom," she says finally.

I take a deep breath, surprised by how easy it is to talk about her. "She was... complicated. Pushy, sometimes over-bearing, but she loved fiercely. She wanted the best for me, even if she didn't always know how to show it."

Frankie listens intently, her presence a balm to the raw edges of my grief. As I talk, I realize how much I needed this—not just to be held, but to be truly seen and under-stood. Almost to know how to process grief for someone I wasn't particularly close to but who I loved regardless.

When I finish, Frankie leans in and kisses me softly. "Thank you for sharing that with me," she whispers.

I cup her face in my hands, struck by how much she's come to mean to me. "Thank you for being here," I say. "For being you."

We fall silent then, content to just be together, to find comfort in each other's presence. The world outside seems distant, unimportant. Here, in this moment, it's just us—two people who've found each other in the midst of loss, forging a connection that seems as crucial as air in my lungs.

TWENTY-SEVEN

Frankie

_____

Tuesday, June 11

10:14 am

MY LAPTOP DINGS with a new email notification, pulling me away from the document I've been working on for the last two hours. I glance at the screen and see Theo Bench's name in the sender line, with Hunter copied. My heart skips a beat as I click it open.

Subject: IRB Approval for Compassionate Use

Frankie, Hunter:
The IRB has granted approval to move forward
with the compassionate use of the pacemaker for
Grace Petit. Let's discuss next steps as soon as
possible. This is a significant achievement. Well
done.

Theo

A rush of excitement floods through me, and I barely suppress the urge to let out a cheer. This is huge. I know how much it means to Hunter and what it could mean for Grace. Not to mention, I can't deny the excitement of putting all these years of work and research to practice.

It's one step closer to making all of this worth it.

I immediately reach for my phone, wanting to call Hunter and share the news. I know how excited he is going to be, how deeply he cares about Grace and her outcome. Just as I'm about to dial, I remember he's in surgery right now. He has a full day of back-to-back procedures, which is why he didn't stay over last night. The first night we haven't spent together in two weeks, and I miss him more than I expected I might.

A mix of anticipation and longing comes over me after I set the phone down. I want to tell him right away, but I also know how important it is for him to stay focused during surgery.

I'll have to wait until he's out. But knowing Hunter, as soon as he gets a break, he'll see the email, and he'll know. I guess selfishly I wanted to be the one to tell him.

We can still celebrate together when he is done with work. I light my lavender candle and bask in the comfort and presence of my mom.

I walk back over to the computer and stare at the email from Theo. A whirlwind of emotions sweeps through me. Relief, excitement, and a deep sense of responsibility all vie for dominance. The past two weeks have been an earnest waiting game—one filled with uncertainty and a growing sense of urgency.

Grace has been in the hospital, her condition deteriorating with each passing day. I know this grueling waiting game well.

She has been in and out of the cardiology ward, where the medical staff has been monitoring her around the clock, since she had the heart attack. The doctors have been doing everything they can to manage her symptoms, but it's been clear that time is running out.

Hunter and Jonah have been on edge since we submitted the compassionate use request. Jonah, who's become something of a guardian for Grace, has been visibly anxious. Every time I see him in the hallways, there's a tension in his eyes that I've never seen before. And, according to Hunter, when he isn't working, he is checking on her or sitting with her in her room.

Hunter, on the other hand, has tried to keep his usual stoic demeanor, but I've noticed the subtle signs of strain: the way his jaw tightens when someone mentions Grace, the way he clenches his fists when he thinks no one's looking. This isn't just another patient for him, this is personal.

And somehow, it's become personal for me too. Grace is my mom. This innovative device will save her life.

Every day has felt like a marathon. I've been pouring over the data, making sure everything is airtight, that there's nothing that could cause this to fall apart at the last minute.

Meanwhile, Hunter has been working with Dr. Calloway, doing everything in his power to keep Grace stable. He has said more than once to me that if we didn't get this approval, we might lose her.

It's been a long two weeks. A long, agonizing two weeks.

But now, with this email sitting in front of me, I can finally breathe a little easier. We have the green light. Grace is going to get the pacemaker. This is it!

It's not lost on me that something that brought Hunter and I together is connected in so many ways. And now, someone he cares deeply for will be the first recipient.

So, instead, I close my eyes for a moment, letting the weight of the past two weeks fall away, replaced by a sense of cautious optimism. We're not out of the woods yet—there's still so much to do—but it finally seems like there might be a light at the end of the tunnel.

———

OVENBIRD

12:29 pm

I STEP into the familiar warmth of our favorite lunch spot, the scent of freshly baked bread and roasting vegetables instantly putting me at ease. It's been too long since Carly and I have had a chance to catch up properly, and I've been looking forward to this all week.

The sun is shining, and I spot Carly waving from the patio, already settled in a shaded spot surrounded by raised beds filled with fresh herbs.

"Hey, stranger!" she calls out, a big grin on her face as I approach. "Thought you'd forgotten all about me with all the excitement in your life lately."

I laugh as I slide into the chair across from her. "Never. Just been a little busy, you know?"

She gives me a knowing look, raising an eyebrow. "Yeah, I can imagine. Between the trial, dealing with your dad's stuff, and a certain grumpy cardiothoracic surgeon, I'd say you've had your hands full."

The waitress comes by, and we both order, opting for our usual salads and iced teas. As soon as she leaves, Carly leans in, eyes sparkling with curiosity.

"So, gimme gimme. Whats the word with Grace? Word on the street is the **IRB** approved the compassionate use. Marijka called me on the way over here."

"Yeah, they did," I reply, a wave of relief washing over me just saying the words. "It's a huge win. We've been waiting for weeks, and it was touch and go there for a while. But now that we have the green light, I'm hoping things will move quickly. Hunter's already got the prototype, so I wouldn't be surprised if they go ahead with the procedure soon."

Carly nods, clearly impressed. "That's amazing, Frankie. It's going to be incredible seeing her get better. And speaking of Hunter... how's that going? As I've mentioned, it's really cramping my after-work stops at your place, but I'm trying not to take it personally."

I smirk, shaking my head. "You can still come over, Carly. It's not like you're banned."

"Please," she laughs, rolling her eyes. "That man's stand-offishness is a force to be reckoned with. I love you, but I'm not interested in trying to compete with him for your attention."

I chuckle, thinking about how Hunter can come across. "He's not that bad, really. He's like a squishy teddy bear under all that brute. And pretty damn thoughtful. It's just a mask."

"Uh-huh," Carly says skeptically, but there's a teasing glint in her eyes. "A very convincing mask, I'd say. But seriously, I'm happy for you. You deserve some happiness, even if it comes wrapped up like Serious Smurf in his blue scrubs."

We both laugh, and the conversation naturally shifts to lighter topics until Carly leans back in her chair, a more serious expression crossing her face. "And how's everything going with your dad's stuff?"

I pause, taking a sip of my iced tea. This is the first time I've mentioned it to anyone, and the words are heavy on my tongue. "There's something I haven't told you yet... He left me an inheritance."

Carly's eyes widen, and she almost chokes on her drink. "Wait. What?! How much are we talking here?"

I glance around, lowering my voice even though we're outside. "Twelve and a half million. Each of the three siblings gets that amount once the closing of the dealerships happens. A national, large car dealership chain is buying them all out."

Carly's jaw drops, and she looks like she might fall out of her chair. "Holy shit, Frankie! That's... that's life-changing! My mind is freaking blown right now."

"I know," I say, a mix of excitement and nerves overcome me as I finally say it out loud. "I haven't met my half-brothers yet, but we're in talks about making it happen. It's kind of surreal. I've always wanted siblings, but now that it's real, I don't know, it's a lot to process. I'm still working through all of it."

Carly reaches across the table, squeezing my hand. "I'm so excited for you, Frankie. This is huge. And I know it's a lot, but you're going to handle it like a champ. You always do. Becoming a millionaire in the process will probably help a tiny bit, too."

I laugh, feeling lighter than I have in days. This is why I love Carly. She always has a humorous perspective to point out. We spend the rest of lunch joking around, sharing stories, and just enjoying each other's company, the way best friends do.

———

SHAIN *Park*

6:38 pm

WE REACH the end of our walk, our usual loop around Shain Park, and that familiar contentment and excitement that always comes with being around Hunter is my constant companion these days.

These evening walks after work are more common than not lately, and I look forward to them. It's a way for us to unwind, connect, and to just be with each other without the pressures of our jobs or the chaos of our lives getting in the way. Honestly, it's my favorite part of the day.

Except, maybe, our morning sex before he leaves me.

Hunter glances at me, a small smile tugging at the corner of his lips. "You're quieter than usual tonight. Plotting something?"

I laugh, nudging him playfully with my elbow. "Who, me? Never."

"Uh-huh," he says, clearly not buying it. "I know that look. What are you up to?"

I pause, turning to face him with a grin. "Wait right here. I'll be back in a sec."

He raises an eyebrow, curiosity piqued, but stays put as I jog back to my car. I pop the trunk and pull out the blanket, cooler with the cheese and charcuterie, and a bottle of wine I'd stashed away for a little surprise. As I make my way back, I see the puzzled look on Hunter's face morph into something warmer, softer when he spots what I'm carrying.

"Wow, you've been holding out on me," he says, his voice tinged with amusement. "When did we turn into those people?"

I smirk, spreading the blanket out on the grass in a secluded spot scoped out the other day. It's tucked away under a canopy of trees, completely hidden from the rest of the park. The late evening light filters through the branches, casting everything in a warm, golden hue. The air is still, the usual hum of the city muted by the thick foliage surrounding us.

"We didn't," I reply, setting the cheese board down in the center of the blanket. "But I figured it was time we did something different. Plus, this spot just seemed perfect for it."

Hunter sits down beside me, leaning back on his hands as he takes in the view. "You're not wrong. This is nice."

"Nice?" I tease, pouring us each a glass of wine. "I'll have you know I put a lot of thought into this. 'Nice' doesn't cut it."

He chuckles, accepting the glass I hand him. "Fine, it's more than nice. It's perfect."

"Damn right it is," I quip, but there's a warmth in my chest that has nothing to do with the wine.

Hunter lays on his stomach and picks at the cheese and salami. He is so handsome, his blue eyes twinkling in the low light. It's all I can do not to jump on him right here and now.

We settle into a comfortable rhythm, chatting and joking as we sip our wine. There's no rush, no urgency, just the two of us enjoying each other's company in this little slice of serenity we've found together. It's natural, easy, like we've been doing this forever.

As the sun dips lower in the sky, casting long shadows over the park, Hunter turns to me, a playful glint in his eyes. "So, what's next on your agenda, Ms. Renna? Do we break out the board games, or is this when you tell me we're going stargazing?"

I roll my eyes, laughing. "Oh, please. Like you'd ever agree to play a board game."

"True," he concedes, taking another sip of wine. "But stargazing, I could be convinced."

"Who says I want to convince you?" I counter, leaning in a little closer. "Maybe I've got something else in mind."

He raises an eyebrow, intrigued. "Like what?"

Instead of answering, I close the small gap between us, pressing my lips to his in a kiss that's soft at first, then deepens as he responds, his hand coming up to cradle the back of my head. The world around us fades away, leaving just the two of us in this perfect, hidden spot in the park.

When we finally break apart, we're both a little breathless, and I can't help but smile. "Like that," I whisper.

Hunter looks at me, a mix of affection and desire in his eyes. "I could get used to this."

"Me too," I reply, leaning back against the blanket. "But I'll keep you on your toes. No promises for the next surprise."

He laughs, the sound warm and genuine, and it fills me with a happiness I didn't expect to find tonight. We fall into a comfortable silence, the sounds of the park around us—a distant dog barking, the rustle of leaves in the breeze— providing the perfect soundtrack to our little escape.

TWENTY-EIGHT

Hunter
___

8:01 pm

FRANKIE'S FINGERS tug at the hem of my shirt, pulling it like a leash to bring me closer. Each touch sends bolts of electricity through me. In return, I slip my hands under the fabric of her top, ensuring it remains in place in case of a sudden need to leave. I cup her full breasts, the warmth and roundness almost undoing me.

The thrill of our surroundings, the risk of being caught, is intoxicating, adding an edge to our desire that's as sharp as it is sweet.

The softness beneath me contrasts with the hardness pressing against my jeans. I can't help but grind against her as a low growl escapes my throat.

I unzip my pants and free my engorged cock, which springs out, looking for work. We're laughing and gasping, the sound mingling with the rustling of leaves and the distant call of a night bird.

Then I pull aside her shorts to find she isn't wearing any panties. She must have planned ahead. I rub my finger over her slick opening. Swiftly and with ease, I place my dick just inside of the opening I created in her shorts and thrust it into her.

The heat of our bodies creates a steam that seems to rise into the night air. It is quick and urgent, both of us obviously turned on by the danger of it all. I'm like a teenager, sneaking it in before someone might catch us.

It's invigorating.

We both come, quietly, but wantonly. Her lace bra presses into my skin. When I pull myself out I'm not done yet. I trace a path down her stomach with my tongue, my fingers teasing the edge of her shorts before pulling them down just enough to lick the top of her opening.

She's panting now, her fingers threading through my hair as I explore her with my mouth, her taste as addictive as the way she quietly moans my name, the sound echoing in the quiet of the park. Her legs wrap around me, pulling me closer, urging me on until she's shuddering beneath me, her cries of pleasure swallowed by our kisses.

Once she shudders, I know I've done my job. I'm growing again, but I don't want to be greedy. We've had our naughty sex without getting caught, foreplay for later. I scoot up to join her, face-to-face.

For a moment, we lay there, our bodies connected, the world around us nothing but a distant memory. The only thing that exists is the two of us, the beating of our hearts slowly returning to normal, the gentle caress of the night breeze cooling our heated skin.

I roll off her and slide one arm under her head, holding her close. We're quiet now, lost in our own thoughts, the adrenaline of our lovemaking still coursing through my veins.

In the distance, the city continues on, oblivious to the intimacy we've shared in its shadow. Here, in this hidden corner of the park, we found another way to make this park a part of us.

———

THURSDAY, *June 13*

UAB Hospital

10:14 *am*

AS I SIT down at the conference table with Dr. Tim Calloway, Jonah Bellinger, and the PA who received training on the new pacemaker, I feel the significance of what we are about to do settling over me.

This isn't just another patient, this is Grace Petit, someone we all care personally about. This is the first time we'll be using the new pacemaker, even before we've conducted the trial. Stressful doesn't even begin to cover it. Thankfully, there's also an undercurrent of excitement humming in the room. We're on the brink of something big, something that will change lives.

Calloway, ever the calm professional, opens the meeting. "I've reviewed Grace's latest scans and blood work. Her condition has stabilized somewhat, but we're still seeing those intermittent arrhythmias. I'm concerned about her ability to tolerate another episode, which is why I'm glad we're moving forward with this."

Jonah, sitting across from me, nods, his expression a mix of determination and worry. "We all know Grace. She's tough, but she's been through the wringer. I want to make sure we're doing everything possible to give her the best shot at a good outcome here."

"Agreed," I say, leaning forward. "The new pacemaker has shown promising results in simulations and preliminary trials, but this is uncharted territory. We need to have a solid plan in place, not just for the surgery, but for the post-op care and monitoring."

The PA, a young guy who's been training with us for weeks, speaks up. "I've reviewed the protocols we established for the trial, and I think we can adapt them for Grace's situation. The main concern will be how her body reacts to the device initially. We'll need to monitor her closely for the first forty-eight hours, especially for any signs of rejection or complications."

Calloway nods, tapping his pen on the table thoughtfully. "We'll need to ensure round-the-clock monitoring, with someone on standby to address any issues immediately. Jonah, I assume you want to stay updated on everything?"

"Absolutely," Jonah replies. "Grace may not be my biological mother, but she's been like one to me. I want to know every step of the way how she's doing."

I glance at the clock on the wall, noting the time. We've been discussing the logistics for a while now, and it's clear we're all on the same page. "I think we're ready to schedule the surgery for tomorrow. Calloway, you'll handle the pre-op checks?"

"Of course," he says. "I'll start her on the necessary medications tonight to prep her for the procedure."

"Good," I reply, relieved that he is on top of it. "I'll be in early to go over everything one last time and scrub in. Let's make sure we're all set before we go in tomorrow. This has to be perfect."

The disquiet in the room is thick, but there's also a shared sense of purpose. We're doing this for Grace, for the chance to give her a better quality of life, and maybe even save it. It's a lot of pressure, but it's what we do, and I trust this team to handle it.

As the meeting wraps up, I stand, shaking hands with Calloway, Jonah, and the PA. "Thanks, everyone. Let's get some rest tonight and come back early tomorrow ready to make history."

Jonah claps me on the back as we head out of the room. "I'm glad we're doing this, Hunter. Grace is lucky to have you on her side. I only feel bad she will have to see that ugly mug of yours when she wakes up."

"The only uglier mug she has to put up with is yours," I give it right back to him, knowing humor is his way to get through this. Grace has always been a fighter, and tomorrow, we're giving her the best shot we can. But until then, all we can do is prepare and hope for the best.

As I leave the hospital, I can't help but think about Frankie. I'll need to update her on the plan and let her know that we're moving forward. Tomorrow is going to be one hell of a day, and I want her to be in the loop every step of the way.

———

FRIDAY, *June 14*

10:24 am

THE ROOM BUZZES with the usual symphony of beeps, each one tracking Grace's vitals with precision. The stakes are higher today. This isn't just any surgery. This is the first time we're implanting Frankie's pacemaker into a human being. The thought sharpens my focus even more, knowing that years of her work and passion have culminated in this moment. And I'm the one bringing it to life.

Frankie stands across from me, suited up and scrubbed in, her eyes locked on the monitors and then on Grace, focused and intense. It's not often you see a researcher in the OR, but there was no way I was doing this without her. This is as much her victory as it is mine—hell, probably more so.

"We're about to place the device," I say, glancing up at Frankie. Her eyes meet mine, and there's a flicker of something between us, an unspoken understanding of how monumental this moment is. She gives me a small nod, her expression a mix of determination and nervous energy.

"Let's make history," she says, her voice steady but laced with emotion.

I turn my attention back to Grace, every movement calculated, every decision precise. "Pacing leads are going in now," I announce to the room. "Prepare for a post-op echo to confirm placement and pacing thresholds."

The PA and nurses move in sync, but my focus is on the device, on making sure it's placed perfectly. Frankie's work, her years of research, all come down to this. I carefully position the pacemaker, checking the leads one final time.

"Leads are secure," I confirm, my voice steady, but my heart is pounding. "Frankie, want to take a look?"

She steps forward, peering over my shoulder as I finish the placement. Her breath catches—this is her baby, her design, now inside a human heart, doing exactly what it was built to do.

"Everything looks good," she says, her voice barely a whisper. But I can hear the pride, the relief, and the weight of the moment all wrapped up in those few words.

"Let's get that post-op echo," I say, more to the team than to her. "I want to confirm lead placement and pacing thresholds before we move her to recovery."

As we close up, I glance at Frankie again. There's something between us that's different now, a deeper connection forged in the heat of this moment. It's like we're the only two people in the room, even though the OR is bustling around us. We've shared something profound, something that goes beyond just work.

In the post-op room, Grace is still under anesthesia, her face relaxed, almost peaceful. I review the immediate post-op orders with the PA and nurses, detailing the importance of frequent vitals checks, ensuring her pain management is optimal, and keeping her on continuous cardiac monitoring for at least the next forty-eight hours.

Frankie stands beside me, her hand resting lightly on Grace's bed. "She's stable," I say, glancing at Frankie. "Pacing is stable, and her rhythm is solid. We'll keep her on telemetry and monitor for any signs of lead dislodgment or pocket hematoma."

Frankie nods, but her eyes are still on Grace. "I can't believe we did it," she murmurs. "I've been dreaming about this becoming a reality for so long, and now... it's real."

I place a hand on her shoulder, a gesture that is both natural and scary. "You did it," I correct her. "My humble job was to put it in, but you made this happen."

She looks up at me, her eyes shining with a mix of tears and pride. "Thank you, Hunter. I couldn't have asked for a better surgeon to do this."

"There was no way I was letting anyone else touch this," I reply, my voice softer than usual.

We stand there for a moment, letting the gravity of what we've accomplished sink in. But then reality pulls me back.

When Jonah and Tim Calloway walk in together, I turn to them. They know I'm leaving today to deal with some things with my mom's stuff in California. I'm torn about it, but it was planned before we got approval and I didn't want to put off surgery until after I returned.

"You know I'll be available any time, day or night, if anything comes up with Grace, while I'm gone."

"We've got this, man," Jonah says. "You go on to Cali and put your legs up, relax. We'll take care of Grace."

"Ha. If only."

"No, seriously, man, you know I'm just messing with you. You did the hard part, now we nurse her back to health. She's in good hands. You've assembled a good team. I really appreciate all you've done."

Frankie looks at me, a flash of concern crossing her face. She wanted to come with me but couldn't make it work with her schedule. I was disappointed, but I didn't make a deal of it because I know she would have made it happen if she could have.

The two men walk out, leaving the two of us alone again.

"Are you going to be okay by yourself?"

"I will be. I'll miss you, but I'll be busy meeting with the attorney, picking up ashes and signing the listing agreement. It won't be fun."

Before we walk out, I turn back to Frankie one last time. "Make sure Grace behaves herself, okay?"

She smiles, a real one this time, the kind that reaches her eyes. "I will. Someone has to take the hard-ass mantle with you gone."

As I walk through the corridors of the hospital, my steps are lighter, like a part of the burden I've been carrying has lifted. We did something incredible today, something that will give people a better shot at health and longevity. But as much as I want to focus on that, my mind is already racing ahead to California, to the past I need to confront.

CALDWELL *& Spencer Law Firm*

4:26 pm PST

I SIT across from the attorney, a middle-aged man with graying hair and an impeccable suit. The office smells faintly of leather and old books, a comforting scent that's at odds with the emotional weight I'm carrying.

The paperwork before me is straightforward. Everything my mother left behind was cleanly organized into a trust. She was meticulous, as always. She handled every detail, leaving no loose ends.

"Your mother made this as seamless as possible, Dr. Parrish," the attorney says, sliding the final document across the table. "All that's left is for you to sign here, authorizing the listing of the house and the estate sale of its contents. We'll handle everything from the listing to the final sale."

I nod, picking up the pen. "She was thorough. No surprises there."

He offers a small smile. "It's rare to see an estate this well organized. She must have been quite a woman."

"Yeah," I say, my voice catching slightly. "You could say that."

I sign the papers, each stroke of the pen another step in saying goodbye. The attorney watches quietly, giving me space to process. When I'm done, he gathers the documents and hands me a card.

"If you need anything else, feel free to reach out. I'll coordinate with the estate company to ensure everything goes smoothly. You mentioned wanting to go to the house yourself?"

"That's right," I reply, slipping the card into my pocket. "I'll go today. Just to pick up a few things, ship them back to Alabama. Whatever's left can be sold through the estate sale."

"Understood. Take your time, Dr. Parrish. There's no rush."

I thank him and stand to leave, the weight of finality pressing down on me. As I walk out of the office, the reality of what's coming next begins to settle in. Going back to her house, the place where she lived and breathed, where every corner holds a piece of her, I'm not sure how I'll handle it. But I have to go nonetheless.

——

1034 BENEDICT CANYON *Drive*

Beverly Hills

5:12 *pm*

THE HOUSE IS QUIET, eerily so, as I unlock the door and step inside. It smells like her: a mix of the perfume she always wore and the faint scent of old wood and polished floors. I close the door behind me, the sound echoing through the empty house. Everything is exactly as she left it, down to the neatly folded throw on the couch and the stack of unopened mail on the entry table.

I wander through the rooms, picking up items here and there, small things that hold meaning—a framed photo of us when I was a kid, a few of her favorite books, the scarf she always wore in the winter. I pack them carefully into a box, each item a thread in the tapestry of her life.

It's when I enter her bedroom that I find it. A letter sitting on the side table with my name written in her precise, familiar handwriting. My heart skips a beat as I pick it up, my fingers trembling slightly as I unfold the paper.

My Dearest Hunter,

If you're reading this, then I'm no longer with you, but I need you to know that I've always been with you, even when it didn't seem that way. I know I wasn't the easiest person to live with or love. I pushed you hard, sometimes too hard, and I see that now. But I always wanted the best for you. I wanted you to be the man I knew you could be—the man you are now.

You were an exemplary child. You were more than I deserved, and I see that now, too. I know I made mistakes. I know I was harsh, that I asked too much of you, and for that, I am truly sorry.

But, Hunter, I need you to understand that everything I did was out of love. Twisted and wrong as it may have been, it was love. I wanted to see you soar, to reach heights I never could. And you did. You've become a man I am so incredibly proud of, even if I didn't say it enough. But please know that in my heart, I was bursting with pride every time I thought of you.

I hope you can forgive me for the pressure, for the distance I created between us. I hope you can find peace knowing that, in the end, I loved you with everything I had, even if I didn't know how to express it outwardly.

I don't know how much time I have left, but if there's one thing I want you to carry with you, it's this: You were always enough, Hunter. More than enough. And I was the lucky one to have you as my son.

Take care of yourself. And please, be happy.

With all my love,

Mom

TEARS BLUR my vision as I fold the letter back up, my chest tightening with the words I so desperately wanted from her my whole life. She wasn't a warm woman, and this letter isn't a warm embrace, but it's huge coming from her. It's closure. It's everything to me.

There's that lingering thought, the one I haven't been able to shake since that last phone call. The way she said goodbye on the phone, the way everything in the house is perfectly in place, this letter left so clearly here—it is almost too neat, too planned.

The ME declared her death natural, but there's a part of me that wonders if she had a hand in how she went. Did she choose to go on her own terms, in a way that she could control, just like everything else in her life?

I don't have any proof, and I'll never know for sure. But

standing here in her bedroom, surrounded by her things, I feel closer to her than I ever did when she was alive.

For the first time I feel a sense of peace and forgiveness. The burden I've carried for years, the weight of her expectation, lifts, leaving behind a strange, comforting emptiness.

I pack the letter away with the other things I've decided to keep, and a strange sense of gratitude comes over me. She's given me a gift, this final act of love, this release from the past. And as I leave the house, locking the door behind me for the last time, I know I can finally let go.

I'm not just saying goodbye to the house or to her things. I'm saying goodbye to the pain, to the pressure, to the unresolved tension that's haunted me for years. And as I drive away, the California sun setting behind me, I realize that by letting go of all that, I now have the space to let someone in.

Epilogue

June 14, 2025

Hunter's Condo

5:23 pm

I SNEAK into the nursery to check on our daughter, Renna Elizabeth Parrish. Her tiny hands curl into fists.

The nursery is bathed in the warm glow of the late afternoon sun, casting a peaceful light across the room. I take a moment to watch her, marveling at the way her little chest rises and falls with each breath.

Carefully and quietly, I close the door softly behind me and head downstairs. Today is a special day. It's been exactly one year since Grace had her pacemaker surgery, and we're celebrating. We are calling it her re-birthday.

Hunter insisted on having a small gathering at our home, just close friends and family, to mark the occasion. It's a mix of celebration and gratitude, a chance to reflect on how far we've all come.

As I walk into the living room, I see Hunter standing by the kitchen counter, pouring drinks for our guests. He looks up as I approach, a smile spreading across his face. "How's our little one?" he asks, handing me a glass of sparkling grape juice.

"Sleeping like an angel," I reply, taking the glass from him. "She's completely out."

Hunter puts his hand on my waist and pulls me to him, leaning in to kiss my forehead. "She takes after you, then. You could sleep through a hurricane."

"Hey, I've been getting up with her every night, thank you very much," I tease, giving him a playful nudge.

His grin widens. "I know, and I appreciate it more than you know. You keep our ship afloat."

I glance around the room, taking in the sight of our friends mingling and chatting. Carly is over by the window, talking animatedly with Jonah, while Grace sits on the couch, her face glowing with health and happiness. Seeing her like this, it's hard to believe she was once so sick. The transformation is nothing short of a miracle.

I turn back to Hunter, my voice softening. "It's amazing, isn't it? To think where we were a year ago... and now look at us."

Hunter nods, his expression turning serious. "It's been a hell of a journey, hasn't it? But I wouldn't trade it for anything."

I slip my hand into his, squeezing it gently. "Me neither."

We stand there for a moment, just taking it all in. The sound of laughter and conversation fills the air, a comforting backdrop to our thoughts. I harbor a deep sense of gratitude—for Hunter, for Renna, for the life we're building together.

My eyes move to Janice, sitting with my two half-brothers, William Jr. and David. It's hard to believe that they are now considered family, but as time has gone by, our relationship has blossomed into something far more profound than I could have ever imagined.

Janice has been a loving and eager grandmother to Renna, and my brothers have embraced their roles as uncles with enthusiasm. It's been a healing process for all of us, learning to bridge the gaps left by years of distance and misunderstanding. I never imagined I'd have this kind of relationship with my father's other family, but now I can't imagine my life without them.

Hunter follows my gaze and nods. "Yeah, it does. And to think, this is just the beginning. The trial is going better than we could have hoped."

The trial has two hundred seventy-five patients enrolled, and four hundred already approved to start Phase Two. "We're changing lives, Frankie. Your work, it's incredible. You're incredible."

A swell of pride fills my chest. "Our work, Hunter. None of this would have been possible without you. Don't forget that."

He smiles, a soft, genuine smile that I've come to cherish. "We make a pretty good team, don't we?"

"The best," I agree, leaning into him.

I put my head on his shoulder, soaking in the joy and warmth of the day. Then, as if on cue, our daughter stirs on the baby monitor, letting out a soft whimper.

"I'll get her," I say, excitedly, handing my glass back to Hunter. I've been waiting to bring her out for the party to show her off.

He takes it with a nod, his eyes following me as I head back upstairs. "Bring her down when she's ready," he calls after me. "Everyone wants to see her."

I smile to myself as I reach the nursery, finding our little girl awake and looking up at me with wide, curious eyes. "Hey, sweetheart," I whisper, lifting her into my arms. "Did you have a good nap? Let's go see everyone, okay?"

As I carry her into the crowd, I hear the murmur of voices growing louder. The love and support that fills our home right now is overwhelming in the best way. I join Hunter in the living room, and as I hand our daughter to him, I feel a deep sense of contentment. This is my family. These are my people.

Hunter cradles our daughter in his arms, gently swaying with her as he talks to Grace. The sight of them together fills my heart with warmth. This is what life is about— these moments of connection, of love, of shared triumphs and even shared losses.

I look around at our friends and family, the people who have been there with us through thick and thin, and I know that we've built something beautiful here. It hasn't been easy, and there's still so much to do, but together, we can handle anything.

Hunter glances over at me, his eyes full of love and admiration. "You okay?" he asks softly.

I nod, as happy tears fill the bottom rim of my eyes. "I'm perfect," I whisper back. "Absolutely perfect."

And in this moment, with my daughter in Hunter's arms, surrounded by the people I love, I know that I truly am.

Afterword

If you loved this book, learn more about Dr. Shep Duncan by checking out the first book in the ***Doctor Feel Good*** series, Doctor Second Chance.

Who knew a trip to the ER in a strange city would bring me face-to-face to the man who shattered my world a decade ago?

A freak accident lands me in an unfamiliar hospital. The last person I expect to see is Shep, my ex from another lifetime.

The moment our eyes lock, the world stops turning. The same burning connection between us is still there, only now I hate him with every fiber of my being.

He chose med school in another city over me, breaking promises and my heart. Now, here in the flesh, there is an intensity in him that still makes me wet.

Stuck in his city for rehab, I can't escape him or my

feelings. Each touch and lingering glance erodes my defenses, devouring my resolve.

As I recover, Shep's unwavering support forces me to reconsider everything. Can I leave the past behind and make it work, or is there too much baggage and distance to undo the past?

———

Download Doctor Second Chance here.

Here is a peak at the first chapter:

Saturday, July 6, 2024

113 Main Street, Birmingham

3:12 pm

"Just another tiny little pull on this ribbon and... engagement party perfection. I believe that's it! What do you think, Sophie?"

I lean back on the ladder and keep my knees on the rung for stability. Surveying the etched crystal vases, with their elegant looped ribbons, on each end of the outdoor mantle, I look at everything with a satisfied smile. I finally feel like we nailed it. Isabella will love it!

Dozens of freshly cut purple, baby blue, and white hydrangeas, my and Isabella's favorite flowers, fill each vase. Greenery trails along the length of the stone ledge, spilling over and literally bringing a tear to my eye.

I can't wait to see her face when she arrives and sees everything pulled together for her engagement party. We've been planning for about six months, and our group Pinterest board for the event now has over two thousand images. As soon as we all got the text, within days of Isabella's engagement, we sprang into planning mode.

"What do you think?" I yell across the yard at Sophie, where she's unwinding a tangle of Edison bulb lights to string across it.

"I told you it looked great thirty minutes ago, Elle! You've been fussing over those vases for too long now. Leave them be and come help me hang these up."

I toss the stem of a broken flower at her. "You know I'm a perfectionist. I do want this night to be absolutely flawless for Izzy. I need to stop fiddling with it, though. You're right."

As soon as the last word leaves my mouth, I lose my footing, and the uneven ground causes the ladder to shift.

In an instant, as if in slow motion, the ladder and I both fall straight toward the herringbone brick floor below.

Reflexively, I grab onto the vase closest to me, grasping for anything to steady me. I meant for it to be on the mantel's edge, but a split second goes by a lot quicker than I imagined it might. The vase is the only thing it grasped.

The thud of hitting the ground reverberates through my body, and then the aluminum ladder, as it pins my arm, makes a metallic clang on the brick. As I struggle to breathe, I'm trying to comprehend everything. It dawns on me that the fall must have taken the breath out of me.

In an attempt to free myself, I try to move and push the ladder away, but my arms feel like jelly, and my vision blurs and darkens.

"Oh my god, Elle!" Sophie's shriek cuts through the ringing in my ears, and dark spots dance before my eyes as I struggle to keep my grip on consciousness. I can't pass out. Not here, not now—

"The party is in four hours." I struggle to get out as several people rush to me and unidentifiable figures stand over me. Someone picks up the ladder, and I struggle to sit up.

"There's still so much that needs to be done..." I need to get up and finish setting up for her engagement party tonight before...before...

Little pastel pompoms are all around me, swimming in the red sea of the blood flowing from my hand. I feel nauseated at the sight. Someone bends down close to my face and says something I can't make out. I feel like I am dreaming. Figures and voices seem to float and echo all around me. Nothing feels right.

Streams of blood are gushing between my trembling fingers as I try to move them, unable to close my hand. I'm too tired.

Bile surges in the back of my throat as the coppery scent of blood slams my senses. The pain crests over me in a suffocating wave. All I want to do is go to sleep, to rest for a bit, then we can finish.

I try to speak, but my lips are numb, and my tongue is a lifeless lump of clay. The tang fills my mouth as my eyes don't seem to work and my vision and dims once more.

Faintly, I hear the sirens wail in the distance, growing steadily louder.

And then everything goes black again.

———

UAB Hospital

1802 6th Ave S, Birmingham

3:59 pm

I slowly blink my eyes open. The harsh fluorescent lights of the hospital room cause me to squint. A dull throbbing pounds in my wrist and hand, emanating all the way up my arm and taking up residence in my shoulder and neck. Everything aches.

What happened? The last thing I remember is decorating for the party at Isabella's house and putting up the final touches. Shit! The party!

I adjust myself in the bed, trying to find a comfortable position.

"Elle? Oh, thank god, you're awake!"

I turn to see Sophie sitting beside the bed, her face drawn with concern. Her eyes are red-rimmed like she's been crying. "Are you okay? Soph...what's going on?" My voice comes out in a raspy croak. "What happened?"

She takes a shuddering breath. "You fell off the ladder at Izzy's house. Cut your hand open badly. You were bleeding everywhere and passed out... You scared all of us to death!"

The memories come flooding back—the fall, the sharp pain, the blood, the feeling of the ground rushing up at me. I glance down at my left hand, now bandaged. It feels heavy, like I can't muster the strength to lift it up off the bed.

"Oh, my God." I am fighting tears as the reality of what is happening hits me. "Where are we?"

"At the UAB emergency room. We decided we needed to call an ambulance since we couldn't get you to stay conscious for more than a few seconds at a time. I was scared for anyone to move you. I rode with you in the ambulance here," Sophie continues.

"I rode in an ambulance?"

"Yes. The paramedics literally just rolled you into this room, not even a minute ago. We are still waiting for a doctor, nurse, or someone to come in and tell us what will happen next."

"This can't be happening right now. Does Izzy know?"

"I texted her on the ride here but haven't heard back. If she isn't already, she should be getting done with her massage any minute."

We sent Isabella off to get a massage while we got everything set up. The point was for her to come home to a magical night to celebrate with our closest friends.

The party is in her gorgeous backyard, which is ideal for outdoor entertaining. It already has an enormous stone fireplace on an expansive brick deck. The centerpiece is a live oak with draping arms and Spanish moss all around.

"Oh, my God. I'm so sorry this happened. I can't even recall what caused me to fall. I'm losing my shit that you called an ambulance! And I missed the whole thing! I've always wanted to ride in an ambulance, watching cars pull over as I zoom by."

"We wouldn't have if you didn't keep passing out. I think we all want to ensure that falling on your head isn't serious. Thank you, God," she says dramatically, looking up at the hospital ceiling. "You landed perfectly on the seat cushion that just happened to be on the ground under the ladder. Someone up there was looking out for you. It was so scary, Elle. I'm so grateful you're talking now! God, I've never been so frightened in my life."

"My mom always said I had a hard head."

Sophie squeezes my arm. I can see the worry on her face and my blood all over her shirt. I hope I didn't make a mess at Isabella's house. I have so much anxiety right now, and none of it has anything to do with my fall.

I look down at my right arm, which is completely wrapped, resembling the end of a giant Q-Tip with the tips of my fingers barely poking out. They are covered with dried blood. My jeans are now a maroon color.

An IV is in my left arm, and some contraption is clipped to the pointer finger of my right, uninjured hand. I feel like I'm tied down to this bed.

All I can think about right now is Isabella's engagement party tonight. A sense of dread washes over me, and an extreme need to get out of here overwhelms me.

"Now that I am awake and apparently fine, I think we should go. I don't need to be here in the emergency room."

"Um, that would be a big, fat no. You fell off of an eight-foot ladder. And you passed out multiple times. You'll sit right here until we hear what the doctor says."

"What is going to happen to the party? I can't let this ruin her night. Is there a lot of blood at the house? Did it get all over everything? Will the yard be ready for the party?"

"Elle, don't worry about all that right now. But to answer your question, everything will be fine. I promise you. Everyone else stayed there to finish up and, yes, there was a lot of blood, but Charity thought quickly and hosed off the brick. Vic put his ROTC experience to good use and made a tourniquet for your hand and wrist, so the blood was limited to just that space on the patio. Everything will go according to plan. We just all want you to be okay so you can enjoy all of your hard work!"

The door opens, and a nurse in light blue scrubs walks in, eyes glued to her clipboard. "Eloise Klass? Good to see you are awake. How are you feeling?"

She is reading something on the clipboard in her hands as she interrogates me. Somehow, it feels like she isn't really interested in how I am feeling, at least on an emotional level.

I grimace. "Like I fell off the top of the Empire State Building."

She gives me a sympathetic look. "Well, the good news is, your vitals are stable. The bad news is that the laceration on your wrist is pretty severe. You're going to need stitches for sure, but we still need to determine if you'll need surgery and if there's any tendon or nerve damage."

Surgery? On my wrist? Panic squeezes my chest. "But..." I am unable to utter any other words of protest as my throat constricts. I don't live here. I have a party tonight. My plan is to go back home to Florida on Sunday and then catch a flight to LA on Monday.

There is no time for surgery. Hell, I don't even have much time to get this stitched up and out of here in time to shower and be ready for the party to start at seven-thirty. Tears are welling up, and I want to tell her I have to go, but I know it will do no good.

My mind races with all the reasons I can't be here doing this right now, except for the fact that she told me the injury is severe. How can a silly cut on my wrist be that bad?

"If I just need stitches, then can I leave here soon? If there is no other damage, I mean, is this a pretty quick fix?"

Please, God, let that be all. I can't stay here in this hospital.

"We'll know more after you get an MRI to assess the extent of the injury," the nurse says calmly.

"MRI?"

"Yes, we want to get images of your hand and your head, since you passed out."

Lord have mercy. Of course, this is happening to me when I'm here to celebrate and have a fun weekend with my friends.

"The sooner we get you stitched up, the better, so we have you expedited for imaging."

I feel lightheaded all over again. This can't be happening —not now. I've been planning this party for months.

Isabella is my best friend, and I can't be the reason her engagement party was ruined.

"Don't worry, Elle," Sophie says as if she can read my mind. She gives my unencumbered hand a squeeze. "Everything is going to be okay, and I will stay right here with you."

I force a smile that I don't feel at all. If only that would make it all better.

———

5:51 pm

I've been in this damn room for almost two hours. If this is the expedited service for imaging, I'd hate to know how long you have to wait for the standard one. The nurse said that the doctor will review them once we finish. It doesn't mean a whole hell of a lot if it takes hours to get the MRI in the first place.

I'm trying to keep calm. Sophie hasn't left my side, but it's becoming increasingly hard to keep my emotions in check. I've gone from desperation over the situation to pure rage at my lack of control over my own body and decisions.

"Soph, you should go. You've got about an hour to get showered and ready for the party."

She is reading the hospital brochure on recognizing the signs of Alzheimer's like it's a *New York Times* Best Seller. "Hmm?"

"I want you to go get ready for the party. There is no reason we both have to miss it. I'll be fine."

"I'll leave soon. I really want to be here when the doctor comes in. There is still some time left. It takes me around thirty minutes to get ready, you know."

I'm so frustrated I could cry. I wish she would leave. Then at least I'll feel like I have some control. Her being here and running behind for the party on my account makes me feel worse than I already do.

"Allow me to take care of you for once, considering you're constantly worrying about everyone else.

"You're amazing. Thank you. But seriously, knowing that you are there and not here trapped like I am will, strangely, give me comfort. Like I'll have some semblance of sovereignty. And I'll live vicariously through you and everyone else at the party."

"Just give it a little more time. Hopefully, someone will be here any minute to tell us what is happening. Okay?"

"Based on their attentiveness so far, I'm not holding my breath…"

"I'm so glad we didn't have to deal with the wrath of Isabella's highfalutin in-laws this time." Sophie changes the subject, realizing I need a diversion. She might be as stubborn as I am, and her redirection is helpful. "That really would have sent you over the edge."

"Oh, don't worry. They will be there in all of their snobby glory tonight. They wouldn't miss an Alabama garden party. But you're right. Thank the good Lord above that Izzy didn't ask them to come help us set up!"

Sophie is alluding to the bachelorette weekend we hosted for Isabella in Miami. For some reason, Isabella invited her soon-to-be sister-in-law and mother-in-law to join us. They were a royal pain in my ass the entire weekend and demanded everything to be over the top.

Since I'm the maid of honor, they treated me like their personal concierge, responsible for turning all their ridiculous ideas about how things should be into reality.

"Speaking of insufferable snobs, how was that double date last night?"

Memories of Wentworth Billings III's arrogant smirk and appraising gaze resurface as I readjust in my hospital bed. I'm convinced I'm getting bed sores in real-time. "I've never felt so annoyed by a hot man buying me a nice dinner and bottle of wine in my life. I couldn't get out of there fast enough."

"That bad, huh?"

"Of course, I enjoyed Izzy, and it was good to catch up with Evan, but why they ever thought to set me up with that man is beyond me. He's exactly the kind of superficial, self-important jackass I've spent years avoiding. I've never met anyone who talks about himself so much."

Sophie snickers. "What did he say? It can't have been that bad, Elle. Come on."

"Let's see... He talked about how he made four hundred thousand dollars that day on stock futures for a client, drives a super exclusive BMW convertible, one of only two hundred and fifty ever made, and has the biggest house in his neighborhood."

"Oh, wow. He got all of that in before the desert?"

"Yep, oh, and he managed to scrunch his nose at the fact

that I scrape crustaceans off the bottom of sedentary ocean objects to study."

"Is that bad? I mean, hanging out at the beach and studying cool Marine life seems pretty amazing to me."

"That's exactly my point!" I throw up my one good hand. "When I told him I have a PhD and work at a biotech firm studying marine life, he scoffed and asked if I work in a non-profit with a condescending look. As if, somehow, that is beneath him."

"What a pretentious prick." Sophie puts the Alzheimer's brochure on the small makeshift tray table. It's beside the large water cup the nurse brought me a lifetime ago, which is now sweating and has a ring of water around it.

"God, you'd think with a face and body like that, he could at least have a decent personality. Why does it always have to be one or the other?"

I hesitate, secretly supposing he wasn't hard on the eyes beneath his off-putting arrogance. But his condescending assumptions instantly soured any physical attraction for me.

"So, how long did you subject yourself to Mr. Moneybags after that lovely first impression?" She quirks an eyebrow. "Based on your tone and the look on your face, I'm guessing it didn't get any better.

"It was the longest dinner in the history of humankind. Unfortunately, I couldn't escape him even after we got back to Isabella's. It's like he thought I would invite him to my room and hook up."

"Eww."

"Finally, around midnight, I told everyone I was turning in. He looked stunned, and I scurried out of the den as fast as possible. Maybe that charm offensive works on some, but not me."

"Geez, I'm so sorry. Are you supposed to see him tonight?" She asks, implying that the hospital will release me tonight. With each passing minute, I am less and less confident that will happen.

"Well, I guess that is one good thing to come out of this. I don't have to be Wentworth, III's date. That is if I am stuck here instead of drinking our signature cocktail and listening to that amazing Tina Turner cover band."

"Well, praise the Lord for that," Sophie chuckles. "That you might not have to see Wentworth, III again."

"A fate worse than death," I deadpan, shifting again in the bed. My lower back is starting to hurt more than my throbbing hand and the growing crick in my neck.

I've worked hard recently to bury thoughts of The Love I Always Dreamed Of. The One. It is starting to look more and more like that isn't in the cards for me. Loneliness is undoubtedly better than deluding myself with impractical fairytale fantasies.

"I'll never understand why you ended things with Justin," Sophie muses, interrupting my reverie. She started to bring this up earlier today while we were decorating, but I was able to walk away and shut it down. Now I'm captive.

"I just knew it wasn't right. It was time. It's not like we're getting any younger. Justin deserves someone who will appreciate all his goodness. He is a great guy, just not my great guy."

I recently ended things with my boyfriend of five years. Justin truly is a good man, and there is nothing I can point out as to why I did it. I was just never head over heels for him. And as much as I keep finding out that head over heels can be an illusion, I am not willing to settle.

When I turned thirty, I suddenly felt I had to make real, long-term decisions. Justin didn't seem like lifelong partner material for me, regardless of how comfortable and easy our relationship was. Once I realized it, it took me a full year to finally pull the trigger and make the break.

"Yeah, yeah. You've told me. You loved him but weren't 'in' love." She levels me with a bewildered look.

"But he adored you, treated you like gold, and God knows that passion stuff fizzles out after a few years for everyone anyway. Wouldn't it have been wiser to just…be happy with that? Most of us would kill for a guy like that."

It's an echo of my own nagging doubts these past few weeks. At thirty-one, shouldn't I embrace security, family, and companionship, even if it isn't the epic romance I dreamed of as a foolish girl?

Ultimately, I keep coming back to the same thing. I'll wait for that epic romance or enjoy my life all by my lonesome. I'm not so bad, after all. Indeed, he is out there. Somewhere.

———

6:09 pm

"I'm going to walk down the hall for a bit," Sophie

declares as she stands and yawns. "I want to stretch my legs. Do you need anything from the cafeteria?"

"No, I'm good, sweet friend. You know you can go, right? I'm going to be okay."

"I told you, I'm staying until we hear from the doctor. So stop trying to get rid of me."

My guess is she's really going out to make a call that she doesn't want me to hear. I love that she is sticking around so much for me, but I just wish she would go. I feel terrible keeping her from everyone. There is no need for both of us to ruin our weekend.

As if on cue, a handsome man walks in wearing a white coat with a stethoscope hanging around his neck. "Hi, I'm Dr. Hampton," he says. "Looks like you got in a fight with some glass shards. Didn't your momma tell you not to play with broken glass?"

I'm not in the mood for jokes, even if he does look like he belongs on the pages of *Vogue*.

"Yes, apparently, that is not a fight I should have picked. Am I going to be able to get out of here tonight, Doc?"

"We are going to take a look at your scans. I'll review them as soon as they come back, and then we can go from there."

"Can you give me some hypothetical scenarios? In case things don't look good, I want to know what to expect. I like to be pleasantly surprised when things go better than anticipated. My life is in your hands. Or, my hand in your hands.

That pun wasn't intentional. I start to babble when I'm uncomfortable. And to say I am uncomfortable would be a massive understatement.

Sophie has been glued to my side all afternoon, but when the moment she has been waiting for arrives, the part the doctor comes in with the "plan," she's out in the hallway on some clandestine call.

I pull out my phone. Speaking of calls, I want to call Isabella right now. But I don't want to ruin her night. She is the one person I would always consult on something like this. And Justin, before we ended things. But now it's just her.

Still, I decide to text my mom instead. I don't want to freak her out, but I want to reach out to somebody.

Suddenly, I realize that Sophie's constant presence has been comforting. Now I have to rethink my whole, "I'll be fine alone if my shining prince doesn't come along," mantra.

"I'll take excellent care of you. I know it is getting late, but if you need surgery, we will aim to do it within the next hour or two. If we can't get everything lined up by nine, then we will schedule it for first thing in the morning. Trina will keep you updated on everything and take excellent care of you until I see you again sometime after you get your MRI."

"Like we might have surgery tonight? Did I just hear you right?"

"Possibly. Let's not get ahead of ourselves. Let's see how the scans look, and then we will know better what we are dealing with."

Great. There are no good scenarios here. I'm fucked either way. Even if it is minor, I'm not getting out of here anytime soon. And if it is more than minor, I have to have surgery.

"Thank you so much. I'll be right here anxiously awaiting your return."

I'm trying not to cry as I absorb all of this information.

"Can I get you anything else?" Trina asks after Dr. Hampton is gone.

The surgeon sweeps in, delivers terrible news before the terrible news, and then sweeps right back out, leaving the nurse to pick up the pieces. I just wish someone would hug me, tell me everything will be alright, and that I'm not alone.

"No, I think I'm okay right now. Thank you so much."

As she leaves the room, I watch her pink scrubs with little bears on them walk out. I'm sure they're supposed to make the patient feel better, but they only make me feel worse. All my friends are getting ready for a party I mostly planned and am financing while I sit here with Teddy bears and Alzheimer's brochures.

Coming to terms with the fact that I'm going to have to have some kind of major surgery alone is pretty fucking miserable. I'm a thirty-one-year-old woman, and I have no one to bask in my misery with.

On top of wallowing in my realization that I am all alone in this world, I don't have time to work a hand surgery and recovery into my already-packed schedule. I'm supposed to be in Los Angeles in less than forty-eight hours for work.

Perfect timing: the International Marine Conservation Congress in LA is next week. I'll miss it if I can't get back to Florida in time to catch my flight Monday morning. The thought sends a wave of frustration and disappointment crashing over me.

This conference is more than just a professional obligation —it's a lifeline. It's where I connect with fellow marine biologists, share my research on coral reef restoration, and learn about the latest advancements in marine conservation.

Every year, I return home inspired, armed with new ideas and collaborations fueling my work. Missing it would feel like an enormous setback, not just for my career, but also for the passion that drives me.

The ocean is my life's work, my escape, my everything. I've dedicated countless hours to studying its mysteries, advocating for its protection, and this conference is where I recharge that dedication.

"Ms. Klass?" Trina's voice breaks into my thoughts. "Are you alright?"

I blink, realizing I've been staring blankly at the wall. "Yes, I'm fine," I manage a weak smile. "Just processing everything."

"It's understandable," she says kindly while she does something with the beeping machine attached to my body. "But try not to worry. We'll take good care of you. I'll keep you posted as soon as I know anything."

I nod, trying to believe her words. But the truth is, I'm scared. I'm afraid of the surgery, of the unknown, of possibly never waking up again if I do go in for surgery.

For a brief moment, I consider picking up my phone to call Justin. I know he would be kind and would probably offer to drive here to be with me. Selfishly, I want to do that just to have someone here—someone to know if I don't wake up from surgery.

But I know it isn't right. I know he would be here for me at a moment's notice, and that is exactly why I shouldn't. Because I know it would be for the wrong reasons. Nothing has changed for me regarding our relationship. I can't do that to him.

He is everything any woman would want in a husband. But I never had those feelings for him, and I could not see myself marrying him. He'd been dropping the hints for a while. I just knew I wouldn't get there because my annoyance and resistance grew every time he mentioned it.

Part of me worried that by staying with Justin, as wonderful as he is, I might end up holding both of us back from finding our true life-partners. So I ripped off the band-aid and broke it off, as painful as it was, convinced it was for the best.

Sitting in a bed in this cold hospital room, I can't help but wonder. Was I throwing away a good thing because I had unrealistic expectations? Maybe Justin was as good as it will get for me, and I torpedoed it out of some misguided search for a storybook romance.

———

8:04 pm

Sophie finally left about an hour ago after I recapped what the doctor said. And how he seemed to be leaning toward surgery, depending on the scans. Even in the best of circumstances, I'm not out of here anytime soon.

Here it is eight o'clock, and I'm still waiting on a prognosis. I'm so grateful Sophie finally listened to me and left.

My phone buzzes on the tray over my bed. I turn it over and see it's Isabella.

"What are you doing calling me? Go enjoy your party, you crazy person!"

"I'm just so worried about you. Have you heard anything?"

"Still nothing. Things move at a snail's pace around here. I've never felt so out of control my entire life."

"Well, we are all missing you here. It all looks amazing. Thank you for everything you did to make this happen. I'm so sorry you're not here with us. Can I come see you tomorrow?"

"Of course. Maybe if we are lucky, I'll be gone. But either way, yes, I want to see you."

I say that, but with each passing minute I'm less convinced that will happen. I try to keep all of my despair out of my voice, hoping to sound chipper and upbeat. But I felt anything but.

"Go to your party. Enjoy. I love you!"

"I love you, Elly-Belly."

I put my phone down, and then I lost it. Just hearing her voice somehow puts me over the edge, and I can't hold it back anymore. I reach for a small box of tissues on the same tray and blow my nose.

That is when I hear a man clear his throat with a deep baritone. I look up to see Dr. Hampton.

"Oh, hi there. Don't mind me. I'm just having an existential crisis over here. All my friends are enjoying the party I was decorating for when this happened," I say, trying to lift my hand to indicate the marshmallow hand that feels like it weighs a hundred pounds.

With only one hand, I blow my nose again and wipe my cheeks. It's more challenging than I might have imagined it would be using only one hand. "Okay, I need some good news. What are we doing, Doc."

He pulls out the computer beside the bed and swivels it to face me. He types something on the keyboard, and black-and-white images of what appears to be my hand pop up on the screen.

"I hate to tell you this, but your scans show what we suspected. You have severed your flexor tendon as well as a few smaller but still important tendons. This type of injury requires surgery to repair. Otherwise, you will not be able to use that hand."

The surgeon's words stay on repeat in my mind. A juxtaposition of Isabella's kind, hopeful words and his harsh ones is like a tsunami in my brain. I want to make all the words stop, but I can't.

His voice feels like the teacher from Charlie Brown's school. "Womp womp womp womp womp." His words are all blurred together, and they don't make sense. The only thing I can process is surgery.

I feel like I am free-falling. My heart is racing, and all I want to do is scream my lungs out.

"You probably can't tell because of all the bandaging, but as it is now," Dr. Hampton keeps droning on. "You will not be able to move your fingers, at least the first three, unless we reattach these tendons where they were severed."

I have so many questions, but I'm unable to articulate them. I feel overwhelmed by everything he's saying. It's too much all at once.

"Will there be any irreversible damage? I mean, if you're able to fix the tendons, what can I expect?"

"It's hard to say for sure if you're going to have permanent nerve damage, but there's a pretty good chance that you will. Our primary aim is to deal with the tendons. Once we are in your hand, we may find that we have to also deal with the nerve component as well. Most of the time, you'll have some degree of both with an injury like this."

That doesn't sound promising. He really knows how to put the patient at ease.

"It's hard to know the impact on the nerves from a scan. We will know more once we get in there with the scope."

Um, okay. There's nothing like assessing a major issue on a prominent limb on the fly. I thought doctors and surgeons were all-knowing. I do not get a lot of confident vibes from this fella.

"Since it has gotten so late, and this isn't urgent, I have pushed surgery off until tomorrow morning, first thing. That way, I will have my vascular surgeon, Dr. Reeves, on hand if we need him."

The sooner, the better, they said. Something about scar tissue forming and tissue dying. But apparently, that isn't the case anymore. So much for getting in there as quickly as possible to get ahead of scar tissue.

The best-case scenario, he says, is that he will be in and out in a couple of hours and only have to fix the severed tendons. After surgery, he will be able to discuss rehab and recovery options.

This all seems like the pretty much worst fucking case scenario I can imagine, no matter what happens in the future.

Also by Blakely Stone

Billionaire Fake Proposal

Billionaire Grumpy Daddy

Billionaire Enemy Roommate

Billionaire Second Chance

Christmas with the Grump

Pucking My Ex

Pucking Dad's BFF

Pucking My Neighbor

About the Author

Blakely Stone is an emerging author of Contemporary Romance. This is Blakely's ninth book.

Join Blakely's newsletter and get insider access to industry new releases, deals + steals and FREEBIES. You'll also get a FREE copy of her novella Billionaire Baby Secret!

facebook.com/blakelystoneromance

instagram.com/blakelystoneromance

bookbub.com/profile/blakely-stone

tiktok.com/@blakelystoneromance

Made in United States
Orlando, FL
26 September 2024

51991066R00209